STOLEN

HEART *of* DREAD

BOOK TWO

MELISSA DE LA CRUZ
MICHAEL JOHNSTON

speak

for BLUE BLOODS:

★ "De la Cruz's Blue Bloods introduces a conception of vampires far different from traditional stake-fleeing demons, coupling sly humor . . . with the gauzier trappings of being fanged and fabulous . . . teens will savor the thrilling sense of being initiated into an exclusive secret society."   —*Booklist,* starred review

"De la Cruz combines American history, vampires and a crew of rich New York City kids, delivering a page-turning debut in Blue Bloods."
                                                                    —*Publishers Weekly*

"Schuyler Van Alen is #9 on the Top 25 Vampires of all time."
                                                                    —*Entertainment Weekly*

for WITCHES OF EAST END:

"Centuries after the practice of magic was forbidden, Freya, Ingrid, and their mom struggle to restrain their witchy ways as chaos builds in their Long Island town. A bubbling cauldron of mystery and romance, the novel shares the fanciful plotting of Blue Bloods, the author's teen vampire series . . . [B]reezy fun."   —*People*

"A magical and romantic page-turner . . . *Witches of East End* is certain to attract new adult readers . . . The pacing is masterful, and while the witchcraft is entertaining, it's ultimately a love triangle that makes the story compelling. De la Cruz has created a family of empathetic women who are both magically gifted and humanly flawed."
                                                                    —*The Washington Post*

"For anyone who was frustrated watching Samantha suppress her magic on *Bewitched,* Ms. de la Cruz brings some satisfaction. In her first novel for adults, the author . . . lets her repressed sorceresses rip."
                                                                    —*The New York Times*

STOLEN

HEART *of* DREAD

BOOK TWO

*For Mattie, who will light the world
on fire one day*

and

*for Josey, whose imagination soars
as high as a drakon*

SPEAK
An imprint of Penguin Random House LLC
375 Hudson Street
New York, New York 10014

First published in the United States of America by G. P. Putnam's Sons,
an imprint of Penguin Group (USA) LLC, 2014
Published by Speak, an imprint of Penguin Random House LLC, 2016

THE LIBRARY OF CONGRESS HAS CATALOGED THE G. P. PUTNAM'S SONS EDITION AS FOLLOWS:
De la Cruz, Melissa, 1971–
Stolen / by Melissa de la Cruz and Michael Johnston.
pages cm.—(Heart of dread ; book 2)
Summary: Nat risked her life to reunite with her drakon in the defense of the Blue,
but Wes, seeking his sister Eliza, is forced to rejoin the military, placing him and
Nat on opposite sides of a war that could destroy what is left of the world.
ISBN 978-0-399-25755-1 (hardcover)
[1. Environmental degradation—Fiction. 2. Magic—Fiction. 3. Dragons—Fiction.
4. Brothers and sisters—Fiction. 5. War—Fiction. 6. Science fiction.]
I. Johnston, Michael (Michael Anthony), 1973– II. Title.
PZ7.D36967Sto 2014
[Fic]—dc23
2014032669

Speak ISBN 978-0-14-751572-8

Printed in the United States of America

1 3 5 7 9 10 8 6 4 2

Men say they know many things;
But lo! they have taken wings,—
The arts and sciences,
And a thousand appliances;
The wind that blows
Is all that any body knows.

—HENRY DAVID THOREAU

Come hell

—THE DECEMBERISTS, "THIS IS WHY WE FIGHT"

THE FIRE AND THE THIEF

THROUGH THE FIRE, THROUGH THE SMOKE
and flame, she saw the boy and the girl huddled in the corner.
Twins. She hadn't known there would be two children. Which one?
The boy looked afraid, but his sister stared back boldly. The girl
had sapphire eyes and a swirl on her shoulder. A weaver.

It was the girl.

A decision was made.

She was the one.

The one they had come to steal.

PART THE FIRST:

THE ARCHIMEDES PALIMPSEST

You drop a coin into the sea,
and shout out,
"Please come back to me"
—STARS, "THE NIGHT STARTS HERE"

1

FIRE IN HER THROAT. FIRE IN HER LUNGS and chest. Nat breathed and the drakon breathed. She exhaled and the drakon exhaled. The drakon roared its fury and the flame was everywhere, a blaze as bright as the noonday sun.

Natasha Kestal was a drakonrydder. She was *Anastasia Dekesthalias, the Resurrection of the Flame.* But neither words nor names could capture the incredible floating, flying, gut-twisting, hair-raising sensation that filled her entire being. Being a drakonrydder was only part of it. Nat *was* the drakon. She was a piece of the creature's soul, a limb that had been torn from its body as surely as a wing or a claw, but now, reunited, they were one as they glided through the clouds, skimming across the water, the wind in her face and hair, its fire burning in her throat. The drakon's fury, its rage, was *her* rage, and she breathed that rage upon the drone ships that flew the flag of the Remaining States of America, setting the entire ocean aflame.

Not everything was so simple. The battle in the Pacific had been only the first victory, as the enemy's might was far more formidable and vast than she or the Council of Vallonis had anticipated. Since the first battle, armadas hidden around points of the globe had tracked and assaulted every possible gateway to the Blue. They'd come with their guns and their rockets, following her with radar and satellite, sending drone aircrafts to track her position and battle cruisers to fire their missiles into the drakon's hide. *Like wasps stinging a hound's coat*, Nat thought. *But if stung enough, the hound will fall.*

It was her job to keep that from happening. But her drakon had suffered many injuries already and it had been a while since they had been able to truly rest.

All the oceans were the same—the frothy waters toxic and black—with the Tasman Sea as blighted as the rest. The gate of Arem had closed, but navy spies discovered the new door-way located north of New Crete that the people of Vallonis were using to rescue their sick brothers and sisters from the dying world. Nat had been patrolling the skies at dawn when she spotted the hulking supercarriers steaming their way to the island.

She urged her drakon downward and they dove through walls of smoke and ash, bursting through flame; a Valkyrie and her mount. The wind from its wings created white-crested waves that sent the fleet's smaller vessels tumbling in the tide, capsizing the drone ships and filling their hulls with black wa-ter that pulled them down into the murky depths, all while Nat and her drakon rose upward on a plume of hot air, disap-pearing into the dark skies and preparing for another volley.

Higher, she urged. *Faster. Fly ahead of their bullets.*

Drakon Mainas flapped its leathery wings, the air gusting

like a hurricane, each mighty wing beat scattering the clouds and creating a vortex, a hole through which she could glimpse the remnants of the latest fleet, the gleaming cruisers and destroyers of the RSA, floundering and nearly obliterated in one breath of the drakon's flame.

One more and they are done.

Nat inhaled. She felt the hot air churning in her lungs, the fire building, heat swirling, rising. *Make this blast the greatest yet—a heat so intense, it will roast their ships into dust.* The fire pulsed in her veins; it climbed up her throat. She let the flame grow until she couldn't control it anymore. The drakon's black and ashy scales glowed hot, red and orange. Nat screamed and a violent blue fireball erupted from its mouth, intense and white-hot in the center, onto the remaining drones.

Now all the ships were burning, their hulls blackened, and they were sinking into the ocean, steam rising and hissing as they slipped into the dark waters. Scorched. Defeated.

Nat felt a fierce swell of joy and triumph, but she had survived enough of these campaigns to know it wasn't over quite yet.

Up, she said to her drakon. *Into the sky, our hunt continues.*

Higher and higher they climbed, rising up until they were above the clouds, above the gray mist. Nat hovered, listening for the engines of the remaining aircraft—the gray drones that swarmed the air above the coast of New Pangaea.

Like the humming snore of a great, sleeping beast, she thought. *Or . . .*

A flock of sleek warbirds ripped through the clouds, their engines screaming, targeting mechanisms whirling, heading straight for them. Only seconds away, a few drakon-lengths at the most.

Dive! Now!

The drakon tucked its mighty wings to its back and fell straight out of the sky, toward the rocky cliffs along the shore. They sailed down into a wedge-shaped valley, passing so close to the stone that Nat thought she saw animals scurrying across the rocks, running away from the great rush of wind that preceded the drakon. But the buzzing drones still followed close behind, and she could see their black-tipped noses from the corner of her eye. *Faster,* she urged her drakon. Down and down they fell, breaking stones and branches, sending rocks and leaves spiraling into the air, coming to a halt a hairsbreadth above the river at the valley's base.

The drakon beat its wings right before they struck the water, and they rose once more, flying in a wide arc before angling up toward the lip of the gorge.

The unexpected move sent a few of their pursuers crashing into the water or the rocks, but others maneuvered faster and continued to trail behind them, spitting out gunfire, and Nat had to dodge the bullets that streaked toward her. She brandished her sword, holding it aloft to direct the drakon's flame, while the bullets bounced harmlessly against her shield.

Get us out of here. Find cover.

There! Nat spied a granite pillar, a tower of rock where they could hide. Soon the drakon was already turning toward it, diving again to an open chasm. The drakon landed on the far side of the rock, talons gripping the stone, breaking chunks from the granite. They hung there, hiding, blending into the dark, listening closely as the roar of the drones' engines filled the canyon.

Shrieking like banshees, wailing like lost souls, the unpiloted drones dove into the valley. *Now. Let's fill this canyon with flame.*

Nat inhaled deeply and the drakon stretched its neck, reaching around the stone to unleash an epic roar, breathing fire into the gorge and turning the rocky crevice into an inferno. One by one the drones flew into the canyon, their engines whizzing, buzzing like enormous insects, searching for Nat, only to find themselves trapped in a heat intense enough to warp their wings and melt their engines. Three crashed into the walls of the cliff while the last one merely sputtered and fell to the valley floor.

It's over. We did it. The canyon was engulfed in drakonfire, and Nat marveled at its beauty, how it swirled around her, dancing. The fire fell like warm rain on her shoulders, as soothing as a cocoon.

She let the flames dim. The battle was finished, or so she believed; she'd been through enough of these to know when it was over.

But just as she exhaled in relief, a lone gray drone soared above the cavern, its dark wings wide as the valley, nose as long as the highest tree was tall, dropping bombs from its belly. It was a grayhawk, the deadliest aircraft in the RSA's arsenal, as large and fearsome as the drakon itself—stealthy and silent, a death machine in the sky.

She could feel the drakon's fear. Like her, it was afraid of iron, of the steel in their bullets and shells. Like her, it was afraid of the grayhawk.

9

Climb!

They rose from the canyon, wings beating. Nat's heels digging into the drakon's side, urging it upward, explosions and smoke chasing them from the gorge as they burst out into the sky, flames nipping at their tail.

Come and get us. Nat waited for the grayhawk to find them in the clouds and smoke, meaning to meet it head-on, to torch it like she had the others.

Come and I will show you what it means to burn.

She waited, but there was nothing but dark smoke that hurt her eyes.

Nat blinked and suddenly she was staring into a black expanse that wasn't ocean or sky, but asphalt—a road with cars racing across its surface. She wiped the tears from her eyes, thinking she was hallucinating, but the vision of the racetrack persisted.

And there, inside one of the cars, was Wes, his face tight with tension, his mouth set in a frown, dark circles under his eyes.

Ryan Wesson.

How long had it been since they had seen each other?

Too long.

He was driving and didn't see her as he maneuvered his car across the track, nearly colliding with another driver but swerving gracefully just in time. Then he looked up, and his brown eyes widened in acknowledgment as they met her green ones.

Nat?

She could hear his voice in her head, and her heart ached and the fire burned white-hot inside her.

Wes! she cried. What was she looking at? Where was he?

But just as quickly as he'd appeared, he was gone. The track and its cars vanished into the mist.

There was only the fat belly of the grayhawk hovering above, its rockets pointed straight at her, and so Nat flew up to meet it, her throat filling with flame, ready to exhale.

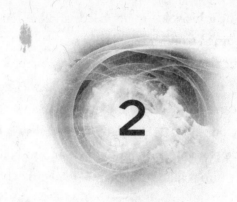

2

WES SLAMMED HIS HEAD ON THE CEILING
of the Mustang, and when he opened his eyes, the racetrack
was gone.

Murky dark water littered with ziggurats of trash the size
of icebergs filled his vision. A burnt battle cruiser slowly sank
into the waves while a grayhawk drone hovered in the sky.
When he blinked again, the roar of a car engine pounded in
his ears, closing in fast from behind. A white Lamborghini
slid past his side mirror, sending a drift of snow over his windshield, blocking his sight.

He turned the wheel sharply to clear his windshield, and
when he blinked, there it was again: the churning waves and
sinking ships. But now he saw something else as well—a great
black silhouette with wings and a tail, soaring through the
gray sky, breathing fire.

Another bump, and Wes was back in the race, past the
bend and into the straightaway. If one of the other drivers was
going to pass him, now was the time. They would approach
from the inside and try to force him toward one of the outer

lanes. *Fine. Let them.* He wasn't trying to win the race, after all. Winning was the last thing he wanted to do. Mostly, he just wanted to stay alive.

Screaming around the turn with the track opening up before him, Wes didn't have to blink this time to see the bow of the drone ship again, and the creature in the air. And this time he saw *her.*

Nat on her drakon, wielding a sword, looking like some kind of god, like a story from a fairy tale, like a hero from the book of legends, her long dark hair streaming like a ribbon in the sky.

Nat!

Wes?

She was looking right back at him, her green tiger eyes flashing in shock and joy.

Nat!

But just as quickly as she appeared, she was gone.

It wasn't real. It couldn't be real. Was it a memory? But Nat looked different—her hair was longer, and she was wearing different clothes. Armor? He could have sworn she was wearing a suit of leather and black chain mail, similar to the black scales of her drakon. It had to be a dream.

But it *felt* so real.

And his feelings for her were as real as the day they'd said good-bye.

He'd done what he promised. He'd taken her out of New Vegas, across the ruined Pacific to the Blue, her home. Together they survived slavers and traitors, chaos and death. Wes had taken her right to the gate of Arem, where she and her drakon had turned the entire Pacific fleet into ash in order to defend their homeland.

An Aston Martin crashed against him with a thunderous crack, sending his car spinning, and Wes quickly refocused on the track. He flew ahead of a pair of black Ferraris, the white Lamborghini close behind. Good. He would lead them for a few laps, before letting them overtake him. The guys in the exotic cars were the ones who were supposed to win, paying top dollar for the privilege. Execs from as far as Xian and New Kong came to the New Vegas track for a chance to race in the last international no-rules speedway. Drivers like Wes were part of the entertainment, to lend authenticity to the experience; he gave them someone to pass, to beat, to outrun, someone to splash with a cloud of snow, someone to send spiraling into the snowbanks. If he made the mistake of actually winning the race, he wouldn't get paid. It was a risky business, driving cars, causing accidents, but it was the only work he could find. He was already blacklisted by a few of the casino bosses for refusing to torch a rival hotel, and then by the military for refusing to patrol the black waters.

His thoughts drifted back to Nat. She had *looked* at him. She had seen him. Her presence made him feel warm for a moment, the way it had on the slavers' ship, when she had kept them both alive. He hadn't thought to question it before, but there was no way they would have survived the subzero weather if one of them hadn't been made of drakonflame.

But she wasn't here anymore. He was alone and the car was cold. The heater on the '77 Mustang didn't work. They'd let him borrow an old heat suit for the race, but the jacket wasn't working, and he was so cold, he could hardly keep his hands on the wheel.

Maybe it was the cold that made him think about her. He'd left Nat at the door to the Blue, left her behind, left her to fight her battles alone. He'd left her to find his sister, Eliza. The girl the RSA had stolen as a child. Eliza was family; Eliza was blood. It had been months since he'd said good-bye to Nat, and during that time he had searched for Eliza. There had been leads here and there, but none of them had led to his sister.

He shivered.

Wes pushed Nat from his thoughts.

The road ahead was open, the track clear. Black pavement stretched in front of him. Wes opened up the gas and floored it, exhilarated from the speed and adrenaline. As he rounded the turn, he saw a mechanic in an orange heat suit waving the checkered flag to signal the end of the race. The finish line was near.

But there was no car in front of him.

Ice. I hadn't meant to do that.

He was about to win the race. He'd let his memory of Nat distract him, and now he was still ahead of the other drivers. His opponents—the heat elite, the global execs and the RSA stooges, the casino lords and gangsters, the rich boys from the heated dome cities—were so inept at driving that he had won without even trying.

Godfreezeit! he cursed, and Wes didn't like cursing. His mother had taught him better. He needed to lose, and he needed to lose now. If he won the race, he wouldn't get paid— not one freezing watt. Those were the rules.

The white Lamborghini flew past him, sending a shower of snow against his windshield once again. *Cretin*. Wes let off the gas a little—he couldn't be too obvious—but he needed to get out of the race and he needed to do it soon. He slammed the brake and his car spun, sideswiping the Lamborghini. Two more cars came flying around the bend, the pair of black Ferraris turning sharply to avoid Wes and the Lamborghini as they careened wildly across the track. But their efforts came to no avail, as the pair rolled over each other and crashed into the embankment. A blue Porsche ran past, gunning to win, but it was too late, and it, too, collided with the Mustang in a flash of blue and a burst of snow. As Wes finally spun to a halt, a black Corvette shrieked across the finish line.

The race was over.

Wes's car skidded into the off-road portion of the track, crashing into a flimsy barrier with an awkward bang. He pushed himself out through the driver's window and fell onto the fresh powder, laughing a little, relishing the look of the other drivers, especially that icehole in the Lamborghini. He couldn't remember the last time he had laughed. Ruining the race for some heatbag was the closest thing Wes had to enjoyment, but his laughter faded quickly. The driver of the white Lamborghini was already running toward the control box, complaining to the track manager about Wes's last-minute maneuver.

Wes shook the snow from his hair. It didn't matter. He had done what was required of him. He would get paid. He would eat tonight.

His back was sore from the impact; the injuries hurt more than he let on. Lately the ice had been getting to him. He felt it in his joints every morning and when he lay awake at night, dreaming of the ocean, his every muscle aching, his mind unable to rest.

Nat was out there somewhere. The nets were full of stories of ocean attacks and images of the creature that was systematically destroying the RSA's armada. First the entire Pacific fleet, then the Atlantic cruisers; now a newly formed battalion of grayhawks and supercarriers was rumored to be headed to New Pangaea to meet the monster head-on. Was that what he'd seen? Was that where she was?

He'd left Nat because he had to, but now he wasn't so certain. She was all alone, one drakonrydder against many drones. He hadn't seen any backup, no sylvan archers, no warriors on horseback. Just Nat and her drakon against the might of the RSA.

Wes pushed his way through the snow, avoiding the other drivers, the victor as well as the losers. He was done for the night. His account would register the watts in a few minutes. When the money arrived, he'd have enough heat for a meal, a drink, maybe two; maybe he'd even be able to share that meal. The wind rose up, the icy breeze rattling his bones, making him shiver. He was only sixteen but was shaking like a frail old man. He was shivering so hard, he hardly noticed the buzzing in his pocket.

When he finally heard the low rumble, he reached into his jacket and pulled out a stolen satellite phone. A text flickered on the screen, green letters glowing on the black display. Wes read the message twice, not quite believing what he was reading.

It was from Shakes. His best friend. His right-hand man. It said:

FOUND ELIZA

Wes stuffed the phone back into his pocket, hurrying from the track, feeling hope spark in his heart again, as warm and bright as drakonfire.

3

THE GRAYHAWK DISAPPEARED BACK into the clouds before the drakonflame could reach it, and Nat shook Wes's warm brown eyes from her thoughts.

Riding high above the ocean, she looked down at the islands below, a stony archipelago covered in blankets of snow and dotted with bursts of bright green foliage. She flew closer to the water, looking for the grayhawk that had chased her from the gorge, but it was nowhere to be found. The drone remained hidden in the misty fog.

As she and her drakon flew closer to land, Nat could see the trees more clearly, hardy brown trunks sprouting from the frost-covered earth, their leafy branches reaching heavenward. Liannan, the sylph who'd guided them to the Blue, told them that one day its magic would cover the world. Here, at the bottom of New Pangaea, along the coasts of the Roo Islands, at the gate of Afal, the deep green forests of the earth were returning, and life was spreading across the black waters once more.

This is what I fight for, Nat thought, seeing the forest in all its beauty. *The land I love.* The words made her fly faster, as if only the speed itself could keep her from the thought she knew would be next. *Is that all you love? The land?* Nat tightened her grip, forcing herself to focus only on what lay ahead of her—just as she always had.

And besides, what lay ahead of her was a truly staggering sight. Closer and closer they came, diving near the treetops, the smell of the sap pungent and heady, the scent of flowers wafting in the air. Nat tried not to let the forest distract her. The drone was still out there, hiding in the fog, waiting. She couldn't let her guard down, even for a moment, even to see this forest, growing where nothing had lived for a century.

When the ice and the floods came, when the world ended and almost everyone and everything died, she had thought these things were lost forever, that vast swaths of the world were too irradiated, the soil too poisoned for any greenery to grow again. But somehow, the Blue was changing everything. The earth was coming back to life. How precious it was: wildflowers and their many-colored blossoms rich with buzzing insects, butterflies flitting while ladybugs crawled. Nat wanted to stop, to smell and touch everything, almost worried the forest would vanish if she didn't. She feared it was nothing but a mirage, like the image of Wes she had just seen, that her mind was soothing her with things she wanted to see. That, like Wes, it would disappear if she blinked or turned away. But it didn't, and as they flew farther and farther, above rich and verdant acres of forest, Nat stopped worrying.

Or so she told herself.

Letting the drakon fly even lower, Nat marveled at the wide

trunks and heavy branches of the trees, at the leafy canopies that soared above her. The trees were over eighty feet tall and would normally have taken a century to grow to this height. Only the power of the Blue could have accomplished this feat in such a short time. Vallonis and its magic was transforming the landscape, renewing what was destroyed.

Nat herself felt renewed in its presence.

During these past months, the days had passed like minutes. The rage and pain, the hurt that had once filled her heart was gone. She had believed she couldn't love, couldn't feel, that she was broken. But she no longer suffered from that hollow feeling of emptiness. In its place she felt a warm, deep sense of fulfillment. She was complete. She had lived half awake, only half alive until she found her drakon. But now she was whole. Ready to live, to fight, to face whatever came next.

She was the last remaining Guardian of the Blue, the first and last drakonrydder of the third age of Vallonis.

Nat inhaled deeply, feeling a tingle from the life all around her. *When the war is over, when the Blue is safe, I will come back here.* Deep in her heart, she knew that her dearest hope was that she would not return alone.

But there was no more time to dream.

As quickly as it had disappeared, it returned. The grayhawk had found her.

And now there were two of them.

Let them come. As the gray-winged planes streaked above the forest, their engines as silent as bird's wings, great gray harbingers of doom and death, her drakon filled the sky with fire, turning the clouds into vapor and the air into flame.

A drone crashed to the earth, burning, dying. *One more,* thought Nat, *one more drone to defeat and then we can rest.*

But Drakon Mainas was slow to move this time, the months of battle finally taking their toll on the great beast. *So many wasps,* she thought. *Too many.* Soon it would rest; soon *they* would rest, she soothed. Just one last push. One more attack.

Breathe, she told her drakon. *Breathe and let's burn this thing and go home.*

No fire came. The last grayhawk set its sights on them, sent its rockets arcing into the air, and she felt a dozen bullets tear through the drakon's hide. Nat screamed, feeling as if her whole body were tearing open as the iron pierced the drakon's scales. Each shard stabbed at her chest, stealing the breath from her lungs, the pain nearly knocking her from her mount.

Breathe, she told herself. *Breathe.*

Struggling against the pain that consumed them both, Nat inhaled as deeply as she could, felt the fire burning inside and out, and before the drone could circle back to fire at them again, she unleashed the drakonfire, bathing the great gray warbird in a pillar of flame that turned the entire body of the drone into a red, glowing cylinder. She watched as the cylinder bent and collapsed, hurtling toward the granite cliffs, shattering into a thousand pieces as it struck the rocks.

They did it. They destroyed the latest battalion as completely as the ones before it. The RSA would have other resources, of course—who knew how many more in its great armada were hidden in the frozen oceans of the world.

But for now, they had won.

Nat's heart was racing as she and her drakon rose once more into the clouds. The sound of the crash reverberated across the island valley. She would bring the news to the Council's Messenger, to tell the Queen that the land was safe once more.

Home now, she urged. *Home and sleep.*

We will have time enough to celebrate.

A sudden strange rumbling shook the air around them. That was no warbird. That was no grayhawk. *What is that?* Nat gripped the reins tightly, waiting, uncertain, and the drakon hovered, flapping its giant wings, remaining in place.

Let's get out of here, Nat told her drakon, but before they could move, a black cloud engulfed them, piercing the drakon with shards of hot iron. They'd been hit with a new weapon, Nat realized. They weren't bullets or missiles, and they were everywhere, painful, hot, and stinging with dangerous silver poison. The drakon moved its body to shield Nat, to protect her from the iron rain, as the iron daggers tore at its hide, searing through scale and armor into the soft flesh of the great beast, drawing rivers of blood.

The pain was too much to bear and they fell, crashing into the earth, the drakon beating its wings to cushion the landing as they smacked into the trees and the rocks, hitting the ground in a clatter of pebbles and a cloud of smoke.

Nat fell from her seat, and when she opened her eyes, she saw that her drakon was weeping, it burned with such pain, and her own face was wet with tears. She felt its pain in her own body, in her own soul, and it was intolerable.

Her drakon was dying. She could feel its pain, its terror, as the iron worked its way into its flesh, into its very spirit, corrupting and destroying with its silver poison.

She screamed and Drakon Mainas rumbled, its voice cutting through the pain.

Stop. Stop. Stop.

What is happening?

You must calm yourself.

Nat took a deep breath and slowed her heart.

Better.

You are hurt. Make it stop.

I cannot. We must separate.

No.

It is the only way to survive. Listen. I will go deep into the earth, deep into the Blue. I will be safe there and the pain will abate for both of us until I am healed.

Already it was digging into the sand, its talons scraping the ground, creating a deep and dark hole.

A tomb. Nat shuddered. A burial site.

Do not let cowardly thoughts overcome you, her drakon thundered. *You must return to Vallonis whole and warn them of this magic that is in our enemy's hands. GO!*

Then the ground opened up, and her drakon disappeared into its depths.

Nat sat still for a moment, exhausted and shaking from the battle, and now from the sudden separation. She was incomplete again, more alone than ever, especially after having known and lived otherwise.

She tried calling to Mainas, but the drakon did not answer.

Where once it was buried in the ocean, now it was underneath the ground itself.

There was nothing to be done.

Nat picked herself up, dusted herself off, and walked toward the gateway hidden deep in the forest.

Home and sleep. Just not the way she'd planned.

4

WES ENJOYED THE ELEVATOR'S WARMTH, the quiet music that tinkled soothingly in the background. Shakes's text message was burning in his pocket. **FOUND ELIZA.** Was it true? He was impatient to find out more, but even if he wished to move faster, he was thankful for the short respite from the cold. When the race was over, he had returned the half-inoperative heat suit. The organizers lent them to the drivers—it was too cold to drive without one— but they took them back after the race was finished. *Cheap bastards.* He missed it even though it barely worked, but was glad to be standing in the wide and well-heated glass elevator. Since he was alone he stood right beneath the vent, savoring the hot air drifting though his hair, tickling his ears. Heat. He could stand there forever. Through the glass windows he saw soldiers patrolling the streets below and posted at every hotel lobby. He was surprised there wasn't an armed guard in the car with him.

Ever since the RSA had lost the battle in the Pacific, the military had doubled their ground troops, making their presence felt in every corner of New Vegas. The brass was on edge, jittery, and dangerous, looking for enemies in every shadow, in every movement. The raids on the marked were more prevalent, and there was no longer any pretense about hospitals or a cure. The white priests were even more visible than before, led by their High Priestess, a madwoman who called herself Lady Algeana Penthos, goddess of pain and suffering. There was no safe harbor for anyone marked by magic. They were considered dangerous, enemies of the state, and anyone caught harboring one would suffer the same fate— there were murmurs that even the military was in collusion with the Lady to get rid of them all. All the more reason to get out of the RSA, out of the crossfire, Wes thought. But where would he go? Where would he live? What kind of life could he dream about for him and his friends on this frozen wasteland of a planet? The time for dreams was long past.

The elevator shot up toward the skyway, to the casinos that floated high above the sidewalks, and it was easy to see that the lights of New Vegas glittered less brightly these days. Two casinos had gone dark this month, one the month before. The big three remained—the Loss, the Apple, and Mark Antony's Forum—along with a few others, but if the downslide continued, the Strip would be dark in a year. An unexpected wave of nostalgia hit Wes. The city's descent had been quick. The diamond in the ice desert was the RSA's last playground, but lately that playground had lost its luster, the bubble was cracking, the snow globe was about to collapse. New Vegas, the city that had shrugged its sequined shoulder at the apocalypse, was about to turn off the lights. He looked down at the lonely black slabs, the abandoned casinos looming like dead trees over the strip. The world was ending, and Vegas had staved off the inevitable for as long as it could, but the End had come to cash in its chips.

Wes only wished he could do the same.

Down below, a group of people were assembling in the middle of the icy sidewalk. Wes held his breath as his phone confirmed what he already suspected. The text read: **LS VGS BLVD + L FLMNGO. ZERO HR.** A protest mob. He'd never heard of anyone protesting anything in the RSA before. No one would have dared.

But that was before 12/12, before the drakon, before Nat. Wes hated the nickname the nets had given the battle, as if it were a tragedy, when only drones had been destroyed. Rumors of what happened on the ocean had spread through the RSA like a swift and wild winter breeze. The soldiers who'd lived to tell the tale were new recruits whom the talking heads on the nets had tried to cast as a group of deluded children spinning stories, perhaps even a Xian conspiracy. Even so, the relentless lore of the mighty fire-breathing creature was becoming popular around the globe. In the outlaw territories, they feared the hydra, in New Pangaea, the *tarakona,* and its rider was named a demon, a devil, a witch, a black drau. Old Vegas hands had dubbed the creature the Black Ace, and its image was everywhere in the city, its serpentine silhouette appearing on T-shirts and graffitied on walls, along with the words THE BLUE IS REAL! THE MONSTER IS REAL! DOWN WITH THE RSA!

People were starting to believe the rumors that the thrillers who haunted Garbage Country weren't suffering from failed government experiments but were dying from a magical disease. Which meant magic was real and the Blue was real.

Of course the Blue was real. So was the Monster, if you wanted to call it that, though having seen it, Wes wasn't certain he would. He just wished he could be as certain of everything else he had witnessed, and he wondered again about the vision he had experienced that afternoon, if Nat had truly seen him as he had seen her. He clung to that memory and to the hope that one day he would make good on his other promise.

I'll come back for you. This isn't the end for us.

Wes flinched every time he played the words back in his mind. They were almost too painful to think about, even for him. He told himself they were true. He needed to believe they were. *As real as the drakon and the stories and the Blue itself.*

The Blue and the girl who belongs to it.

He'd left Nat to find his sister, to answer a question that had occupied him for nearly a decade: *Where was Eliza? What happened on the night she disappeared?*

Did Shakes have the answer to that question at last?

The elevator chimed, the music faded, and the doors opened to a blast of cold air. He'd reached his destination. The thirty-second floor. A girl in a slim-fitting, whole-body heat suit stood at the door. She was wearing one of the new ones, with the fancy hoods, the bootstraps, and the matching balaclava that left only her eyes visible. Her eyebrows were tattooed pink and her eyelids were covered with gold glitter and swooping waves of blue eyeliner. "Welcome to Ice. Are you on the list?" she said automatically, checking the tablet she held.

He coughed and she looked up at him. "Oh, hey, Wes."

"Nela," he said, letting her press her cheeks against his. "How are you, gorgeous?" He winked.

"How am I gorgeous? How am I *not* gorgeous?" His friend Nela smirked. She was the hostess at Ice, and he'd shared many a can of Nutri with her and her girlfriend, the equally stunning Vixen, while waiting for Shakes to finish his shift.

"He's over there," she said, pointing to the empty portion of the bar where a familiar solitary figure was clearing snow from the glass floor. "Seems more cheerful than usual, and that's saying a lot."

Wes nodded. "Any crazy stories tonight?" Like him, Nela was a New Vegas native and had juicy anecdotes about growing up among the gamblers and the gangsters. Last week she told him how she'd heard about a pair of kids who'd jumped off the ice bridge with parachutes strapped to their backs. One of the packs hadn't deployed, but the boy had been lucky enough to land on his friend's chute and had made it to the ground unharmed. That friend had landed beneath him and lost a mouthful of teeth. That was the price of friendship in a city like theirs.

"Not yet but the night is young." Nela smiled, showing her gold grill.

"Isn't it ever?" Wes pinched the edge of her heat suit playfully.

She batted him away.

Wes smiled and pushed through the crowd in the direction she'd indicated. Guys like him couldn't get into a place like Ice unless they knew someone important or, better yet, were friendly with the ice princesses at the door. Like all decent Vegas hotspots, it was guarded by beauteous young things who knew every mover and shaker in the frozen city—along with whatever it was that happened to be moving and shaking. If they wanted to, they could tell you the secrets of the universe. But in general, they were as cold as their suits were warm. Only Nela had ever shown him anything like affection, and Wes was careful not to abuse it.

The all-glass bridge bar was the hottest place around. Ice stretched across the Sky Strip, joining a pair of casinos that afforded the best views in town. Patrons toasted with cocktails as they floated three hundred feet in the air, with nothing beneath their feet but an inch of glass. Heat suits and heat lamps kept the clients warm, but they couldn't keep the snow from collecting on the bridge, so the bar had half a dozen full-time employees tasked with shoveling snow from the floor. Their official job title was "snow manager," a moniker that never failed to make Wes chuckle, and one he constantly teased Shakes about.

Shakes spotted him and nodded in greeting, but continued to work, clearing the snow from a glass rail and tossing it to the sidewalks below.

Wes wanted to barrage him with questions but decided to play it as cool as his friend was acting. "Hey, man, how's the snow?" he asked, sliding up next to his friend.

"Cold," Shakes said, shivering in his cheap down jacket. Flaky crystals dotted his beard and eyelashes. The two of them were the only ones on the bridge not wearing heat suits or heat vests.

"But you're managing?" Wes tried to wink at his friend, but his eyelashes stuck together.

Shakes sighed. He looked far from the young, scrappy recruit Wes had met in Texas when they were both new recruits. He was thinner now, his neat goatee scruffy, and his clothes threadbare. The heavy lines on his face made it look like he hadn't smiled in a month. Wes knew the source of his friend's unhappiness, but there was nothing he could do about it. Nothing either of them could do.

"Pick up a shovel and help out, will ya?" Shakes groused. "If you can manage that."

"You know I'm not management material." All the same, Wes picked up a trowel and chipped at the ice. "So, about your text . . ."

"Give me a minute, can't be seen talking to customers, or lowlifes like you," said Shakes with a wan smile. "My shift ends in fifteen."

Wes nodded and hacked at the snow that had clumped on the side of the bar, sending it flying. Four months and now he had to wait another fifteen minutes.

He'd been working side by side with Shakes for a while when the sound of sirens filled the air. A helicopter hovered between the two towers, spraying snow and ice in every direction. A blinking casino sign failed as the sound of a car crash echoed in the distance. A portion of the Strip suddenly went dark, just as a large crowd appeared in the middle of the street. They could be anybody—casino workers, military, vets, tourists.

Wes checked his watch. It was midnight.

The protest was on.

The crowd didn't say a word, didn't scream slogans, didn't hold signs; they were a silent, moving, amorphous shape. On cue, they stopped, and when they did, the people clustered on the sidewalks and up on the sky bridges all gasped. Wes pushed closer to the bridge to see.

The mob had formed the shape of some sort of beast, only with short arms and legs that bent down the street, and a longer shape trailing down the Strip after it.

Now he could make out shadowy larger protrusions on either side, near the vacant buildings, almost as if they were . . .

Wings.

A drakon.

It was unmistakable, now that he saw it all at once, with its long body and heavy tail. The people who formed its mouth released a cloud of red dye that covered the snow in scarlet. Without making a sound, they made their message heard:

Down with the RSA!

We believe in the Blue!

The monster is real!

Wes snapped a picture and hurriedly put away his phone as the slick, smug patrons of Ice gathered by the rails to watch the commotion. But the protesters dispersed just as quickly as they'd appeared, blending back into the crowds, shedding coats and hats and swapping jackets and wigs to evade the security cameras. The entire protest lasted for just a heartbeat, then it was gone, swallowed by masses and the snow, and when the military police arrived, there was nothing to see but a plume of red in the snow, no one to arrest, as if nothing had happened at all.

Except, of course, that it had. Tomorrow, images from the protest would go viral on the nets, and similar protest mobs would spontaneously gather in streets all over the world.

Something had happened because something was happening. *Something is happening,* Wes thought. The idea occupied him as he continued shoveling his part of the bridge until Shakes tapped him on the shoulder to indicate they were done. They picked up glasses of Nutri from the bar and found an empty table. Underneath their feet, through the glass, and down thirty-two stories, they could see more patrol cars arrive. Meanwhile, the bar's heat lamps melted the icicles on the top of the rails, sending pellets of warm rain falling onto their faces.

Shakes took a big gulp from his drink and avoided Wes's eyes.

A group of kids jostled their table, spilling his drink. Wes ran his fingers through his thick brown hair in annoyance.

"Icebags," Shakes muttered as the kids shuffled past.

"All right, stop messing around," Wes said.

"What are you talking about?" Shakes looked anxious.

"You said you found Eliza. So where is she?" Wes asked, the light catching his face, illuminating a stubbled chin and chestnut bangs. "Come on, man."

"Might not be anything." Shakes scratched his goatee. "Can't be sure." He shrugged.

"Try me," Wes said, taking the drink out of Shakes's hand.

He sighed. "I mean, the guy who gave me the intel makes you look like a rocket scientist and me look like a, a—you know . . ." Shakes couldn't even think of the right word.

"An honest person?"

Finally, and probably only to get back his drink, Shakes gave it up: One of his contacts, a friend who knew Wes and Shakes were searching for Eliza, had found her name on a list of prisoners being held in a facility in El Dorado, a domed city floating on what was once the Great Salt Lake.

"El Kiss-My-Golden-Dorado." Shakes finally spat it out. "That's all I got."

Wes exhaled. Thank god. His sister was alive, and they finally knew where she was. El Dorado was a haul, but he could get there in a day; he just had to find some wheels.

"You boys want anything?" a waitress asked, stopping by their table, cocking an eyebrow and pursing her lips. She wore long golden blond extensions, a look they were calling "sylph-style."

Shakes was about to demur when Wes nodded to his friend. "Yeah. But not here."

The waitress rolled her eyes, moving on.

Wes stood up. "Come on, let's get something to eat. I got paid today." He'd waste his entire paycheck if they had more rounds of Nutri at Ice, and even Nela couldn't front them that much. "We gotta celebrate."

But Shakes didn't move and his frown deepened.

Wes slapped his friend on the shoulder. In happier times

the two often sparred, trading punches as easily as they exchanged quips, but when he slugged Shakes, the boy didn't
move, he didn't even respond. "What is it?" he asked.

"About Eliza," Shakes said, not quite meeting Wes's eyes
again.

"What's with all the drama?" Wes said. "El Dorado, I got it.
We covered this already."

Shakes bowed his head. "The list she was on that my friend
got. It was part of a job." When he saw the dark look on Wes's
face, he continued hurriedly. "You know the type—high paying, off the books, like the stuff we used to get. He didn't take
the gig, but someone else will . . ." He trailed off.

"A job?" Wes stared at him in disbelief.

Shakes shrugged.

"A *job* job? Like, one of our old ones?" Wes could feel the
adrenaline race through his body. They had been mercenaries
once, but they never took those gigs anymore. It was why
Shakes was working as a snow janitor and Wes was racing
cars to lose. Which basically made him a professional loser, a
thought that wasn't lost on him. Still, it was worth it, to get
out of the work they used to do.

"You're sure?"

"Looks that way."

"Go on," Wes said, his voice flat and toneless.

"Eliza's on a transfer list. They're moving her out to the
Red City. Which can only mean they're done with her and her
next stop's the flesh markets where she'll most likely be sold to
the temple of the white priests. And you know what they do
there: the bone charms, the unguents made from the essence

of the marked, the wigs woven from sylph hair. We don't have much time. The brass are eager to keep their hands clean on this one, so they're looking for an outside contractor. Pretty sure they would've found someone to take it by now. I mean, with that kind of payout."

Shakes sounded as miserable as Wes felt, but he kept going. "Not everyone's a hero."

5

HER HEART HEAVY AND HER ARMOR still smoking from the battle, Nat left her buried drakon and stomped through the mud toward the archway of trees that marked the gate. Pilgrims called it the Blue, but its true name was Vallonis. As Nat slipped through the gate of Afal, she entered a world where the breeze was sweet as honey, the air ripe with the scent of blossoms. Just like the first time, she was overwhelmed by the brightness of everything around her. The sun was so strong that she had to shield her eyes from the glare. Here, the sky was an eternal, endless cerulean, nothing like the perpetual gray and fog of New Vegas. Vallonis glowed with color in every soft and velvety leaf, every glorious flower, every mossy rock and pebble. It looked like pictures from the net archives, of the times before the Big Freeze.

It was paradise, and today, for the very first time, it meant nothing. *How could it? Paradise bought with the blood of my own.* Her drakon was gone; it could be dying. *And I am alone.*

The words repeated themselves on an endless loop as she walked. She hadn't gone far when a shadow fell across the forest floor.

Faix.

You are alone, he sent. Sylphs rarely bothered to communicate with spoken word. *Where is Mainas?*

"In the ground," she replied. Unlike the drakon's, Faix's voice in her head was very much an *other,* and she resisted his ability to speak directly into her consciousness.

The sylph raised a pale eyebrow. Faix was the first person she had met in Vallonis and was a member of its ruling council. He had welcomed her in the name of Queen Nineveh, the immortal mother of all the marked. Faix of the Green Island was the Queen's trusted adviser, an ageless sylph, the most beautiful boy she had ever seen. Like Liannan, he was unnaturally tall and thin, with iridescent eyes and hair the color of starlight that fell to his shoulders. Faix was the one who had gifted her with armor, who sent her on patrols, who told her which gate was under attack. He was also the one teaching her how to use her newfound power. She should really be used to him by now, but each time she met him was like the first—she was taken aback by his beauty, by the sound of his silky soft voice in her mind. *Usually.*

Just not today.

Today the sylph's beauty meant nothing. All beauty was nothing. Today was a day of blood.

"Your blade," he said aloud, a concession, since she had replied to him by conversing instead of through telepathy.

During their initial meeting, Faix had explained that there was no need to speak, since he knew what she was going to say before she said it, but Nat insisted. His voice had a different timbre when spoken—deeper and less uncomfortably intimate.

She removed her sword from its sheath and handed it to him. He narrowed his almond eyes at her before taking in the sight of the sword.

He weighed it, examining the black corroded markings on its surface where the iron cloud had hit it.

"Can you fix it?" she asked.

"Yes."

But can you fix what has wounded you? The sylph sent the words almost as quietly as she ignored him.

"Mainas was hurt badly and told me to come back here." Already she felt weaker, lesser, without her drakon. She was not complete, not without it, and when she thought of her great magnificent beast bleeding and dying in the ground, she felt the tears start to come, as if from the very center of her chest. As if her heart itself was weeping.

She said none of this to Faix, but he nodded, as impassive and implacable as ever. "A wise choice, to return. Do not weep. Vallonis will keep your drakon safe."

"It wasn't just that. It was different this time. They attacked us with an iron bomb, a new weapon, a *magical* weapon," Nat said.

"That is ill news indeed," said Faix, his lips barely moving, his eyes trained on some distant horizon.

She nodded and a wave of exhaustion overtook her. It was

too much, all of it. She wished she were already home so she could remove her armor. *Maybe that would help with this immense weight.* It was lighter than it looked but still heavier than the clothes she preferred to wear—her black jeans and boots from New Vegas, the homespun shirts she'd been given when she first came to the island. Faix had set her up in a little cottage near a river, where she had a bed and a table, a small kitchen, and a few books. "What if the enemy returns with more ships while Mainas is in the ground?" she asked.

She knew Faix had heard the real question: *What if I alone can't protect us? What if I am too weak without my drakon half? What happens then?*

He held up his hand. "The threat from the gray lands is contained for now. It will take some time for them to return with a new battalion." It was his way of acknowledging her victory on the seas today. Faix was not given to praise, only direct statement, and she tried not to let it bother her.

When she first met the sylph and was remanded to his care, Faix had cautioned her that the war was far from over, and that they should prepare for the next attack. As they sat by the fire that first night, Faix told her that the kingdom of Vallonis had many enemies throughout history, and the RSA was only its latest opponent. "Being a drakonrydder means that your life will be one of war, and your heart will forever be consumed with fire and rage."

"I understand," she had said, though she hadn't then, and wasn't sure she believed it now—even now that she had felt that rage deep within her own soul.

Faix had made her listen. He had said it again and again,

until she could practically recite the words back to him: "The place of the drakonrydder is not inside Vallonis but outside its peaceful haven, guarding the door, part of it but apart from it at the same time."

When she had only nodded, he had sighed.

"It is a terrible honor, and now it is yours."

In so many ways, Faix had been right. It was a solitary life. Nat didn't need much, but she had hoped for more from the Blue, had hoped to find a community of the marked where she belonged. Liannan had spoken of the White Mountain tribes, and the villages filled with smallfolk. A basket of food was left at Nat's door every morning, but she never even caught a glimpse of her benefactors. She understood she had to live on the outskirts, since she was the land's first and best defense, but she hoped that one day she would be able to explore and enjoy her new world. Of late, she had begun to think Faix was right. Perhaps warriors like her could never rest.

Now she thought of Wes, hunched over on the steering wheel of that car. *He didn't look like he got much rest, either.* She struggled to keep her mind focused on Faix.

"I will take you to Apis so we can report this new development to the Queen. The drakonslayer weapon is not our truth to conceal." He spoke without expression, his voice flat, and his features unreadable. Faix's perfection—his calm demeanor, his rigid posture—often unnerved her. Nat felt as if she were facing a statue, not a man.

"No," Nat said miserably. "It's not," she murmured, the howl of the wind nearly swallowing her words. The forest was cold; she longed for the sky, for her drakon. She felt trapped without her loyal steed.

"Besides, it is high time you were introduced to Nineveh and saw more of the place you are sworn to protect," Faix said slyly. "As well as the benefactors of your solitary life."

Of course.

It was his way of reminding her that her mind was open to him, that they had no secrets between them. If so, did he see her think of Wes? Faix never asked about her old life, and never asked if she was happy in this new one. He was her guide to her new life as a drakonrydder, but he was far from a friend.

"You are wrong, Anastasia. I am your friend," he said. *I am your friend and I feel the weight you carry with you now,* he sent.

She colored. "Do you?" It was one thing to be a telepath, but quite another to be rude about it.

Faix's eyes flickered in his impassive face. "I apologize," he said. "It is difficult to shut out the thoughts that I hear. I will make more of an effort not to eavesdrop in the future."

"Thank you, Faix," she said. "And like I said before, please call me Nat. Everyone does."

"I know what you are called by your intimates, but I find it is not enough for you. It is rather like the name of a small insect."

She smiled inwardly, remembering what Wes had said to her when they first met. *Nat, like the insect?*

Faix continued. "Names carry power, Anastasia Dekesthalias," he said.

But I have no power. My power is bleeding out beneath the

earth. She thought the words before she could take them back. Mainas had been certain that Vallonis would cure what ailed it, but what if it was wrong? What if it succumbed to its wounds?

Faix only shook his head. If he was listening, he didn't let on. "You must learn that in Vallonis, you have no need to disguise your strength. Names carry one's history and identity."

"Then what of yours?" Nat asked, wary of any more talk about herself or her drakon.

A hint of a smile appeared on Faix's handsome face. "I am Faix Lazaved, Messenger to the Queen. Faix was my father's name and his father's name and his father's name before him and so on until the beginning of time. We share a common name but we earn our surnames; they are titles that are determined by our talents, by the skills we have honed, the positions we have achieved."

"Is that pride I hear in your voice, Faix?" It was a rare thing for a sylph to venture any sort of personal information about himself.

"Our names *are* a source of great pride. My father was Faix Lumeras, weaver of light, and long ago, his father before him was Faix Paean, healer of wounds, and our direct ancestor was Faix Drakaras, herder of drakons."

"He was a rydder?"

"No." Faix touched the necklace he wore, a slim chain holding a small ruby-colored charm. "He was a shepherd. During the first age of Vallonis, when the mighty clans of drakonborn kept the land and waters safe."

Clans of drakonborn. She could see them for a moment, through his eyes. A blaze of drakons and their rydders, mighty and proud. People like her. But they were gone now, and she understood why his smile was sad. She was the last and the only, and right now her drakon, the last drakon, was buried in the ground, weakened by an unseen and dangerous enemy. She was all alone, and so was her drakon self.

Nat leaned against the trunk of a mighty oak, running a hand over its gnarled and knobby bark. Birds chirped in the distance, their calls echoing through the trees. The sun was rising, its first red rays casting long and elegantly dappled shadows on the forest floor, and the ache in her chest throbbed.

We are powerless now. Alone.

You didn't have to be a sylph to know that.

"Not alone, Nat," said Faix with a hint of an apologetic smile.

"You're doing it again." Nat sighed.

"And you may as well be shouting." Faix raised an eyebrow. "But even so, you must understand, you are not alone. Not even when your drakon is apart from you."

"Because I have you?" Nat said skeptically.

Faix stared at her with unblinking eyes. "Because you carry the hope of all Vallonis with you."

With that, he turned and walked deeper into the forest, and Nat followed.

You realize you just called me Nat, right?

If the sylph was listening, he didn't say a word.

6

WES DIDN'T WASTE ANY TIME MOVING
on Shakes's intel, and by morning he had arranged their transport to the golden city of El Dorado, which was a day's drive
from Vegas. When Shakes insisted on coming, Wes had tried
to talk him out of it at first.

"So maybe I got a death wish," his friend said, shrugging.
Dark circles ringed Shakes's once-bright eyes. His messy hair
fell across his forehead. Wes knew he was thinking about
Liannan.

"And maybe I have a stupid friend," Wes answered, clapping
his hand on his friend's back. After that, Wes had given up.

They were leaving that night. Sitting in a restaurant, waiting for their pickup, he hoped the meal would improve his
friend's dark mood. But not even the fact that they were eating something other than glop could put a smile on Shakes's
face. As luck would have it, Wes had been paid twice the usual
fee for racing the speedway and there were more watts than
he'd expected in his account. It appeared his bosses had enjoyed the little trick he'd pulled, the way he'd swerved and

crashed into that Lamborghini, causing the five-car pileup. Crashes made for good entertainment as long as no one got hurt, and Wes had been lucky in that respect.

The crash bonus came in handy for bribing his way to Eliza. In a matter of hours, Shakes's contact had been able to pass on a few more details—the name and exact location of the facility, and Eliza's identification number. Wes sent her information to a hacker, who was able to glean her room number and schedule. By the time dinner was over, Wes had gotten word that the hacker had also confirmed her transfer order. The transport to the Red City was scheduled for later that week.

It had been nine years since he'd seen Eliza. They were both children when she disappeared. She would be sixteen now; would she still remember him? It didn't matter. She was his only remaining family, his sister, his *twin*. He wondered what kind of life she had led, what kind of girl she had grown up to become. Her childhood hadn't been easy, she'd found her power at a young age, it had made life hard for her. Wes shrugged off his worry. It didn't matter who she had become, she was still his sister, his kin—he needed to help her.

Shakes had an all-tofu plasti-burger shoved so far into his mouth, it looked like he might choke. *You'd think the guy never saw a burger before,* Wes thought, although he himself couldn't remember the last time they'd spent the watts on one.

"Slow down, man," Wes reached for his own sandwich, "or you'll yak that mess onto the floor and they'll charge us extra to scrub out the vinyl." He grinned. "I'm sorry, I meant *manage* the vinyl."

In answer, Shakes took an even bigger bite, his cheeks

bulging chipmunklike. When he saw the look on Wes's face, he laughed through his food and spit a chunk on his plate.

Wes shook his head as he bit into his own plasti-burger. But he was glad he'd splurged on the burgers. It was good to see Shakes laughing. There hadn't been a lot of occasions to laugh lately. They'd been evicted twice in the last four months and were currently living in a ramshackle trailer outside the Strip, stealing power from the grid to heat and light their home, but it was only a matter of time before they'd get busted and kicked out again. With the sudden and unexpected recession crippling the local economy, the credits Nat had paid them for the trip to the Blue hadn't lasted as long as he'd hoped. While Wes was scraping together a few watts racing, tourist season would be over soon and the track would close.

More darkness on the Strip.

Shakes put his burger down. Wes could tell he wanted to talk about Liannan and the Blue, and Wes just didn't want to go there. Thinking about the Blue made him think of Nat and thinking of Nat made his stomach twist. He couldn't keep the image of her from his mind. Nat astride her drakon, her green eyes flashing, looking dangerous and beautiful, and he missed her so much. So he kept his feelings buried deep inside and he didn't want to hear his friend talk about his own. To be silent and miserable together was enough.

"They're dead, you know," Shakes said suddenly. "They have to be. I can't believe Liannan would just . . ."

Wes was alarmed at the level of his despair. "No—no. We'll find them. We will. Especially now that we've got the watts. After we get Eliza, we'll—"

"Nah. I'm done hoping. You know what they say . . . gone longer than a month and god knows what's been done to them. If they were taken, they're dead, and we failed them."

"You don't know that." Wes tried to console him, but there was no use. He needed comfort himself. He took a second bite of plasti-burger and looked away. The diner was a far cry from the fancy bar where Shakes worked. There were no clear glass walls or glass floor, no snow concierges to make sure a dusting of powder didn't fall into your cocktail. The place had a roof that leaked and walls patched with crooked sheet metal. It was the kind of nondescript place frequented by runners like them; the restaurant had no identifying markers, no signs out front, no lights that you could see from the outside. It looked like an abandoned building, a disguise that worked well for its patrons.

Wes and Shakes weren't exactly wanted men, but they weren't always legitimate hardworking citizens, either, so they kept a low profile. As far as he could tell, no one knew that his team had been on Nat's side when the Pacific fleet sunk beneath the black waters. Make that *almost* no one. There were slavers out there who worked for the RSA and knew what really happened. Wes guessed he was safe in New Vegas for now, but he wasn't taking any chances, not when he was planning another grab-and-go job, this time from a military hospital prison. He finished his burger, fumbling for his napkin.

"We'll find them," he said, trying to sound confident.

Shakes nodded but didn't answer.

Wes checked his watch. "Our ride should be here by now. Wait till you see it." He hoped a familiar face might cheer them both up.

They picked up their trays and stumbled through the darkness of the diner, Shakes knocking into a table on their way out. Did they really need to keep the place so dark? Paranoia drove the hunted to extremes—there was no limit to what runners would do to stay undercover. Wes had seen some pretty bad plastic surgery and dye jobs on a couple of their colleagues.

Shakes opened the door and the two of them huddled in the cold for a while. "He said he'd be here by now," Wes muttered.

"Who? Prince Charming?" Shakes stamped his feet in the snow.

"More or less," Wes sighed.

A few minutes later a vintage white stretch limousine pulled up to the curb. It was a behemoth, a boat, like one of those old ocean cruisers, from when people still took vacations on the sea. The car was a relic, most likely rebuilt half a dozen times, the body made from flimsy white plastic, but through the front window he could see it had black leather seats, and the engine purred.

Shakes snickered when the limo stopped in front of them. "Let me guess. This monstrosity is our ride to El Dorado?"

"You're welcome," replied Wes, feigning hurt.

The front window rolled down to reveal the smiling mug of one Farouk Jones, a member of their former crew and fellow survivor of the battle of the black water. The kid held a screen in one hand and the steering wheel in the other. The loud beats of a reggae mash-up thumped from his headphones. He was listening to music, playing a video game, and driving all at the same time. Typical Farouk.

Farouk's long, thin face broke into a huge grin. "You guys call a cab?" he asked, getting out to open the back door for his friends. When they'd returned to New Vegas after ferrying Nat to the Blue, it had been difficult for Wes to get work for his crew, and so after a few weeks kicking around waiting, Farouk left, taking a job as a casino driver. At thirteen, he had the battle-hardened face of a thirty-year-old and the temperament of a kid not older than nine. He brushed back a face full of dreads as he opened the door.

Wes pushed into the backseat, Shakes nudging him aside as he shoved in behind him. The door slammed and the limo pulled out, music blaring, Farouk spinning the wheel to avoid almost colliding with a pedestrian. He turned around and his smile faded. "What's with the long faces? Just you two? Where's the pretty lady and my bros?" he asked. The last time they'd seen him was a month ago, when the team was still intact and Liannan, Brendon, and Roark were still part of it.

Shakes remained silent as he sprawled on the backseat with his hat on his face, and Wes also ignored Farouk's question. He ran a hand across the leather seat. Luxuries of this sort were rare these days; even his Mustang from the racetrack didn't have this sort of juice. "Who owns this white elephant?" he asked. "Must be a big shot if he can pay for the gas."

"Nope, this thing runs on electric, man, and the casino bosses pay for everything," Farouk said. "Like I told you on the phone, I run daily routes between the El Dorado domes and the Strip, sometimes Ho Ho City if we have an armed escort. Everyone's leaving New Veg, what with the casino wars and now with the protests, the place is a mess. Wait till we get to the domes. Good stuff. Hot in there for sure. Chicks in bikinis even." He winked. "Talk about domes."

"Which nobody was," Shakes groused, rattling empty bottles in the minibar.

"Sounds like paradise," Wes joked, kicking his legs up to the seat while Shakes poked around, rooting for treats. "This ride have any heat, vids, tunes?"

Farouk bobbed in his seat, his fingers running across the stream on the screen, playing some video game Wes couldn't see. He was the youngest of Wes's former team members and a know-it-all. He could fly or drive anything and was better on the nets than any other kid they'd worked with. "Yeah, this baby's fully loaded, but you need a key card to turn on the goodies. That's why I carry portables. Gotta ride in the cold and can't use the toys. I don't even get to chauffeur the bigwigs. My job is to drive the cars back to El Dorado after I drop off the tourists." Farouk adjusted the rearview mirror as the enormous New Vegas perimeter came into view. "Fence is coming up, you guys know what to do."

Wes and Shakes made for the trunk, pulling down the seat and clambering into the dark space, then pushing the seats back into place. The casino bosses paid the right bribes, so the hotel logo on the side door meant they were waved through the checkpoint without a word.

"Might as well be invisible." Farouk beamed. "Like I'm not even here."

"Yeah? That pickup line work for you?" Wes asked as he edged his way out of the trunk and climbed back into his seat.

"Man, this whole ride is my pickup line," Farouk said, snapping his fingers.

"This ride is your pickup *truck*," Shakes said. "Only not as nice."

But they were relieved to scramble back into their seats as the car pulled away.

So far, so good. But getting out of the city was only the first step. Wes still had to figure out a way to get *into* El Dorado. The holes in his plan were big enough to fly a drakon through, but there was no use worrying the boys right now. He would figure things out as he went; he always did. He always had.

I'm not going to let Eliza down now.

The roads heading north toward Salt Lake were white with snow, stark and gleaming against the black lines made by the cars ahead. Traffic was infrequent, the sky gray, the air white and alive with snowy flakes. But in the distance Wes glimpsed patches of green—a sight that might have been unthinkable a few years back. The world was changing, little by little. Whether the earth was coming alive again because the Blue was spreading as Liannan said, he didn't know, but he hoped she was right. Maybe once all the lights went out in every casino in New Vegas and every city in the RSA, they would be able to see the stars again. A new world could begin. He smiled. One trip on the black ocean had turned him into a pilgrim, but unlike many, he had actually seen Nat's drakon, had seen the Blue with his own eyes. The world was changing, whatever that meant. He just hoped to live long enough to see it happen.

As they drove, the only noise came from Farouk's head-phones, a small tinny sound. Wes was used to the rowdy camaraderie of soldiers, of blasting music, screeching punk-metal-rap mash-ups, the blaring of video games, Shakes laughing; he found the quiet downright depressing.

Apparently he wasn't the only one who thought so.

The limo suddenly braked hard, making both Wes and Shakes lurch forward. Farouk swung his arm over the seat and turned to them, annoyance written all over his face. "You two going to tell me what's wrong or am I going to have to dump you on the side of the road? Come on, spill."

"You trying to kill us?" Shakes rubbed his head where he'd hit the window.

"Yes. Kill you, and then talk to you." Farouk looked at them expectantly.

"It's Liannan and the boys," Wes said finally. Because in a way, it was. It was Nat, of course, and Eliza. But as far as Farouk needed to know, it was also the issue of their comrades, the rest of their crew—the beautiful sylph who was Shakes's girlfriend and the pair of smallmen, Brendon Rimmel and Roark Goderson. Everyone was gone now.

"I knew it." Farouk slapped the steering wheel. "Where the ice are they?"

"That's the thing. We don't know. They just disappeared one day. We don't even know if they're dead or alive. That's what's wrong."

As he said it, Wes just wished it was the only thing.

7

NAT HAD TO RUN TO CATCH UP TO Faix. His footfalls made only the softest sounds—not because he was weightless, but because his every step was carefully considered. He stepped *over* twigs and leaves, never cracking a fallen branch or crunching leaves under his feet. She felt like a large, lumbering fool next to him. It was as if time passed more slowly for him, allowing him to choreograph his every movement with graceful and delicate balance, to ponder every word before he spoke. Nat remembered how Liannan had been able to walk across the water. The sylphs were gifted: quick, light, living in harmony with the world around them.

In comparison, Nat might as well be made of mud.

But she followed in his shadow, trying to stay close. He was moving quickly, leaping over rocks and logs like a gazelle. It reminded her of Wes. Fast-moving, quick-thinking Wes, who only had his wits and good humor to help him survive the cold. She missed them all—Shakes with his jolly demeanor, Liannan's warmth, Brendon's and Roark's staunch loyalty, Farouk with his wide-eyed enthusiasm for the world.

Wes had promised to return to her, but it was difficult, somehow, to picture him, in his worn fatigues, gun belt slung low on his hips, with that sardonic smile on his handsome face, accepting the somewhat mystical nature of Vallonis. What would he think of Faix, she wondered, and his ability to read minds?

Nat . . .

A faint voice echoed through the forest.

Nat . . .

"Did you hear that?" she asked.

Faix turned around and shook his head.

Perhaps it was Wes? But it wasn't. She knew the sound of his voice. She wished she knew how they had been able to see each other earlier, so she could do it again. Nat decided to ignore the voice for now. Maybe it had just been an echo.

They came to the edge of the forest and Faix pointed to the distance, where a tall white city floated high in the air, casting a deep shadow over the land, hovering above sandstone cliffs that seemed to reach toward it but just stopped short of meeting its foundation. "When the city was called Atlantis, it floated above the ocean. During the second age, it was called Avalon and its walls were hidden in the mist. In Avalon's Mirror, a relic from that age, we can see the past and sometimes a hint of the future. This is Apis, our city in the sky, and it is more splendid than any incarnation before it. It is the home of our queen and her court."

Nat marveled at the city of stone high up above the clouds, defying gravity, defying reality. *But how?* she thought, knowing Faix would answer.

He gestured at the great empty expanse of nothingness below and around the city. "Those in the gray world only see emptiness, but here in the Blue, there is no such thing as a void. Your scientists call it the dark matter of the universe, that which does not reflect light and cannot be touched or sensed, but is nevertheless real. Your world also calls it 'magic,' but I assure you the ether is as solid as the ground we stand upon. Our power comes from being able to use and control that invisible matter. We harness the power of the ether, of the very wind that bends the tree, the force that tosses leaves into the air. You've used this power your whole life. You used it when you were three years old and you pushed that little boy across the living room."

It didn't surprise her that he knew about her past, but it was still disconcerting to hear it spoken about so casually.

Yes, I've known about this power, but not how to control it, she thought.

"This is why you are here now, why I must teach you," he replied. "The people of Vallonis are able to channel this power to their will. We call it 'sculpting the void.' Weavers use the ether to make illusions, to manipulate reality, while others use it to move objects or to render themselves invisible. Along with the ability to create fire, drakonrydders are usually gifted with what your world calls telekinesis, hence your ability to move things without touching them. You have the ability to learn other skills as well as honing the ones you already possess."

Other skills . . . what other skills?

This time Faix's smile was wide and full. "With the power of the ether at your command, you can do anything you can imagine. We are artists of the unseen. Like any art, you must possess raw talent, but you must also practice. Our medium is the ether; our tools are our minds. We sculpt with our imagination, our thoughts. This task requires a strong will and a clear mind. In Vallonis, to be marked means we are blessed by the ether. We use it to build, to create, to imagine a different world from the one we know. If we do not exercise our power, if we do not use it correctly, we suffer, like you suffered." Pain flashed on his face for the briefest moment.

As I know you suffer now, Faix sent.

The doctors had made her believe the mark was a curse, and the flame on her chest was a symbol that nearly cost her life many times. Nat had been frightened and ashamed of her power; it had warped her, it had filled her thoughts with helplessness and destruction, but now she understood the source of that rage. It was the passion of an artist unable to paint, a poet unable to write. Denied a true understanding of the gift she'd been born with, she was unable to express her power, and so she had turned it inward, and lived with anger in her soul.

She had been groping in the dark, but now, looking at that tall white city suspended in the sky, Nat felt as if she had stepped into the light at last.

8

IF FAROUK WANTED A STORY, HE WAS going to get one. Wes started talking and didn't stop—almost as if he couldn't. He began with the part that Farouk already knew, about how when the team had returned to New Vegas from the Blue, they found the city taken over by the military.

It had been dangerous for anyone who looked like Liannan, Brendon, or Roark to move around in daylight. The beautiful Liannan had disguised her golden hair with dye and her violet eyes with contacts, but it was harder for the smallmen to conceal their nature. Since they couldn't stay anywhere legally, Wes decided it was safer for them to squat in one of the old burned-out casinos, where they could blend in with the junkies, homeless vets, and burnouts. No one was supposed to live in the abandoned towers, but hundreds occupied it anyway. The place used to be one of the casino's fabulous penthouses, and although it was dirty and abandoned, it still had working lights powered by stolen electricity, a kitchen with a real stove, and enough insulation to keep out the worst of the cold. It wasn't the best way to live but it was far from the worst; there was a room for each couple, and Wes didn't mind sleeping on the ratty couch next to the kitchen. If Wes and Shakes had to work outside the city for a couple of days, they hired runners to send supplies to the suite.

It wasn't exactly a home, but it was something like it. Given the circumstances, it was their own imperfect paradise. Some days were harder than others; Roark and Brendon started to catch a little cabin fever, and once in a while Wes would find them up on the roof. He told them to knock it off, someone would see them and report them, but they kept doing it. One day they finally showed him why they were up there. Wes couldn't believe it at first. The smallmen had rigged a tent to make a sort of greenhouse, and in the boxed garden they had planted turnips, squash, cabbage, and carrots from seeds Liannan kept from the Blue.

Small magic indeed, Wes marveled. That anything could thrive in Vegas was nothing short of a miracle. The toxic floods had poisoned the entire planet, and there were compounds in the water that no filter could clean. It was why everyone drank Nutri—the "nutrition" process countered the worst effects of the toxins with chemical vitamins. But up here, on an abandoned rooftop, a garden was growing.

More than just a garden began to flourish. Wes missed Nat, but he had his friends, and that was something. Liannan would sing, Shakes cooked, and Brendon and Roark would always find something during their scavenger hunts around the abandoned hotel—little treasures like a bar of chocolate or a bottle of wine from a forgotten minifridge. Every so often a flock of brightly colored birds would arrive at their windowsill at dawn, with offerings of fruit for Liannan. Animals of all kinds were devoted to the sylph. Wes still remembered the taste of the fruit they brought—tart and fresh and unlike anything he'd ever eaten before—real fruit, not grown in the domes or under a heat lamp. Liannan said the birds and the fruit meant that life was returning to the gray lands. Wes knew more than anything how badly she wanted to believe that.

Then one day it was over, as suddenly as it had all begun. Wes and Shakes had been running a weekend job over in Little Tijuana, and when they returned to the suite, their friends were gone. There was no evidence of a scuffle—no blood, no footprints or bullet casings. Nothing. The suite was just as they had left it. Neat. Tidy. The garden was the same. No smashed tents, no planters turned over, no sprouts or seedlings uprooted. Wes thought they might have gone out for a walk, but Shakes was worried.

They waited for them to come back. Maybe the others had gone on a scavenger hunt in the hotel; they did that sometimes. But night came, and still they didn't return. It was eerie and quiet, and Wes began to get a really bad feeling that Shakes was right, that their friends had been stolen.

When they didn't return the next day or the next, Shakes went on a rampage, up and down the tower, kicking down every door, pummeling neighbors with questions. He suspected that one of their runners had turned on them, that the MPs caught one of them making a supply run to their squat. There was no way to be certain.

They searched every port they could, called up every favor, every shady connection in Garbage Country and beyond, but it was as if their friends had disappeared into thin air. No one had seen them anywhere, on any ship or any list of prisoners or refugees. Not even at the morgue.

Maybe they'd left, maybe they'd had enough of the crew, of New Vegas, of the two of them. Who knew? But Wes couldn't believe they would just abandon them without a word or a note. Even so, he didn't know what to think.

It was hard to make sense of—and even harder to speak of, usually—but today, when Farouk had asked, Wes couldn't shut himself up. As if he had done something to drive them away, as if these were his sins to confess.

Wes told Farouk everything in a quiet monotone, while Shakes kept his hat on his face and remained silent. They missed the little guys, and losing Liannan had hit Shakes the hardest, of course—seeing as the sylph was the closest thing he had ever known to love—but in his own way, Wes was just as bereft. Liannan was their last link to the Blue, and to Nat. Sometimes Wes thought the journey over the ocean was just a dream, that he had made it all up, but Liannan was living proof that Nat was real. Having the sylph on his crew gave him hope that he would find his way back to the Blue and see Nat again. But that hope vanished when he lost his friends.

"That's messed up, man," Farouk said, sighing heavily. He didn't ask any more questions. Wes could only imagine how his friend was now regretting having forced the story out of him.

"Yeah, well," Wes grunted. Because really, what else was there to say?

At least he had a chance, however slim, to save Eliza. If he couldn't be with Nat, if he couldn't find his crew or his friends, at least he could do what he could to save his only sister. The information he had was solid, but the odds of success were still long. When he was a runner for the casino bosses, there'd been unlimited resources at his fingertips, money for bribes, inside contacts. On his own, Wes had a few watts and two soldiers. He was counting on his luck and wits to come through.

So she was being held in a RSA hospital. Where had she been all these years? He'd always assumed she'd been taken because she was marked, but he wasn't sure. His memory of the night she was kidnapped was fuzzy at best. Wes wasn't sure he even wanted to know.

He just wanted her back, like everyone and everything else that had been taken from him.

From all of us.

He tried to put the image of the crowd surging into the form of the drakon out of his mind. He wasn't Nat. He wasn't here to save the world, or even New Vegas. He wasn't a hero. He was just some kid who grew up in the casinos, someone who lived on the scraps and the leftovers.

Just get the job done. In and out. Like the old days. As if anything was the same as it was then.

Wes closed his eyes and tried not to think at all.

They'd been driving for a few hours when Farouk stopped the car again. "Flood," he said, annoyed. "Come on, help me get the chains on." The snow had melted into a giant puddle in the middle of the road.

Wes and Shakes got out of the car and helped Farouk rig

the wheels with a couple of rusty chains. As the car churned slowly across the slush, Wes asked Shakes if he ever wondered where the ice came from.

"My ass." Shakes snorted.

"I'm being serious. You never thought about it?"

"He thinks about his ass all the time, man. This is Shakes you're talkin' about." Farouk was enjoying the conversation.

"What do you mean?" asked Shakes, in a surly tone. "It got hot, then it got cold. Second Ice Age. Duh."

Wes rolled his eyes. He knew the facts like any kid in the RSA. It was 111 C.D., one hundred and eleven years after the Catastrophic Disaster destroyed the earth and wiped out 99 percent of humanity. Global warming supposedly melted the polar ice caps and caused ocean temperatures to drop dramatically, and the massive earthquakes and tremendous blizzards that followed were similar to the severe cold spell that occurred in the last Ice Age, almost ten thousand years ago. The Big Freeze turned oceans into sheets of glass and buried cities under impenetrable layers of ice.

And now here they were.

Wes shook his head. "Yeah, that's what they say, but it happened so fast, you know? And it's just a theory. The world ended and that's what everyone knows; no one cares about the reasons anymore, no one cares how the end of the world began."

"So?"

Wes guessed his friend wasn't in the mood to ponder the universe, but he kept pressing. "Don't you wonder? Don't you want to know?"

"No. Staying alive and staying warm sort of gets in the way of a lot of 'wonder.'"

Wes looked from Shakes to Farouk, who only shrugged. "Don't look at me, I just drive the car."

Wes didn't respond, knowing Shakes was impossible to talk to when his mood was this bleak, and Farouk couldn't care less about the world beyond New Vegas.

"Remember what Liannan told us," Shakes said finally. "She said it was happening in her world, too, everything breaking down. Magic was supposed to return to this world, but something is, I don't know, blocking it."

"And she unblocked it for you?" Farouk winked into the rearview mirror. Wes glared at him.

"Her people sent her out so she could find the source of the corruption." Shakes shrugged. "Maybe that's where she is now."

"So she just up and left?" Farouk looked skeptical.

Wes thought about it. Anything was possible. Maybe Shakes was right. Maybe Liannan had decided it was time to pursue her quest again and had taken off before Shakes could talk her into staying with him.

But there was no more time to wonder about it anymore, because Farouk whistled from the front seat. "Heads up, kids, we're here." Over the rise, a collection of domes looking like bubbles over water glinted in the failing sunlight. Salt Lake was the last liquid lake in North America, as the toxic salt in its depths naturally lowered the freezing temperature of the water, and El Dorado's developers also kept the lake pumped full of antifreeze to keep it liquid.

Why fill a poisoned lake with more poison? Wes didn't get it, but the developers were quite proud of their achievement. Brochures touted its rarity. *Live above the water, away from the snow! Live the old life, pretend the ice never came!* The developers christened it El Dorado, after the mythic lost city of gold, and had given their domes a golden tint, but to the consternation of its wealthy inhabitants, most people called it Soda Pop City, after the lake waters that bubbled and fizzed softly underneath the domes.

As they approached the bridge that led to the first dome, Farouk shifted in his seat. "We're on the manifest, right? You guys can't hide in the trunk this time. They'll comb this limo with a laser. Dorado security don't mess around; they'll fire if we don't have the creds. This place is locked up tighter than your mama's ass."

"Leave my mother out of it," said Wes, bemused. "Your ride's legit, what are you worried about, man? It's no problem, we have it handled—right, Shakes?" He nudged his friend.

Shakes shrugged. "Don't know, boss, you took care of the bribes and logs, right?"

Wes nodded. "Smooth as this limo's cheap plastic doors. I got our suits in my bag. We'll be on the manifest. It cost us, but we should have no problem at the checkpoint." It sounded good, and for a minute, Wes almost believed it himself.

Farouk seemed satisfied with the answer and didn't ask further questions; nor did Shakes. They trusted him, which made Wes feel even worse. He hated lying to his guys. It was the one thing he had sworn never to do, but in truth, he hadn't had the watts to pay the required bribes. He was counting on the limo providing enough cover to get them through the door, where he could sweet-talk his way in like he always did. He was hoping the guards would cut Farouk some slack since he ran this route nearly every day.

Those were a whole lot of ifs.

It was a long shot, but Eliza would be gone if he'd spent another month working the races, trying to earn enough for the bribes. If he'd waited, most likely she'd already have been sold to the temple, to the High Priestess who, it was rumored, fed on blood of the marked, sucking all the life force out of them for her own immortality. And if Eliza was dead on top of all of this—leaving Nat, losing Roark, Brendon, and Liannan—there would be nothing left for him.

Wes had to trust his fate to chance, and hope his luck wouldn't fail him. And then that he wouldn't fail everyone else.

9

LEAVING THE FOREST BEHIND, NAT stepped toward the cliffs that led into the clouds where the white city began. There were stairs carved into the rock leading upward. *Where is everybody?* she wondered. There was nobody on the stairs. This was the capital of Vallonis and yet she and Faix were the only two people at its entrance.

There are other ways into the city, but everyone must come through this entrance the first time he or she approaches Apis, Faix sent, as if he were merely a piece of her mind that contained knowledge she did not yet have access to. *You will travel this route only once.*

They started to climb. A soft breeze blew. Birds fluttered in the great void beneath the city. The blue- and red-winged creatures looked familiar, like the birds that came to her on the black ocean when she was alone with Wes in a cargo container on the slave ship.

She climbed, eyes downcast, focusing on the steps, careful not to trip or lose her balance. She had no thought but not to fall, and even her telepathic conversation with Faix ceased.

After what felt like a long and arduous hike, she felt the air getting colder, and when she looked up, she saw that they were nearing the top and that the city was coming into view. The stairs terminated in a great promontory, a stone outcropping that extended outward from the cliff to the gates of the city.

Nat walked right up to the edge and stopped. There was a gap of about ten feet between the cliff and the doorway to the city. It was too far to leap across.

She turned to look at Faix, who had been walking behind her, but he wasn't there—and when she looked across, he was standing at the doorway, underneath the stone archway, his bright hair almost as white as the city stone.

"How did you do that?" Nat frowned. She was fairly certain she didn't want to know the answer, whatever it was.

"Simple. Just walk across."

"Yeah, right." She looked at the great chasm below. She had once leapt from a hospital window, falling many stories without injury. She had flown on the drakon's back, had soared at greater heights than these. She was not afraid of heights, but something about the gap made her hesitate.

"Walk across the bridge, Nat," said Faix. "Every pupil of mine has succeeded in doing so."

"But I'll fall. There's nothing there."

"It only looks like there is nothing," he said. "You must walk on the ether, must command it to hold you upright. One cannot simply enter the city; the city must admit you. To prove you are worthy of Apis, you must step upon the ether and cross the void."

"A leap of faith."

Faix nodded. "So it appears."

"But if I fall, I'll die."

"You will not fall if you believe you can cross." He stared at her for a moment and tapped his chin. "There is a story from your world, a tale of a king who conquered a land and wished to know its people. He wanted to understand their customs, what they would and would not do. He asked about their burial practices. He asked what sum he must pay to induce his new subjects to eat the bodies of their dead. *No sum*, the people said. Their dead were burned. They could not imagine consuming the flesh of their mothers and fathers. This same king asked the opposite question of the barbarian tribesmen that lived outside the kingdom. How much must I pay you to *burn* your dead? *No sum*, the barbarians said. In their culture, they consumed the flesh of their dead. To burn the flesh of their loved ones was inconceivable."

Nat saw the images Faix was sending her, of two ancient peoples and their revulsion for each other's death rites. The dead that were burned and the dead that were eaten.

"Do you understand? The two cultures, the 'civilized' people and the so-called 'barbarians,' understood their world in completely different ways. You and I suffer a similar misunderstanding. In the gray lands, your people see the material world, the things you touch, the possessions you collect. But in Vallonis, we see the ether, the void. We do not build cars and ships, guns and planes. We build music and theory, ideas and visions, all crafted from the ether. To enter Vallonis, you must believe that the ether, the void, the nothingness, that which you cannot see, is as real as a table or a chair. Trust in your power, Nat, and enter Vallonis." He held out his hand. "Take your place as a member of the Queen's Council, a citizen of the White City."

But instead of stepping forward, Nat took a step back, fear and doubt on her face. "I can't. I'm not one of you. Where I come from, nothing is nothing. I'll fall."

"You will not. You must shape the ether into a walkway. Imagine it into being and it will be as sturdy as the stone steps that you stand on. Trust me. Learn to live in Vallonis."

"Do you eat your dead here?" she asked. "Who is the civilized man and who is the barbarian—the one who takes the leap or the one who does not?"

Faix stared at her, unblinking. *No one has ever asked me that, young Nat. You have the mind of a drakonrydder. Within and without.*

"That's not an answer," Nat said, crossing her arms.

Faix sighed. "From our perspective, yours is the cruder sensibility. A world that only trusts in what can be seen feels very vulgar to us."

"Why am I not surprised?" Nat raised an eyebrow.

"I understand that from your point of view, a world that prizes what is unseen might seem primitive and backward, like the people in your world who believe in nonsense such as astrology. I hope to show you that our world is rich in intellect and history, that there is reason and logic in our 'magic.'"

Nat looked down at the gap again. Wind whistled across her face. At this particular moment, she wished to be anywhere else in the world. *Even under the world,* she thought, *with my drakon.*

That would be safer for me than this.

But here she was.

She looked up at Faix. "If I were to try—and I'm not saying I am—how would I start? A little help, here?"

"Picture the water that fills the glass, instead of the glass that holds the water. See the shape of nothingness, feel the presence of the void."

Nat shook her head. She didn't understand. She didn't know how. Her power was unpredictable, uncontrollable. She looked across to the open doorway where Faix stood. There was light beyond, and people, the sounds of a market, the chatter of a crowd, laughter. She had come so far from that living room in Ashes, from her first trip into Garbage Country and her stay at MacArthur.

She had flown upon the back of the drakon, but this simple step, this leap of faith, was an even greater hurdle. Faix had taught countless pupils like her, and each one had been able to accomplish this step.

So what am I so afraid of?

The air? The gap? Falling? Oblivion?

She stared across the void, trying to sort out the chaos in her mind.

No. She did not fear the air or the gap. The risk of falling from the sky, of sudden death, those possibilities were with her always. Those were familiar fears, almost comforting ones. At least, consistent.

What is it, then?

She stared across the void until she knew the answer.

She feared Vallonis itself, feared that she was not worthy

to join a world she had spent her whole life searching for. She was anxious about finally meeting the great Queen Nineveh. She was afraid of disappointing her.

What if the city did not allow her admittance? What if she was left outside forever?

What if her search had been meaningless, after all?

Nat looked at the void, tried to will the ether into some shape—a bridge, or a wooden plank—but nothing happened. She tried again. And again. And again. Sweat glistened on her brow. Her legs felt heavy, her fingers tingled, then became numb, her eyes twitched. She tried again. Nothing happened. Long minutes passed. Faix reached out to her mind but she pushed him away, silenced him. She had to do this on her own.

She had to clear her thoughts, to take control, but her head throbbed with resentment and confusion. With dark memories of her past, and an aching sadness at parting from Wes. With endless anxiety, even guilt, about her drakon.

I am made of shadow and unsettled darkness.

There is nothing so steady as a bridge inside of me.

Nat looked across the gap at the warm light, the people, the city beyond, everything so close and yet so very far away. The beautiful queen she had never met, but only glimpsed in Faix's memories and thoughts. She belonged in Apis, she only had to believe it to make it true, but she couldn't.

The fear was too great.

10

IN THE BACKSEAT OF THE WHITE limousine, Wes had changed into a cheap black suit with fake heat buttons; Shakes wore a similar getup. He tossed Shakes a pair of mirrored sunglasses like his own and peered anxiously at the narrow one-laned bridges as the gold domes loomed in the windshield. The pair of bridges extended from the mainland to the domes and back, like a pair of tendrils floating above the water. They were the only way into and out of the floating city of El Dorado.

Shakes turned to him. "You all right, boss? You're pale."

Wes grunted. "It's cold. What do you want?"

Shakes studied him. "Screw you 'it's cold.' Like I don't see your face every day you freeze your ass off back home. You paid the data hacks, right? Manifests are good? What, you think we might've been ripped off?"

Wes could never keep anything from Shakes. His friend knew something was up. "Maybe," he finally admitted. *Maybe we'll get out of this alive, or maybe we won't, because maybe we're not on any manifest and maybe I haven't paid anyone off.*

"Maybe, huh." Shakes sighed, knowing that Wes's "maybe" meant he hadn't been able to bribe anyone and they were headed toward disaster. "And maybe you're a bigger idiot than I thought."

"I find that hard to believe, after all this time." Wes raised a finger to his lips. He didn't want to have this conversation with Farouk, not yet. He glanced up front. "Slow it down, Farouk. Let's not look too eager."

Farouk hit the brakes and the limo skidded to a stop.

Wes grabbed the side of the car. "Easy, man, try not to look scared, either. Take it slow. Cool. You've done this a hundred times, right?"

"Yeah, yeah, no sweat," Farouk said, picking up the speed, trying to drive as normally as possible. "A hundred times before I was dumb enough to bring you two iceholes." He shook his dreadlocks at them.

Snow blew in waves across the lake, sending ripples drifting toward the causeway's concrete pillars. Red bubbles rose to the lake's surface, gathering and popping. Wes thought the gurgling water looked like his stomach felt: anxious and boiling.

"Like I said, a little slower," he said, trying to postpone the inevitable as much as he could, but the limo was already at the dome's entryway, right at the golden arch.

"Like I said, make up your mind already," Farouk groused.

The shiny half loop of gold-plated steel glistened, its surface newly polished. Guards flanked the arch in front of the checkpoint, weapons raised, robo-hounds held back by leashes. El Dorado was a paradise for those who could pay to get inside—Vallonis for the wealthy. The people of El Dorado didn't suffer from military raids or eat processed glop; here in the domed cities, they could pretend the apocalypse had never happened. Who wouldn't want that?

"Boss," Shakes said, nudging him. "Boss."

"A minute," Wes said, trying to figure out what he would say once the guards asked for his ID and told Farouk they weren't on the manifest.

"You need to look at this," Shakes said, pointing to the tip of the dome.

A plume of black smoke drifted from the far side of the golden hemisphere. Cracks appeared across the face of its glass shield.

"Damn. What is that?" Wes fumbled for his field binoculars. "Looks like they're venting smoke." Enclosures needed an exhaust system; otherwise a simple fire could clog the dome with smoke and threaten the lives of everyone inside.

Wes lowered the binoculars.

They were next at the guardhouse. One of the soldiers raised his weapon; the robo-dogs howled. The limo slowed to a stop. A security officer wearing a crisp white shirt, red tie, and blue blazer with a gold dome embroidered on the pocket stepped out of the booth, radio in hand and dark glasses on his face as he approached the front window.

"Hey, man, where's Rolf?" Farouk asked, handing over his ID.

The security guard tipped his hat, gestured back toward the booth. His radio buzzed and he put the receiver in his ear, nodding as he listened.

"Passengers?" he asked.

"Casino bosses from the Loss. They should be on the manifest," Farouk said, offering the fake IDs Wes had given him earlier.

The guard nodded and studied the IDs, radioing in their names.

Wes looked from the guard to the dome and back to Farouk. Smoke continued to pour out of the vent, creating black clouds around the dome. More guards appeared, surrounding the limo, listening to headsets, hands pressed to their earpieces.

Something was happening. Someone screamed, and the guards whipped around, watching smoke billow out of the entryway.

"Repeat, I need clearance for a Dr. Jekyll and a Mr. Hyde," the guard said into his radio, waiting.

Shakes rolled his eyes. Wes tried not to smile. They were two of his favorite aliases. No one read books anymore, so no one would get the joke.

The guard's radio buzzed.

"Turn around," he said. "Turn around, the domes are closed for today." He made a spinning motion with his index finger, indicating the act of turning the limo in a circle.

"Are you serious? I can't turn this beast around." Farouk gestured to the limo.

"Turn around now." The guard stepped back, a hand resting on the grip of his sidearm.

In the distance, sirens boomed, and red and blue strobe lights reflected off the dome. Wes turned around to see as emergency vehicles approached from behind, blocking the causeway. Even if Farouk could turn around, the fire trucks and ambulances were blocking the bridge. There was no going back. A convoy of high-tech Humvees carrying armed soldiers rolled behind them as well.

Why would a fire draw military vehicles? Something else was happening, something bigger than a crack in the dome and a plume of smoke.

Maybe something as big as a drakon on the streets of New Vegas, Wes thought. *Something unstoppable.*

"Come on, man, I'll get in trouble if I don't deliver," Farouk said, pleading with the guard.

The guard shook his head. "Pull to the side, please."

Farouk sighed, shifted the car into drive, and angled the limo to the right. "Bad luck, boss," he said. "Looks like no one's getting into Dorado today."

"We'll wait it out," Wes said. "Try again when they open back up."

"There's a way station not too far—I guess we can stay there. Godfreezeit, I was looking forward to the domes," Farouk replied.

They watched as the conclave of emergency and military vehicles made their way inside, when a group of guards suddenly surrounded the limousine, and the young security officer led the pack, holding his gun. "Out of the car," he yelled over the sirens. "Out of the car now!"

"What the ice?" Farouk cursed and shot an accusatory glance at Wes.

"Out of the car!" the guard ordered.

"Stay in the limo," Wes growled, picking up his own weapon.

Farouk rolled down the window. "What's this about?"

"Your passengers aren't on any manifest. No one's expecting them. Out of the car now."

"No way, man. It's a mistake. Ask your people to check the roster again. Can you get Rolf out here? The man knows me. Help me out—you know I'm going to lose my job if I don't drop off these iceholes. Come on, man."

"Hold on," the security officer said, looking annoyed and confused.

When the guard left, Farouk turned to Wes. "What's going on, boss? Looks like we're getting screwed by your guys—they bungle the job or something? Why aren't you on the manifest?" Then realization hit. "You're not on the freezing manifest, are you?" He cursed. "You could have told me."

"I didn't have the watts," Wes mumbled. "Sorry. I thought we'd be able to talk our way in. Thought you wouldn't take us here if you knew."

"I wouldn't take you here? Of course I wouldn't take you here—" Farouk began to argue, but the rest of his words were muffled by the sound of more ambulances rushing past.

Wes watched as they sped through the gate, pulling the smoke behind it, leaving the gate clear for an instant. A girl stood in the archway, dressed in a blue hospital gown, shivering in the street, her hair a mess, her eyes flashing scarlet. Shards of gold littered the street, and gunfire mixed with the sounds of shattering glass. Smoke billowed through the air.

"Was that a girl?" Shakes stared at the surreal scene.

"What the . . . ?" Farouk said as a shiny new car shot through the face of the dome, arcing through the sky, and crashing into the guard booth, exploding in a giant burst of glass and steel and flame.

The guards left the limo and ran toward the booth, yelling and cursing.

"Hit it!" Wes yelled. "Go! Now, Farouk."

Farouk didn't hesitate; he jammed the accelerator, spinning the wheels, careening past the stunned guards who were still staring at the burning booth, and blasting into the entrance of the smoke-filled city.

They were inside.

Farouk slid into a tangle of alleyways, turning deeper and deeper off the main road and into the heart of the city. As far away from anything like law enforcement as possible. Only then did he slow down and choke a few words out. "You both can go to hell."

"Think we just did, brother." Wes clapped him on the shoulder.

Shakes looked like he was going to puke, which was just another way Wes could rationalize the positive side of having no watts for breakfast today.

"See," Wes said, nudging Shakes. "Told you we'd make it."

"What he said," Shakes muttered back.

Wes smiled.

But getting inside was one thing, and getting Eliza out was something else entirely.

11

HER PARALYSIS MADE EVERYTHING harder—and Faix more exasperated.

So Nat stood at the edge of the cliff, trying to shape the ether, to sculpt something from nothing, to use her power to control the void. She closed her eyes and tried to find the voice of her drakon. Its voice in her head had guided her all her life, and she needed to hear it now. *Where are you?* In her mind's eye she saw the forests of the Blue, she explored the clouds and trees, the mountains and the gorges, and from there she traveled to the ruined Pacific, to Garbage Country, New Vegas, Ashes, and everywhere in between. She searched and she listened, hearing the buzz of a honeybee, the rush of river below, but she could not hear her drakon. Its voice had gone silent, resting somewhere underneath the earth, somewhere she would not be able to feel its pain.

Imagine a bridge, Faix had told her. *Build a wooden plank. The nothingness is as real as the stone you stand on. In Vallonis we see what cannot be seen.*

I need you, she called to her drakon. *Can you hear me?*

Hear me, hear me, came an echo. Nat startled. That wasn't her voice but someone else's she heard.

Nat opened her eyes with a start. She had heard the voice earlier when she had crossed the gate of Afal.

"Do not be distracted," Faix scolded. "There is no voice. I hear nothing." *Stop stalling,* he sent.

Nat frowned. "I can't do this. I don't see anything."

Faix sighed. "I had hoped that since you were able to ride your drakon you would know a little more than you do."

"How about you try to ride my drakon and then we'll talk?"

Enough, he sent. The look he gave her was particularly piercing. Then he tried again. "The children of Vallonis begin when we are young. From the time we are three or four years of age, when we first sense our power, our lessons begin. We learn through games and play, we discover our power as naturally as a young child who learns to imitate the voices of her parents."

"Is there a point here?"

"When we are older, we learn focus and concentration. Control doesn't come from emotion, my father once told me. We have noticed that the uninitiated—people your world call marked—have discovered that strong emotions can access their powers, but it is not the correct way to do so. Emotions are a crude and unpredictable way to access one's power. Emotion can be overwhelming, and ultimately destructive," said Faix.

Nat nodded. She knew from experience that Faix was right. She recalled the slave ships, how she had torn the mast and toppled the slave crates. She had lost control; she'd nearly sunk the boat and killed all of them. But here was the thing—she had enjoyed it. There was a thrill to giving into the rage and fury inside her.

"Once you lose your sense of self, you allow the corruption to take over. It happens to everyone."

She looked sharply at Faix, who sounded as if he was speaking from experience.

Yes, I am, he sent. But he did not elaborate. She only sensed a brief flash of grief, and then it was gone.

You cannot let the darkness overcome the light.

Faix continued, "In art, there is always emotion, but we cannot sculpt from emotion alone. If we did, our work would be chaotic; it would lack focus."

"I'm not an artist," she said. And for good reason. Chaos was all she knew. When she was a prisoner at MacArthur Med, the doctors and her superior officers had told her to use her emotions, to let her hatred build. They'd turned her into a weapon—their weapon. She hunted her own people, used her power to bring in those who were just like her, marked by magic, marked for death. Her mentors had bred that fear, that pain, and like a bomb they'd primed her to explode.

But now Faix was telling her that she needed to forget what she had learned. "They lied to you. They tortured you. They wanted your power, but they did not know how to teach you to control it. They only knew how to make a fire, but not how to keep it burning steadily. It will take time to move past what you have learned."

Nat tried again. Nothing. "I can't . . . I can't do it without . . . ," she said.

Faix raised his voice and bellowed into the air, something she never thought she'd hear, especially not spoken aloud. "You think you are the only one to have lost a drakon?"

She stared at him. He came from a line of drakon herders, the mighty clans of drakonborn. She should have remembered.

"Yes, I was born a rydder. I have felt the same pain you have, the grief that comes from separation," he told her, his voice now once again as calm as ever.

"Where is your drakon?" she asked, her voice trembling, afraid of the answer.

"Gone from this world," he said, touching his necklace again. "During the first breaking, when Vallonis fell the first time."

Gone? But then . . . how is it that you live? Her drakon had gone into the ground; the creature was wounded, but alive. Its temporary absence pained her, but they would be rejoined one day, whereas Faix had lost that bond forever. The possibility of losing her drakon seemed suddenly very real. She had thought she was invincible as she soared through the sky, as she battled the drone army astride her great drakon. Now, she felt foolish. Perhaps she had been in far greater danger than she suspected.

I live because I have to. You will hurt, you will bleed, you will be betrayed as I have been betrayed. You will survive. And you must learn to control your power.

"Teach me," she said. Now that she knew Faix understood her pain, had experienced it himself, she felt closer to him.

She believed him.

He nodded. "We will start with my father's exercise. A practice I learned as a child. Pick an object."

"Any object?" she asked. *What does he want me to say?*

Say anything. This is not a test.

"A violin?" she said. It sounded like something a sylph would picture.

"Good enough. Picture the instrument. The strings, the neck, the scroll at one end, the chin rest at the other."

"Okay," she said.

"Now take a piece of the object, the scroll at the tip of the neck. Picture the spiral, the grain of the wood, the fibers within that wood."

She was trying, but she couldn't see the point of his father's exercise.

"Go deeper. Within those wooden fibers, try to see the cells that make up the strands, and the molecules that compose the next layer. Imagine each step, smaller and smaller until there is nothing, just the void left within all things, the atoms whizzing through space. Imagine the thing until you've exhausted its essence, until you've reduced it to nothing, to the void, the ether. Only then can you *shape* it into anything you want—you can turn a violin into a cello, or a bridge."

"I'm trying," Nat said.

"It's not about trying. It's about repetition. Don't expect results. Expect to fail and fail and fail. Once you are accustomed to failing, once you've made a habit of it, then you can *shape*."

Nat pictured the violin, the wood, the fibers, the molecules, electrons swirling in the void. Nothing happened. She understood the idea: All things are made from the void, so reduce each object to the void and she could shape that void. "I don't know, I can't do it, I can't make something out of nothing."

"It is not nothing; that is what you don't understand," said Faix sadly.

As if a light had turned on inside her head, Nat gasped. She understood. The void was not a void at all, *not nothing*—and all at once, there, right in front of her, was a wooden bridge that stretched from the cliff to the city entry.

She'd done it!

She'd willed it into being.

Nat took a step on the wooden plank, and as Faix had promised, it was as real as the stone behind her. She took another step, her confidence growing—she could do this, she could harness the ether, control her power—she took a third step—

And fell, screaming, into the void.

12

EL DORADO WAS BURNING AND THE
whole city was in chaos. From the marginal safety of the car,
Wes stared at what should have been a beautiful metropolis.
He'd never seen a city that was intact like this, with sidewalks
and trees, manicured storefronts, even if today it was on fire.
If not for the billowing black smoke, the whole place would
look like a photo snapped in the time *before*—the days before the ice and the snow came, before the world froze. Shiny
condominiums stretched ten, twelve stories above the street,
sprouting upward between cinemas and restaurants, sidewalk
cafés and fancy clothing stores. There were even flower shops
and supermarkets—two things Wes hadn't seen in years, at
least not with actual flowers or food to sell. It was a snapshot
stolen from paradise.

Or it had been, before the fire and the shattered glass.
And the people—so many people—running around in a
panic, but Wes hardly noticed their stricken expressions;
he was staring at them because they were running around
bare-legged, dressed in what the typical New Vegas resident

wore as underclothes. It was so hot here in the dome, he was sweating already.

Farouk pulled out of the alleyway and zigzagged down the main thoroughfare. "Which way?" he yelled.

"Take your time. Apparently we're just here to see the sights," Shakes said, elbowing Wes as hard as he could.

"Ow." Wes snapped out of his reverie. He scrolled through his phone and found what he had paid for with the last of his watts: a map to the facility where Eliza was being held.

"Left," he said, and the limo squealed left. "Now straight," he said, looking out the window to the street, trying to orient himself. "Up ahead, turn at the next light."

"Left?" Farouk asked.

"Right!"

"Which one?" yelled Farouk, confused.

"Left!"

The limo turned just as a shower of glass hit the street, tinkling like bells, like broken music. The scene was even more confusing, more people running out of their houses, out of office buildings, away from the smoke and the flames.

But not everyone was running.

"Look!" Farouk pointed. Scattered throughout the crowds were kids in hospital gowns, in white robes or orange jumpsuits. They walked slowly, deliberately, and their faces were set, concentrating, focused. They were *marked,* all of them.

A boy in a half-zipped jumpsuit pushed past the car. His eyes were flashing yellow. He stared into the window of the limo.

"What are you looking at?" Farouk growled, pressing the gas pedal.

Wes watched out the rear window as the boy turned to the car immediately behind them.

The boy picked it up in his arms and hurled it into the air, as effortlessly as if he were tossing a toy.

"Maybe I'd drive a little faster," Shakes said, his eyes fixed on a girl across the street who was blowing fire down the street with the wave of two bare hands.

Wes watched as a child with glowing purple eyes in a torn robe raised two hands upward to the dome, forcing the panels to shatter, one by one. She seemed indifferent to the rain of glass all around her.

Even in the chaos, one thing seemed increasingly clear. The marked prisoners had escaped, and now they were having their revenge.

But where's Eliza? Has she escaped, too? Was she one of these silent, angry children? He would never find her in this crowd. He had to check the hospital first.

"Turn right, turn right," Wes ordered, and Farouk swerved hard to avoid the burning cars in the intersection, and the limousine skidded on its side; if they had been going any faster, it would have flipped over.

"There!" Wes said. A few blocks ahead stood a white building with rows of black windows. It was nearly as tall as the dome's golden ceiling, with a sign in front that proclaimed it the Eisenhower Medical Facility. Typical. The RSA liked to hide in plain sight, to call their prisons "hospitals," their military bases "peace centers." The hospital's street-level windows were cracked and smoke poured out of its open glass doors.

Steel barricades blocked the street entrance to the hospital, so Wes told Farouk to pull into the alley and park. The limousine crashed into a pile of trash cans before stopping. Wes grabbed the pack that held his equipment. He might need it if they lost the limo. He kicked aside the cans and was out on the street, the boys right behind him. Wes didn't even bother to look over his shoulder when he heard two sets of footsteps. "You can stay in the car, 'Rouk. You didn't sign up for this."

"Screw you, icehole," Farouk panted. Shakes shoved him as he ran beside him.

They ran toward the hospital, the smoke darker and thicker as they neared it. Looking up, Wes saw enormous fans built into the dome's structure, the massive blades drawing waves of smoke toward the vents. It was a clever system, but it wasn't enough to clear the air entirely, and soon, everyone in this section of the city would perish from smoke inhalation.

A public announcement system blared: *ALL* RESIDENTS TO THE *EASTERN* EXIT. *ALL* OTHER EXITS CLOSED DUE TO SMOKE CONTAINMENT.

Shakes coughed into his hand. "We've got to get out of here before they shut the doors."

Wes nodded, as the panic around him grew and the screaming grew louder.

EASTERN EXIT WILL CLOSE IN ZERO MINUS *TEN* MINUTES.

El Dorado was going to cut off this dome to save the others

lest the smoke and fire jump to the next enclosure, consigning everyone who didn't make it out to their deaths. Meanwhile, the marked prisoners were everywhere, bending street lamps, causing explosions, creating havoc. Wes wanted to help them— hell, he wanted to *join* them—but he needed to find Eliza first.

Wes wanted to feel sympathy for the frightened people running through the streets, towels held to their mouths, fear in their eyes. He wanted to pity them, their homes aflame, but he could not ignore their richly tailored clothes, the fabric shiny and gaudy, their restored vintage cars now blackened by smoke. The residents of El Dorado were the lucky ones. They had literally walled themselves off from the End, living a life that hadn't existed for over a hundred years. It was warm inside, and flowers grew in boxes and grass. The air was moist. The domes were trapped in a time capsule, and their citizens lived in a fantasy. Maybe it was good for the citizens of El Dorado to smell the smoke, to shiver from the cold wind that was starting to blow through the broken glass, to feel fear for a change.

Wes had known fear his entire life. He had lived with fear, with cold, and with hunger, so maybe it was time the people of El Dorado learned how the other half lived.

You're full of ice. You had the watts, you'd live here, too. Wouldn't you? A girl about his age ran past him, blood dripping from her head; she was crying, holding a young boy close to her side. *No one deserves this, no matter how they live.*

"Boss?" Shakes and Farouk were up ahead and confused to find their leader behind them. "You dreaming, man?"

He *had* been dreaming, just as he had been when he was racing at the New Vegas speedway. He found himself doing it more and more since he'd left Nat, since the black ocean and all that happened on those dark waters. When he dreamt, it was as if he could see into another world.

"Sorry." Wes ran to join them and took the point position, leading them past rows of polished sports cars toward the hospital doors. Gunfire thundered in the dome, the sound amplified by the hard surface of the gold hemisphere. Soldiers roamed the streets, taking up defensive positions, helping people out of their buildings, guiding them toward the last remaining exit.

EASTERN EXIT WILL CLOSE IN ZERO MINUS *NINE* MINUTES.

"Look. They found the limo." Farouk pointed to the alleyway where they had parked. Shots rang out and peppered the limo's plastic doors and its tires deflated.

Freeze it, that was our only way out of here.

The security officer appeared, the one from the guard post; he was the one who had shot at the car. He lifted a pair of high-tech binoculars and spotted Wes and his team.

"HALT!" he ordered, dropping the lenses and picking up his automatic.

"RUN!" Wes yelled, and the boys ran.

"We'll draw him off," Shakes said. "Head for the hospital. We've got your back. Find Eliza, we'll meet you back at the alley in five—if not, we'll see you at the way station tonight. We know the drill."

Wes nodded his thanks and waved as he parted ways with his friends. He watched them scramble between a line of parked cars, shooting over the guard's head, drawing his fire away from Wes and forcing him to find his own cover.

The gunfire stopped; the way was clear. Wes bolted for the hospital entry, dashing between the open doors, through the smoke and fire, and into the hospital, calling his sister's name.

13

WHEN NAT OPENED HER EYES, SHE WAS standing at the edge of the forest again, and Faix was with her. The gleaming white city in the clouds was gone. "What happened?" she asked. "I made the bridge—I saw it, I felt it—and then . . ."

"You fell," Faix said, looking deeply troubled. "That was not supposed to happen. It's why I brought you here after I caught you."

She looked around and saw fields of flowers growing around the skeletal remains of broken cars, and broken, burnt trees standing next to healthy ones. They were at the border, where Blue land turned into gray.

"Do you see it?" asked Faix. "Two worlds, overlapping each other, one dead and one alive?"

Or one dying, and the other coming into being, Nat thought.

"Exactly," he said, nodding.

"What does it have to do with falling from the bridge to Apis?" she asked.

But Faix smiled inscrutably again, and instead of answering, he walked over to stand between two gray oak trees, one withered, the other lush with life. *Here.*

She stood next to him.

The air was dead in one spot and alive in the other, electric. One part it was numb and destroyed, and the other was alive, vibrant, exultant. Nat stood in the middle, excited and alarmed.

Can you feel it?

Yes.

"When you fell, I believed at first that you had lost your hold on the ether, but then I realized that I saw the bridge as well, and it is the *ether* that failed you. It has happened before, but not at this intensity."

"The ether failed? But I don't understand . . ."

He nodded solemnly. "Your world is dying," he said, "and the Blue is returning, or so we had thought." He gestured from the muddy forest floor to a wall of light, glimmering and magnificent. Faix whispered an incantation underneath his breath and a vision appeared in the light, that of a dark and infinite sky. "To understand its failure, you must understand the history of Vallonis."

In the beginning was the word.

And the word was made flesh.

A world was born from a bright light. Mountains rose from the oceans, rivers snaked through barren valleys, a dark land was covered with green vegetation. Brilliant white castles appeared on the horizon, villages full of every kind of creature, from smallmen to sylphs, centaurs, and flying horses.

This is Atlantis. The first iteration of the binding spell, the one that would cover the world with magic. *In Atlantis, the worlds of science and magic existed peacefully together.*

Nat watched as the shining white city was swallowed by the ocean.

But the spell was weak, and the magic failed.

Next, a green island glittered in the middle of a lake.

This is Avalon. The second iteration. The second attempt to unite the world of magic with the gray lands.

A young girl with fiery red hair stood on the shore and stared out at Nat before the island disappeared into the mist.

Then the image showed her and Faix's reflection as they stood in the forest. *This is the third age of Vallonis, or the Blue, as it is known in your world. The third iteration, the third attempt to bring magic back into the world.*

Faix cleared his throat and the vision faded. He turned to Nat. "The spell has been cast several times now, and every time it does not hold. Atlantis disappeared into the depths. Avalon survives, but is closed to the world around it. And as for the Blue . . ." Faix shook his head. "When the third spell was cast, the ice came with it. The cold was born on the same day. The spell that was supposed to transform this world is also destroying it. The magic turned against itself."

"It's broken," she said quietly, thinking of the corruption, of the sickness that had turned the marked people into thrillers, living corpses, their magic rotting them from the inside.

A spell that was meant to heal the world, to bring magic and wonder back into existence, had brought death and destruction instead.

"The very nothingness from which everything is made has been tainted," said Faix. "Some believe that when the spell was cast, it was broken because the earth was too full of poison, that the oceans were too polluted, that the very foundation of life had already begun to crumble."

She stared at the lush green trees of the forest and past that, into the countryside, covered in gray ice, at the world where the stars couldn't penetrate the veil, where the sun was just a memory.

"So there's no hope then?" she said, gazing into iridescent eyes. "No refuge for the marked?"

"Are you asking if there is a way to escape the rot and the ice? Since Vallonis itself is corrupted?"

"Yeah." Nat had fought for Vallonis, she had bled and her drakon was broken, for the dream of a place that did not even exist.

"The spell can be recast, the damage undone," Faix said. "Vallonis can rise again."

"How?"

"In the beginning was the word," Faix reminded her. "There is a codex, a scroll or a book called the *Archimedes Palimpsest* which contains the instructions for the binding spell. I have studied its history. The spellcaster, the one who reads from its pages, must hold the power of Vallonis in their very soul. The spell requires a sacrifice in its casting, but it also carries a reward."

"A reward?"

"The caster becomes king—or the queen—of Vallonis."

"What's the price?"

"The spell demands the greatest sacrifice of its caster. When the spell was cast three times before, each time the magic faltered because the caster failed to provide a sufficient sacrifice. Queen Vallona, first ruler of Atlantis, cut off her hand to bind the spell, but it was not enough. Atlantis sank. Arthur gave up his love and his wife, but the power of Avalon faded. Our queen gave her own son's life to cast the spell, but still it was not enough. The spell did not hold and so our queen has sought to cast the spell once more."

"And did she?"

Faix shook his head sadly. "No. The corruption froze the book inside the Gray Tower, and the key to unlocking it was stolen from us by one we thought was a friend. Without the key, the binding spell cannot be unmade nor recast."

"What happened to this friend?" she asked, remembering his words. *You will be betrayed as I have been betrayed.*

"We don't know. Only that the tower still stands, and the world is still broken."

"So find this key, get the book, and fix this broken world? Is that it?" She smiled at her confidence, but she was a drakonrydder; this was what she was meant to do.

"Yes, but it is not as simple as it sounds. Even if we find the key and its thief, and are able to rescue the book from the tower, there is still no guarantee we can find the source of the corruption to set the spell to rights." The charm on his necklace glowed.

"What is that?" she asked.

He smiled. "It is a pendant that contains a portion of the first tree of Atlantis, preserved from the time before the first Breaking. This necklace has been in my family for thousands of years. There were ten pendants at the start, but now only a few remain. The pendants are used in the recasting of the binding spell. When the last piece of Vallonis is gone, we will no longer have the ability to remake this world."

"Can I see it?"

Faix lifted the pendant from his neck and it hung in the air, a red sphere held by what looked like a tiny gold drakon claw, and inside the sphere Nat could see a silhouette of a tree. A whole universe inside a charm.

They were silent.

Nat, Nat, Nat.

Faix cocked his head. This time, he'd heard it, too.

It was the same voice she had heard when she first entered the forest, the same voice she'd heard when she stood on the cliff.

The voice was stronger now, louder, and it hit her like a punch to the head. Someone wanted her attention. Someone was in pain. Someone needed help, someone she knew. The voice was familiar. Over and over she heard it until she had to put her hands over her ears.

Nat! the voice called, screaming and full of terror. *Nat! Nat! Don't let them—! I need you!*

14

THE HOSPITAL LOBBY WAS EMPTY.
There was no one at the security desk, no one at admittance,
no one at the nurses' station. The floor was black with ash,
the air was filled with smoke, and strobe lights flashed as the
fire alarms rang. Wes removed his phone again to check his
notes. Eliza was in room 712. He needed a map, some kind
of directory, but the computer on the nurses' desk was dead.

He burst through steel doors that separated the lobby
from the rest of the hospital and immediately plunged into
darkness. A bright strobe flashed, lighting the corridor to the
stairway, blinding him for a moment before vanishing again.
Wes had seen enough to orient himself, and he made for the
stairs, groping in the darkness, and the light flashed again, but
too late this time as he slammed into a cart filled with sharp
instruments. Steel and glass clattered to the floor.

The hospital was nearly empty, and outside, he could hear
the countdown. *EASTERN* EXIT WILL CLOSE IN ZERO
MINUS *SEVEN* MINUTES.

When the strobe flashed, he saw the door to the stairway

and opened it, just as a boy with a star mark on his cheek and black hair stumbled past him. A doctor in a white coat appeared in the hallway, and when he saw the marked boy, he ran in the opposite direction. Wes kept climbing up, waiting for the light to flash again, and when it did, it revealed the walls were pocked with bullet holes. He passed more doctors, running away, running down.

"Eliza Wesson! Do you know where Eliza Wesson is?"

But the doctors only shook their heads and ran, fearful and mute. Wes understood their fear; he was afraid, too. The building felt as if it might collapse at any moment. He was running in the darkness; the only light came from the emergency strobes and the occasional ripple of flame. The structure—the walls and floors—was starting to creak. The higher he went in the building, the hotter it got. The floors beneath his feet began to buckle.

EASTERN EXIT WILL CLOSE IN ZERO MINUS *SIX* MINUTES.

Wes ran up the dark stairway until he made it to what he thought was the seventh floor. Eliza was in room 712. He stumbled over a body, then another. A shaft of light illuminated the floor from a hole blown out the side of the building. A bright golden shaft—Wes supposed it was beautiful, but given the circumstances, he didn't pause to admire it. Eliza's floor was littered with the bodies of dead prisoners and dead soldiers. He checked every face but didn't see his sister's. Outside, the screams of the crowd were fading. The dome was emptying.

EASTERN EXIT WILL CLOSE IN ZERO MINUS *FIVE* MINUTES.

"Eliza!" Wes called, thinking she might hear him if she was still in the hospital. "Eliza!" he called again, but there was no reply.

He heard footsteps echoing in the stairway, heading up, not down. Soldiers. Crap. He'd given himself away by shouting.

At the far end of the corridor, Wes saw the same security officer from the guard booth who had chased his team from the entrance to the alley and now the hospital.

"YOU! STOP!"

Wes opened the nearest door and crashed into an office, plunging into desks and Nutri coolers and computer screens. Where were Shakes and Farouk? Had they made it out? They knew the drill. They'd give Wes five minutes and that was it. There was no waiting. They should've gotten out, hopefully made it to the way station somehow. Too many people had been hurt or lost while trying to help him find Eliza: Liannan, Roark, Brendon, and now Shakes and Farouk. His team. His family.

The footsteps faded. Wes pushed through a door on the other side and found himself in a different corridor, a long white passage, lined with doors on both sides. He'd found the prison cells.

The strobe flashed. Wes checked the room numbers. 702. He was close. More flashes. 708. 710. Finally 712.

Eliza's room. Wes kicked the door open.

The strobe flashed in the hallway, illuminating the room. It was tidy, but empty. He had expected nothing less. All the rooms were empty; everyone was gone. But he had wanted to go inside the hospital on the fleeting chance that she might still be there. The strobe flashed, freezing an image in his mind's eye. White linens. White robe. A desk covered in paper.

Heavy footsteps outside, coming closer.

Wes lifted one of the manila folders on the desk. The strobe flashed. He saw her name typed on the front. A pink rabbit sat on the desk, the fabric faded, the fur worn. He had no memory of the toy. But it had to be from her childhood. He took the rabbit; it was something. If he never found his sister, he would have this one token, he thought as he stuffed the rabbit into his coat pocket. Had she been transported out already? Or was she one of those marked prisoners tearing apart the domed city?

He was about to leave when the door clicked open and he felt the barrel of a gun pressed against his back. Wes raised his hands, placing his palms on the back of his head and weaving his fingers together. He knew the drill, he knew how to surrender—he had been a soldier once.

"Turn around, slowly."

Wes did as he was told. The light flashed, and he saw the security guard's gun aimed at his chest.

"Ryan Wesson?" the guard barked.

How did they know his name?

"ARE YOU RYAN WESSON?"

"Yes! Yes! I surrender. You can put that down."

The light flashed again.

EASTERN EXIT WILL CLOSE IN ZERO MINUS *TWO* MINUTES.

The guard nodded, reached into his pack, and produced a pair of plasti-cuffs.

"What's the point, we're both dead," Wes said as the officer snapped the cuffs on his wrists.

"Don't worry, icehole, they'll get us out," the guard said, pulling out his radio. "I got him. Yeah, he confirmed. Meet us at the front." He pushed Wes out of the room, to the corridor, toward the hole in the building where a blackbird heli was waiting, hovering.

The security officer pushed Wes out the opening and onto the floor of the chopper, and that was the last thing Wes remembered before the building exploded, crumbling to the ground, and everything went black.

15

THE VOICE WAS A FORCE THAT PUSHED her into the ground. Its terror was overpowering, and it washed over her entire being, coming in waves and threatening to drown her. It was like being attacked by that iron bomb again. Nat put a hand on her forehead. She was shaking. Her head throbbed and there were tears in her eyes. "Someone's calling me. Someone needs my help. I don't know what to do. It hurts."

"Let me help," Faix said quietly. "Open your mind to me. I believe I can amplify the message and take away the pain. Trust me, Nat. Let me help you."

Nat considered his offer, relieved to discover there were limits to his ability to tap into her consciousness. If he needed permission to enter deep into her mind, it meant she could also keep him out and must have been successful in closing herself off before. But that didn't matter now. Only the pain mattered. She needed relief. Now. If Faix could help her, she would let him.

Sensing her acquiescence, he came closer, his white hair brushing her face as he whispered in her ear, "Relax. Clear your mind. Don't resist. I will do the rest."

She sighed. "Okay."

He put a hand on her forehead.

Nat tried not to think, not to do anything. It was easy enough; the throbbing in her head was overpowering. She took a breath and told him to start, to do whatever he could.

His forehead touched hers. She felt his presence in her mind, like a ghost, like a shadow on an overcast day. The pain faded and an image appeared.

Walls of pristine white marble. Steel doors. Cries echoed through the darkness. A chorus of pain. Cell after cell after cell. Prisoners, pilgrims, huddled together, cold and afraid. In one cell, heavy iron chains hung from the wall, sapphire blood pooled on the floor, and a girl in a white robe cowered in the corner.

A girl she would know anywhere.

Liannan! Nat screamed. *Where are you?*

Nat! Listen! Don't let them—

With a jolt, Nat snapped awake from the dream, pushing Faix backward, severing their link, sending him tumbling. He looked surprised, shaken.

"Did you see?" she asked. "Did you see her?"

He nodded, his face aghast.

"What was wrong with her—" Nat shuddered. Liannan's robe was covered with her bright sapphire blood. What happened to her? Where was she being held? Where was everyone else? Brendon? Roark? Wes? Shakes? Farouk? Were they prisoners, too?

Nat kneeled in the dirt, shaking. She had to help Liannan, but how? Without her drakon, without her power, she was useless.

"You must learn to believe, Nat," said Faix, reading her mind as always. "We found you once before, when you were a prisoner on the ocean. Do you remember the birds who visited you when you were on the deck of the slave ship?"

Nat nodded slowly.

"Those birds traveled from Vallonis, and so shall we. We will find them. Let me see what you saw, one more time."

She let him touch her forehead with his hand again, felt his power soothing her anxiety.

The image returned, the stark white rooms, long corridors full of soldiers and prisoners. It was all a fast-moving blur.

Concentrate, sent Faix.

Nat focused on any markers she could see, anything that would give away the location. But all she saw were alabaster walls, concrete floors. No signs, nothing that would indicate a specific location.

There's nothing, she sent Faix.

You are still attached to the material world. Concentrate on what you cannot *see.*

Then she understood. She focused on the source of the call; if she could hear it clearly, Faix could take them there, wherever that was. She focused her energies. *Nat! Nat! Listen! Don't let them— Save—*

Don't let them kill us! Save us! That's what Liannan was telling her before the connection was severed. She wouldn't. Nat opened her eyes. She knew where to go now. "Show me the way."

"In the gray lands, the doors to Vallonis are few as we must protect our country, but a door from Vallonis to your world can take us anywhere. However, once we pass through the door, we cannot use it to travel back here. We can reach your friend, but the return journey will be long and difficult."

"I understand." It wouldn't be her first trip across the black waters; she had survived the ocean before and she could do it again, even if she had to do it without her drakon. Liannan needed her.

And I need Liannan. The two had survived the black waters, she had helped bring Nat to the Blue, and she had taught Nat to understand her power and commune with her drakon. Liannan was one of the few friends Nat had in the world.

Faix waved his hand in a circle, and the ground shook, and the entire forest before them whirled as if it were a great stew and he was stirring the pot, weaving the grass and rocks and the very sky into a hole in the air. He was shaping the void, sculpting the ether, creating a doorway where none had stood before. The hole was no larger than a pinprick at first, but it gradually widened, larger and larger. Soon the circle was as wide as Nat was tall. Faix put his hands together and drew them up close to his chest, then pushed his fingers forward and turned the ring into a tunnel, a passage made from the earth and sky of Vallonis.

This battle would be different from the others she had won. With no drakon at her command, she had only herself, her sword and shield, and the sylph by her side. It would have to be enough to save Liannan. Nat followed Faix into the passage. There was no time to waste.

16

HIS HANDS WERE SHAKING UNCONTROL-
lably. Wes wedged his fingers between his arm and chest,
trying to stop them from trembling, but the tremors would
not abate. The room he was in wasn't cold or damp. Something was wrong with him. At first he'd thought it was the ice,
since the snow got to everyone eventually. The cold got into
your bones. They called it ice disease, even though it wasn't
a real disease, like cancer or even rickets or scurvy, which the
vitamin-deficient populace suffered from due to the lack of
sunlight and citrus fruits, no matter how much Nutri they
drank. Ice disease was just a name given to a common set of
symptoms, an ailment everyone got eventually, like the flu.
Only it was worse than influenza. There was no cure, no vac-
cine, and it never went away.

When he started losing his vision a few years ago, and his
hands started trembling, Wes just assumed he had the same
thing everyone else did. But lately, he wondered. Usually when
his vision went white, he would be blind for a few moments.

But on the speedway he hadn't gone blind. He'd seen *Nat*. There was something wrong with him, all right, but maybe it wasn't the ice.

He couldn't worry about it now. He had other, more pressing concerns. He had woken up strapped to a bed in the back of an ambulance. The explosion had taken out the hospital, and he suffered some burns to his face and smoke inhalation. His lungs had been at minimum capacity for keeping him alive. Every breath he'd drawn felt shallow and desperate.

He had no idea where he was, and only vaguely remembered being flown to an air base, then bundled up and taken somewhere else. He could be anywhere in the world, in any one of the RSA's secret military detention centers. Wes recognized the lime-green walls that denoted a military prison. Someone had once told him the pale color was chosen for its calming effects, but the green just made him nauseous. Green floor. Green walls. Green ceiling. Green lights.

He had failed. How badly, he had no way of knowing. Not yet.

Eliza was dead or she was not. She had escaped or she had not. Either way, it had nothing to do with him.

He had been too late.

Wes didn't know what happened to his boys; he hoped Shakes and Farouk had gotten away, but the limo had been under fire when they last saw it. For all Wes knew they were dead, or locked in another cell. He hadn't been allowed out of his cell since he arrived, and hadn't spoken to anyone but himself.

If it was meant to drive him crazy, it was working. Then

again, he could have told them they were wasting their time. He'd been crazy a whole lot longer than this.

Wes counted the days by the lights in his cell. The room went black for eight or nine hours each day. The room had gone dark seven times, so he guessed seven days had passed. He couldn't be certain. For all he knew a month had gone by. His mind was foggy, disoriented, and now he was trembling all over.

What do they want from me?

When the guards came one day, he overheard them talking about the lockdown. No one was allowed out of their cells. There had been some kind of riot the other week, and everyone was on edge.

Food arrived, with some regularity, through a slot in the door. Heat drifted through a grille in the wall. The light in his cell was greenish, but constant. These were the good things. So his captors wanted him alive; there was that, at least. Wes didn't try to think about why—there were too many possible reasons, and none of them were comforting.

Your comfort is not the point, he reminded himself.

Your sister is. Your friends.

Or at least they were.

The slot opened. A tray passed through the hole. He wondered if the prison designers had modeled his cell on old vids downloaded from the nets, or if prisons always looked like this—green and empty, with a slot in the door for food.

Wes took the tray, which contained a bowl of a gray viscous pudding—vitamin-infused soy cake, if you used the proper name, or VISC, as it was called down at the Fo-Pro lines. He sat down and took the plastic spoon and napkin from the tray, laying the napkin on his lap and the tray on the napkin. No sense making a mess.

In old vids, prisoners threw their meals across the rooms, but that made no sense to Wes. He was hungry, and if he threw the tray across the room, who would clean up the mess? No one. He'd just be eating off the floor instead of from a bowl.

He had to close his eyes, had to pretend the food looked like something other than gray slime, to get himself to swallow. He was halfway through the bowl when the door squealed on its hinges. Soldiers stood in the doorway.

"Time to go," said one, a square-jawed, square-headed grunt with a shaved head.

"I don't get to finish my gourmet dinner?" he asked.

"C'mon," said the other, his eyes flashing with anger, black flames tattooed on his neck.

Wes put the tray aside with a sigh. He'd actually enjoyed the taste of gray slime. He should tell Shakes, if he ever saw him again, that it wasn't too bad if you closed your eyes and didn't smell it.

The soldiers escorted him out of the room and into a small metal room, with a table and a chair on either side of it, and everything bolted to the floor. Wes had been in a room like this before, except then he'd been on the other side of the table.

He sat on a chair, the metal cold against his legs, sending a chill up his back.

The guards uncuffed him and left him alone.

It was a long time before the door opened again.

Wes caught a familiar scent and heard low whistling that accompanied footsteps on the concrete. He knew that whistling, that cheap cologne. How long had it been since he'd sat down with Bradley at the restaurant? He remembered the cold beer, the Wagyu steaks with hot butter, the meal he turned down when he last spoke to his old commander. He wished he'd had even one piece of that steak, just a taste, but he'd just left it there, getting cold.

"Wesson." Bradley slid smoothly into the chair across from Wes. "We meet again. Another table, a different location. I hear the food's not as good here. How's the slime?"

"Not bad," Wes lied as he shifted in his chair. The processed glop was starting to curdle in his stomach. "How'd you know it was me?" he asked, remembering that the guard knew his name. "At the hospital?"

"Would you believe we were waiting for you all along?" Bradley asked, his eyes crinkling with amusement, as if he knew a secret. The commander had grown a mustache, his uniform looked starched, and there were a few new medals pinned to his pocket, a pair of gray flags Wes didn't recognize.

Wes grunted. He knew what Bradley wanted from him before he even asked: the same thing he'd always wanted. For Wes to work the black waters. Round up the pilgrims to sell to the traders and the slavers, the priests and the masters. It was likely the only reason Wes was still alive, because he was still useful. Wes gritted his teeth; he would rot in prison before he took the job.

"You like it here? You like the view?" Bradley asked with a soft smile, knowing Wes's cell had only four walls and no window.

"Let's skip to the job, Bradley. Tell me what you want so I can say no and you can send me back to the cell."

"Now, don't get too excited, boy. And don't think you're so smart, either. I'll tell you what, Wesson. Let's make a bet."

"A bet? You're going to bet that I'll take the job? Okay. I'll play," Wes said, rubbing his hands together.

Bradley smiled. "Good. Tell me. How am I going to get you back into the service?" He opened the file in front of him. "I could pin all the damage in El Dorado on you, you know. You were seen at the hospital; I could have witnesses saying they saw you set the fire. Arson. But what's another mark on your criminal record?"

Wes shrugged. "Do I look like a guy who cares?"

Bradley smirked. "No. And that wasn't the way."

Wes frowned. He guessed Bradley was intimating they had a hostage, someone close to him that he could hurt. Maybe Shakes, maybe Farouk, too. Bradley knew he and Shakes worked together. Or if not the boys, then who? Liannan? The smallmen? But Wes wasn't sure Bradley knew about the marked on his team. Eliza? But hadn't she been transferred already? The notion was too painful, so he pushed it from his thoughts.

"You don't want to guess?" Bradley asked with a twinkle in his eye, so smug that Wes wanted to shove an icicle through his brain. "I'll tell you what. Let's just cut to it like you've asked. I'll tell you how we'll motivate you. *We've got her.*"

Her.

Does he mean Nat? They have Nat?

"She's been with us for a very long time," Bradley said lazily, and Wes realized he meant Eliza. Of course, they still had Eliza. Wes felt as if he had been punched in the gut. "I didn't realize she was your sister, or I would have used her as leverage earlier."

Wes glared at him.

"We flew her out to the Red City this morning. Took her home, shall we say." He was clearly enjoying himself. "We've got a base out there, a great place to get rid of those we no longer need. You've heard of the flesh markets, haven't you? The Temple of the High Priestess of the White? Lady Algeana has a soft spot for her kind. Unless . . ."

"Unless I work for you," Wes growled. "It just gets better and better."

"Bingo." Bradley smiled. "Do I win the bet?"

Wes didn't reply.

"I think I do, because you're not going to let that happen, are you? You know what I think? I think you were in El Dorado to break her out." He smirked. "So predictable. So ridiculously honorable, coming from someone like you."

Wes looked at him. "Foreign concept, eh?"

"Not really. Just a luxurious one. And luxury is something you don't have."

Wes said nothing.

Bradley smirked. "But don't worry. She's alive and safe. And you're going to keep her that way—aren't you? I'm pretty sure I win our little bet. Because from now on, you work for me and you do everything I say. Deal?"

Wes flexed his fists as he contemplated his lack of options. He had never felt so powerless.

Bradley sat back in his chair. "You know, you really should have taken me up on that steak."

PART THE SECOND:

RYDDER AND SYLPH

To a surrounded enemy,
you must leave a way of escape.

—SUN TZU

17

HIS UNIFORM WAS WARM BUT ITCHY.
Wes wasn't a uniform person. He scratched his neck underneath his collar, still a bit shocked to find himself back in gray
wool synthetic, RSA badges, and stripes on his shoulders. He
wasn't cold anymore, but that was little consolation for the
task they'd sent him to do.

The military had been through a few changes since his
time in the service. They'd suffered major losses during a
recent conflict in the Tasman Sea, and their resources were
stretched beyond limit. Now they needed sailors who could
navigate the trash-filled oceans without getting lost or sinking
their ships, so they were recruiting ex-runners, former coyotes
who knew the oceans and the pilgrim routes. Wes was the
best runner in Vegas, the one who had the most luck evading
the naval scouts, helping pilgrims cross the waters. Now they
wanted him to use his skills against the same desperate souls
he used to help.

After accepting the commission, Wes was flown to a naval
outpost in New Java for a perfunctory training session, where

he was schooled in the routes and procedures of patrol. Wes commanded a ship that was part of a team of two search vessels, light cruisers working in tandem around the seas surrounding the South Asian islands. Wes's every move would be tracked by satellite from the base, and there were quotas to fill, expectations to be met.

"Don't think you can go out there on surveillance and come back empty-handed, Lieutenant," Bradley threatened that morning before Wes left to take command of his crew, a few days after he had been released from his cell. "We fish out two dozen pilgrims a month, so don't think you can bullshit me. With your record, I expect double, triple our usual intake. Happy hunting," Bradley said with his skull-head smile.

Wes stood alone at the helm of the *Goliath*, watching the waves roll, lapping around rust-colored towers of trash. They had been at sea for a few days now, and had reached their designated patrol area, the heavily trafficked straits where pilgrim boats were usually found on the way to New Kandy, where supposedly there was another gateway to the Blue. Back in New Vegas, Liannan had mentioned that the original gateway to Vallonis was closed, and lately he'd heard no one headed for New Crete anymore; they all wanted to go to KandyLand. Wes didn't think that was such a great idea, as everyone knew the Red City was overrun by the white priests, and they even had their temple there. But pilgrims were stubborn, unable to give up hope, and if so, he was more like them than ever. Over the radio, the captain of the other cruiser had reported sightings of boats on the north perimeter and went to check it out.

Yesterday Wes had noticed pockets of light winking through the trash, probably a pilgrim boat or two, so he steered clear, or as clear as he could without deviating from his search path. To pass the time, he made the crew practice drills and review the new procedures on how to approach and take control of pilgrim vehicles, how to shackle prisoners safely. The recruits manning the boat were a bunch of hardened kids who were only too happy to collect the extra watts paid for each pilgrim they found, and Wes worried for anyone unfortunate enough to run into them. Maybe if he was lucky he could keep his ship from running into refugee boats, or at least postpone the encounters till he could figure out how to get out of this mess.

A few minutes later the captain of the *Colossus* reported picking up two pilgrim ships. One was in particularly bad shape, and had already lost half its passengers. They'd been floating on their own for miles, lost on the black ocean, abandoned by captain and crew. Con men promised passage across the black waters, but didn't know how to find the doors to Vallonis. Once they collected their fees, they left the ships—floating wrecks—in the dark of night. Others were just in over their heads, inexperienced sailors who should never have set out from shore in the first place.

"We're heavy and returning to port to drop off our cargo," the other captain said smugly, and Wes could tell the icehole was already counting the watts in his kill fee. "Hold on, looks like we've found another floater, we'll go check it out."

Wes acknowledged and ended the call.

It was quiet on the ocean, and he was remembering that the last time he had been on the water Nat was with him, when Shakes entered the bridge with a portable screen in hand and a dark look on his face. "Hey, boss, you gotta take a look at this."

"What's up?" Wes asked. His deal with Bradley had brought one perk, at least—Shakes and Farouk. Wes had been able to convince the general he wouldn't be able to do his job correctly if he didn't have his team with him; Bradley didn't seem too surprised, as all runners felt the same way about their crews. The boys had been captured fleeing the dome—really, it was a miracle the shot-up limo could even move—and had been thrown into the same prison where Wes had been held. Like him, the most they had suffered were meals of gray slime, but they weren't too bad off otherwise. Farouk was down in the engine room, and Shakes was first mate.

You couldn't really call it luck, but the days had gone by without incident so far. But the look on Shakes's face gave Wes the feeling that everything was about to change. "You found something."

"Yeah." Shakes grimaced as his eyes darted to the black waters.

"We knew this was going to happen sooner or later," Wes said, taking the screen and checking it out.

"I know," Shakes said, "but how come with you it's always sooner?" He cursed under his breath.

Wes didn't really have an answer for that one.

He had promised Shakes that no matter what happened,

when the time came, they would do the right thing, somehow. No one was going to get hurt under his watch. Not Eliza, and not the pilgrims they captured on the black waters. Shakes had to trust him, and usually he did, but it was obvious his friend was feeling skeptical. Wes didn't blame him, since he wasn't sure how he was going to get them out of this, either, but a little faith would have been nice.

A green mark blinked on the monitor. "Think it might just be junk?" Wes asked, hoping, squinting at the monitor.

"Not the way it's moving. Look how fast it is; it's got a motor for sure. They might have spotted us, too; look, it just changed course." Shakes leaned against the rail, glancing between the monitor and the trash-strewn ocean, searching for the ship, but seeing only the gray sky, the murky waters packed with floating debris.

The radio blared and Wes picked up the comm. "Wesson here."

"You on this?" It was Callahan, the fleet commander in charge of the patrol teams.

"Yeah, we got it." Wes thought he saw the ship in the distance, but couldn't be certain.

"Bradley said you were hot shit, so let's see what you can do in the black water. Reel 'em in."

"Roger that," Wes said, and dropped the comm. He turned to Shakes. "You heard the man; guess we can't ignore this one. Hit the sirens and tell the guys to get out the inflatables like we taught them. We'll take the pilgrims in the small boats, it'll be less intimidating. Turn on the lights, the big floods, to let them see us coming so they don't panic. Tell Farouk to take the helm, bring us in nice and slow." Wes searched once more for the pilgrim vessel, caught sight of a distant ship, jutting between ziggurats of trash, trying to avoid detection.

"Then what?" Shakes asked, sounding irritable.

"Then we'll figure it out. We always do, don't we?" he snapped back.

Wes watched as the crew dropped the black inflatables into the water as they neared the pilgrim vessel. The pilgrim craft was a good-sized ship, bigger than most, and its passengers stood on deck, their arms raised in surrender. They didn't fire any weapons; there would be no scuffle. Wes watched from the bridge, trying to keep his face impassive as he watched them being herded into the rafts that would take them to his cruiser. The pilgrims knew their journey was over, they were caught, they would never cross the ocean, they would never find the Blue.

Wes knew how that felt.

He remained on deck as the inflatables returned from the pilgrim boat loaded with passengers. Shakes saluted him, standing guard over a group of smallmen, who huddled together, looking sickly and pale. The rafts pulled up alongside the cruiser, and Wes and his men helped them on board. *No guns*, he'd warned his guys. *You fire and I'll fire on you.* But their sullen hostages accepted their fate quietly, and there was no need for weapons. There was no rebellion, only grim stares and red-rimmed eyes.

Wes followed the captives down to the hold. He'd warned his men not to abuse or harass their hostages, and he went from cell to cell, bandaging wounds, handing out Nutri and

Meals Ready to Squeeze. If his men found his behavior odd, they didn't comment for now. More captives arrived, and he heard a cry from the next cell.

"Leave me alone! I know your captain, I tell you! Let me go!"

Wes bolted from the cell, locking the door behind him and running into Shakes. That voice sounded familiar. He raised his eyebrows and Shakes shrugged. They burst open the cell door where the screams were coming from.

Inside, one of the young soldiers had a smallman pushed up against the wall. The smallman's face was swollen and bloody, and it looked like he had taken the worst of the fight as the soldier battered him with his fists.

"Shut the ice up! Lying bastard! Shut up!" yelled the soldier as he punched him in the jaw.

"Hey, hey, what's going on here?" Shakes demanded.

The soldier whipped around. "Lieutenant!" he cried when he saw Wes.

Wes cleared his throat and his voice was murderous. "I gave everyone explicit instructions that none of the hostages were to be harmed."

"But, sir!"

"Let him go."

The soldier did as told, and the smallman slumped to the floor. "He says he knows you," the soldier said bitterly. "He's a liar. You don't know him, do you, sir?"

Wes stared at the smallman. He hadn't recognized him earlier, but he did now.

Of course he did. It was Roark.

The last time he'd seen him, Roark was tending his garden

and humming a song. Wise and sweet Roark, who could make a delicious meal out of random scraps, and a joke out of the direst of situations. Maybe one day they would laugh at this, too.

Roark, his dear friend. *Alive.*

If Roark was alive, then maybe Brendon was, too, and Liannan . . .

Wes saw the elation starting to show on Shakes's face, but if they made the wrong move now, all of them were trapped. Eliza would be sent to the priests, and the rest of them, including Roark, would be dumped into the ocean like just another piece of trash.

"Wes," Roark whispered. "Thank Vallonis, it really is you. I saw you from the deck, Wes . . . tell him I'm right. Tell him you know me."

The soldier glared at Wes. "Sir?"

Wes stared at Roark, nodded to Shakes, and turned to his soldier. "Never saw him in my life. Carry on."

18

THE PASSAGE OPENED UP TO A DESERTED beach and the vortex closed behind them. Nat looked back at it, wondering if she would ever return to Vallonis, if she would ever see her drakon again. There was a ship far off in the distance. Liannan's call was even stronger here than in Vallonis.

Nat! Nat! Can you hear me?

I'm coming. I'm here. Hold on! Nat sent back, but there was no reply. She wondered if Liannan heard her, if the sylph was actually communicating with her or merely sending out a distress call. Either way, she had never heard Liannan sound that terrified before, and it made her feel panicked and helpless.

"She's in there," Nat said urgently, pointing to the navy cruiser. "But how do we get there without a drakon? Swim?" She bit her words when Faix lifted his hands and whispered a quiet incantation.

This time, the vortex whirled and instead of opening up a black hole, it created something—*something out of nothing*—he had sculpted the ether, and in front of them was a small motorboat, floating on the waves. Faix waded over to claim it and helped Nat climb inside.

"It's no drakon," Nat said. "But I guess it beats swimming."

"It's made to look like a pilgrim's vessel. We will let them think we are defenseless."

Faix steered the boat, his every movement full of grace. Someone like Faix didn't belong here, Nat thought, in a place where the air stank of garbage and the long-dead carcasses of animals. Was she like him? She was a drakonrydder, too, but she had been born in the gray lands. Where did she belong? It was a shock to be back in the middle of the black waters, back in the gray world, where everything was dying.

We will recover the palimpsest, Faix sent. *We will search for the source of the corruption and we will fix what is broken and return Vallonis to its glory.*

Nat nodded to let him know she'd heard, even though he probably knew anyway. She looked out anxiously at the ship they were heading toward. It was a small cruiser, flying RSA flags, COLOSSUS engraved on its side. This wasn't a slaver ship; these were soldiers, and soldiers were organized. If they lost this fight, she'd be back in shackles and kept in an iron cage or, worse, sent back to Bradley and forced to work for them again, stealing children, setting fires, killing their enemies.

Do not fear them, Faix soothed. *We will find your friends. We will not let them take us.*

But his words were little comfort. Faix didn't know, didn't truly understand. He had never fought against them. Once they made contact, she would need to act quickly. She would need to tap into her power and use her anger once more. If only she were past such things. She had stood at the door to Apis. She longed to use her power to build, to create, to make things—not destroy them. But she was headed toward battle once more. Would she die out here, fighting on the ocean? Would she die as Faix's drakon had died, as Mainas had almost died? What would happen to her drakon if she did not survive?

Head winds blew onto their small boat, and Nat shivered. She was cold without her drakon, but Faix neither shivered nor complained about the cold and the wind and the ice. She wondered if he missed its warmth, the sense of drakonfire in his lungs.

He glanced at her and she knew he had read her thoughts.

"I miss it every day. Like a missing limb." He touched his necklace, as if for luck.

"You're very attached to that charm," she said.

"Am I? It is just a habit," he said dismissively, and the corner of his mouth quivered slightly.

Nat wouldn't have thought anything of it except that it was so strange to see him perturbed, and she realized, all of a sudden, that he was lying. Faix was keeping something from her about the charm, so she tried to think about something else so he wouldn't know she knew. She imagined herself burrowing into the earth with her drakon, erecting a wall between her thoughts and his.

Then she pictured their boat, its hull made of fiberglass, the strands of white glass, the resin between the fibers, the filaments in the white strands, and the tiny molecules that made up those fibers. She pictured smaller and smaller structures until at last they were only particles spinning in the void.

"STOP," Faix said, as the boat flickered in and out of reality.

Nat gasped. "I'm sorry—I was just—practicing."

He smiled. "Good work, but perhaps you can keep the boat real until we reach the ship? I do not wish to drown."

They reached the cruiser and floated close by. "We will allow them to take us," Faix said. "Once we are inside, we will look for your friends."

They didn't have to wait long. Nat heard the familiar sounds of drones in the air, cutting through the clouds, hovering out of sight, alerting the ship to their location. Faix shut down the motor. They stood back to back, Nat holding her sword and shield, waiting. The plan was to surrender, but she wanted to be prepared to fight anyway. She missed her drakon. Missed the feeling of the creature's fire in her lungs, of the power at her command as they rained death from above. She could have vaporized the drones, taken the ship in seconds, and freed her friends, if only she were whole.

The sleek navy cruiser cut across the mist, its guns trained on their position. Soldiers stood on the bow, pointing their automatic rifles straight at them. More soldiers were dropping smaller rafts in the water to take them prisoner.

As the small boats came their way, Nat braced herself to be captured. The cruiser followed close behind, its shadow drifting across her vessel.

"We surrender," Faix declared when the boats floated by their starboard side. "We come peacefully."

In answer, a bullet came whizzing through the night, striking Faix in the arm. Then came another, and another. Nat ducked under her shield and used her sword to fend off the bullets. "Are you hurt?" she asked.

"No," Faix said, his eyes flashing dangerously. They had offered peace and had been attacked instead. His wound flared, then healed; Nat saw the skin regenerate and become smooth again. "But I will show them what it means to hurt."

"Faix!"

The sylph seemed to grow to twice his size, his white hair shone brightly, and his entire being was covered in a brilliant white light. Faix clapped his arms together and in an instant, the small black boats were gone and the bullets clattered harmlessly on the water.

The soldiers on the deck of the *Colossus* yelled, scanning the waters, astonished. The boats had vanished so quickly, it was as if the ocean had swallowed them up. They answered with a barrage of artillery. Nat crashed to her knees, covering her head with her shield. She couldn't see her attackers, but she knew they could see her. They had infrared lenses, scopes that peered effortlessly through mist and clouds, through darkness and smoke. There was nowhere to hide. Something hot scraped her shoulder, tearing a hole in her armor, burning her skin. A bullet had ripped a hole in her jacket, exposing her arm to the bitter cold. She flinched, covering the wound as a second projectile screamed past her ear, deafening her momentarily.

Use your fire, Faix sent. *Burn them.*

But I don't have any fire, Nat replied.

He shook his head and turned back to the cruiser, facing

the bullets, standing and unafraid, and brought his hands together once more. A fiery projectile exploded from his palms and ripped toward the cruiser, setting it on fire and sending frothy black water bubbling through the newly formed hole in the side.

The fire is within you.

The ship was burning, even without a drakon. The soldiers had scattered, the snipers abandoning their positions.

When she first met Faix, he had reminded her of Liannan, with his beauty and his soft voice, but he was nothing like Liannan at all, and what she saw scared her—the mighty power at his command, his indifference to pain, to emotion, to humanity. But Faix wasn't human, he was a sylph. *Who are you?* she sent. *Who are you really?*

I am Faix Lazaved. Messenger to the Queen. Drakonrydder of Vallonis. Protector of the Realm. Guardian of the Blue. I am like you, Anastasia. I am made of fire.

Then he turned away and steered their quickly sinking boat toward the side of the ship. He motioned to the knotted ropes that stretched from the water to the deck of the cruiser at regular intervals. "When our boat hits the side, reach for the ropes," he said, preparing to jump.

The burning ship bobbled in the water, sending waves rippling across the ocean, its wake threatening to capsize their already-waterlogged craft.

Nat nodded, eyeing the approaching vessel. The fire was concentrated on the starboard side and a few soldiers were rushing to put it out with fire extinguishers. But the port side was empty, and she nodded to Faix to take them there.

Faix rushed toward the edge of the boat, his foot poised on the rail. He leapt across the water, grabbed hold of a rope, and pulled himself up. Nat followed, almost falling into the water as she caught hold of the rope. Faix was nearly at the top of the rope when he leaned down and pulled her up by her wrists, strong and fast.

Leaping over the rail, he turned to face her, offering her his hand to help her cross the railing.

"I'm good," she said, not wanting his help a second time. It was strange to be so close to her enemies, to stand onboard a navy cruiser not unlike the ones she had destroyed in the past. She couldn't help but think that these frightened children in uniform who were running from them now were no more responsible for their actions than she had been when she was still one of them. When she, too, answered to an unforgiving commander.

Nat! Nat! cried Liannan's voice in her head.

"It's coming from over there," she said, pointing across the burning deck. "Let's go."

Together they ran across the deck to answer the call.

19

THE SOLDIER SMILED AND RAISED
his fist to punch Roark in the face again, but he fell to the
ground before he could land the blow. Shakes stood behind
him with a grim smile, holding the blunt edge of his gun.
"Next time, pick on someone your own size, icehole."

"You jammed his radio?" asked Wes, making sure.

"Easy as stealing watts from a tourist at roulette," Shakes
said with a grin, showing Wes the broken comm he'd filched
from the soldier's pocket. "No one can hear us."

Wes knelt down, dabbed his handkerchief in Nutri, and
passed it to Roark. "Sorry about that, man. I told the guys to
leave you all alone, but some of them aren't so obedient."

"Took you two long enough," Roark said, putting the hanky
to his eye. "Thanks a lot—I'm sure I'm quite a sight."

Wes gave him a few of the fried chicken wafers he carried
in his pocket, and the smallman calmed down.

"What happened? Where have you been? How'd you get
here?" Wes asked.

"It was the garden," Roark said sadly, his dark hair falling in his eyes. "You were right, Wes. We shouldn't have done it, but we were tired of hiding in our rooms—we wanted air. Even if the sky was gray, it was something. I wanted to feel the open space, to stand in a place without walls."

"For a few damn vegetables?" Shakes shook his head.

Roark just shrugged.

"I loved that garden, too. I get it," said Wes.

"How'd they find you?" Shakes asked.

"Drones. We heard buzzing the day before they came. The drones must have spied us on the roof. We should have fled that night, but we decided to wait till you got back. Besides, we didn't know where to go, and Liannan didn't want to leave without finding a way to tell Shakes what had happened."

"Really?" Shakes asked. His face was turning red. "She didn't want to . . . to leave me?"

Roark rolled his eyes. "Which turned out to be the wrong decision, as the soldiers came for us the next day. Brendon and I were downstairs, in the kitchen, and suddenly they were everywhere; we didn't even hear the door open, we looked up and they had surrounded us. They had some sort of weapon that blocked our hearing." He winced at the memory.

"We told them there were only two of us, but they knew there was a third. They found Liannan on the roof. They took us to the detention center in K-Town first, then New Java."

"We were just there!" Shakes yelped.

"How'd you get on a pilgrim boat, then?" asked Wes.

"There was a riot, and we escaped."

Wes nodded. He remembered the guards talking about a breakout, which was why they had kept him in solitary. The whole place was still under lockdown when they arrived.

"We found a runner taking pilgrims to the Blue and took a chance on it again—where else could we go? We wanted to get a message to New Vegas but didn't think we could trust anyone after what happened. And by bad luck Brendon and I got separated. He should be on the other boat that got picked up hours ago; we heard their distress signal. I thought our boat would be able to escape until you caught us just now."

"The *Colossus* must have picked them up," Wes said, thinking about the pilgrim boat the other captain had bragged about finding.

"What about Liannan?" Shakes asked. "She on that boat, too?"

"I don't know."

"What do you mean? You don't know?"

Shakes looked ready to pound the smallman even smaller.

"They took her away the moment they found her on the roof. We asked around at the DC, asked the prison network, and when we got out, we asked again, but no one's seen her. We haven't seen her for weeks, maybe longer . . . ," Roark said, rubbing at his eyes with one fist. "But I can't believe she's dead . . . and I won't."

Shakes nodded, turning away. He slumped against the cell wall.

Wes reached out to put a hand on his shoulder but Shakes pulled from his grasp. "It's okay," Shakes said, his voice hoarse.

"When we lost her, that first day, I knew it was over. I knew I would never get her back. But when we saw you, Roark, I hoped . . ." The words trailed off.

Roark looked as miserable as Shakes sounded.

"She might be on the *Colossus*. There might still be time, man," said Wes.

"Wes is right, there is still hope," said Roark. "I had lost mine until I saw Wes on the deck and you on the other lifeboat." He looked at them as if he had only now realized the significance of the situation. "Are you going to tell me why you're suddenly working for the enemy?"

They had only just finished filling him in on El Dorado and Eliza when Wes's radio crackled to life. "Hold on," he said, and picked up the comm. It was the other carrier. "Wesson here."

"This is McCleod from the *Colossus*. Hostiles are firing on us, request backup, converge on our location. Repeat, we are under attack!"

Wes confirmed the order, put down his radio. "All right, listen up, looks like they caught some heat. You said Donnie's on the other cruiser, right?"

Roark nodded.

"Okay, we'll get him out, and maybe we can sneak away while they're firing at each other. Take one of the inflatable boats."

"What about Eliza?" asked Shakes.

"Bradley mentioned a base in the Red City. That's in New Kandy, right? We'll go there," Wes decided. "Try to spring her out."

"What if they kill her before we get there? When they find out you went AWOL?"

Wes bit his lip. "I'm counting on us working faster than their bureaucracy. We can't stay here. If this icehole wakes up, knock him out again," he told his small friend.

"Gladly," replied Roark with a bloody smile.

Wes left Shakes to deal with the rest of the prisoners and ran to the bridge, where he ordered Farouk to plot a course toward the other cruiser. They traveled as fast as their vessel would allow, riding toward a cloud of smoke that gradually expanded on the horizon. Wes radioed the ship's captain again but didn't receive a reply. He had no other way to communicate with the sinking ship, and the smoke grew darker and denser as they drew nearer.

He picked up his binoculars and saw the vessel aflame, smoke rising from the deck, soldiers scrambling in the dark, some escaping in lifeboats, others staying to fight. The ship was not moving; the hull was pierced and taking on water.

Wes ordered Farouk to run parallel to the other ship, to come up slowly. "*Goliath*, this is your captain, Lieutenant Wesson. Stand ready. Do not fire until ordered. Repeat. Do not fire until ordered."

He told Farouk to slow down and kill the engines, so they could drift toward the flaming vessel. The cruiser was on fire, but Wes couldn't spot the hostile ship that had attacked them.

"Boss," Farouk said. "We've got a problem."

"What?" Wes snapped, watching with horror as one of the soldiers on the burning deck of the *Goliath* just *burst into flame* when his fire extinguisher hit the blaze. This was magic, all right; whoever had attacked the ship was marked, powerful, and dangerous.

"One of the boys below just armed our rockets."

The kids must have panicked. They'd seen what he had just seen—and probably thought it best to sink the entire ship, since that's what the brass always did. Cut losses. Close exits. Kill everyone inside.

Wes scrambled for the override and hit the button, but it was too late.

A rocket sailed through the air, a brilliant orange arc. It would tear a hole through the deck and the ship would sink, taking everyone down with it.. Godfreezeit, Wes sure hoped Brendon and Liannan weren't on that ship. He looked through his binoculars again.

A pair of figures on the deck were running from the missile aimed their way—a tall male figure with shocking white hair, and the other—female, slim, raven-haired, and so familiar.

Wes almost dropped the binoculars.

It was Nat.

20

NAT WAS RUNNING BEHIND FAIX WHEN she heard it—a low hum that echoed all around, the sound of engines, the dull churn of the waves. Over her shoulder she saw a second cruiser burst out of the mist and a flame shoot upward from its deck. They'd fired a rocket, and the gleaming missile was heading right for them.

Without hesitating, almost without thinking, she turned toward it and raised her hands as she had seen Faix do, and the missile exploded into the air all around her. She accepted its flames, accepted its destruction, took the heat into her body to join the fire inside her, and shattered it into a million molecules, so that it fell harmlessly around them like a rain of white light. Nat hadn't yet learned how to shape the ether, but turning something into nothing—*that* she could do.

"You're learning." Faix smiled.

"Baby steps." Nat acknowledged it with satisfaction, but their work wasn't done. "Come on, Liannan's voice is coming from down here," she said, running to a door in the bulkhead. It was secured with a large wheel and she spun it, unwinding the hidden mechanism, the locks clicking open. But when she pulled on it, the door remained stuck, and she braced herself against the wall and pulled again.

The door ripped free from the bulkhead, hurtling through the air, crashing into the dark waters, splashing black filth in all directions.

Nat felt a certain grim satisfaction at her capacity for destruction. She had obliterated the missile and torn open the door. Whatever she was, she was good at breaking things, and she was proud of it.

Faix peered into the hole. Stairs spiraled down into the darkness.

Nat, Nat, Nat.

Nat slid down the stairs, Faix right behind. There were dozens of cells and prisoners clamoring for release; they had heard the sounds of gunshots, of battle, and worried they would be left to drown in the bottom of the ship.

Faix gestured with his hand and all the doors opened at once.

The pilgrims swarmed out, haggard and dirty, running up the stairs toward the lifeboats. "Liannan! Where are you? Liannan!" Nat called. She couldn't hear the voice in her head anymore. "Liannan!"

"Nat!" A hand was pulling on her shirt.

She looked down.

"Brendon!"

"Nat!" he exclaimed joyfully. "You're here! You've come to rescue us!"

She grinned. It was good to see her friend. Brendon was

thinner, and his beard was ragged and filthy, but his eyes were shining brightly. She handed him a dagger from her boot and he accepted it gratefully. "Oh, you look lovely," he said. "Is that leather? The craftsmanship is spectacular." She thought only Brendon would notice what she was wearing at a time like this. Then she realized he was talking about the knife.

She had to smile. "Where's Liannan? Isn't she with you? Roark? Shakes? Wes?"

Brendon shook his head. "No, it's just me. I don't know where anyone is. Roark and I got separated a few days ago, and I haven't seen Liannan in weeks." His eyes grew wide when he saw Faix.

The sylph approached, lurked, half in shadow, his face slowly emerging from the dark, his pale skin and bright eyes glowing in the dim light. "She is not here. I don't understand it. But we must get away. The other ship will be upon us."

Nat nodded. Brendon followed speechlessly.

They ran back up to the deck to find chaos, as soldiers scattered and fled, shoving pilgrims off the lifeboats or jumping into the water.

They fear my people as they feared the drakon. All those years I lived in fear, and now I am feared.

Nat looked across the water, at the gray hull of the second cruiser approaching fast. Would they fire another rocket? The ship was coming alongside their vessel to board it.

I will sink their ship. I will tear holes in its hull. I will crush it into nothingness. I will burn it to ashes. Destroy them before they destroy you.

Was it the drakon's voice she heard or her own?

She stared at the ship, feeling the fire begin to build inside her, swirling and beautiful, and she smiled.

I feel almost whole again. When it burns.

"What are you doing?" Brendon asked, watching in horror. The black armor she wore turned hot as coals, and she was covered in orange flame. "Roark could be on that ship!"

Roark. Liannan. She was still looking for her friends. What was she thinking? There were people on that ship. She had been about to kill everyone on board. Her flame died as quickly as it appeared.

NAT!

She looked up and saw Faix at the corner of her eye, slipping into the shadows. But why? Then she saw—a secret boat—an inflatable from the other cruiser—and its soldiers had snuck up onto the deck to secure it while she and Faix were down below.

Nat was about to move toward them when there was a *click* by her ear. She felt the barrel of a gun pointed right at the back of her head.

"Brendon's right, Roark *is* on that ship," said a voice behind her.

A strong voice.

Brave. Unwavering.

And very, very familiar.

She turned and saw the face of her captor for the first time.

It was really him, unless her mind was playing tricks on her. And given all of the tricks she had been trying to get it to play lately, that was a real possibility.

Maybe I've formed him out of the ether.

Something from not-nothing.

But the longer she stared, the more she knew he was real.

Wes stood in front of her, his face grim and his mouth set in a hard line. He was wearing a uniform, with officer stripes on his shoulders, and his shaggy hair had been cut short, close to the scalp, making his face even more striking. *Like a warrior,* she thought. *Something ancient. Something rough. There are other kinds of power besides mine and Faix's.*

While her heart leapt at the sight of him, she was afraid as well. Slowly, she tried to piece together the reality of the situation.

He was a soldier again? Wes?

Wes was the enemy? He was on board the other ship? He had fired that missile? Why was he pointing a gun at her?

She stared at him, her heart beating so fast in her chest, she felt dizzy. *Wes . . .*

Her mind was muddled with thoughts, memories, feelings, but she didn't want to think too much while Faix was around to read her thoughts. She didn't want him to know what she felt for Wes. That part of her was sacred, private, something only she and the boy standing in front of her in the gray uniform could know.

If it's still there. If he still feels it, too.

When she had seen him on the racetrack, he was a runner, but what had happened between then and now? Why was he in uniform? The last time they'd been together he had kissed her, and the memory of his kiss was still alive in her mind, in her heart, in that promise he had made. *This isn't the end for us.* She wanted to throw her arms around him, wanted him to hold her again, wanted to feel his body next to hers.

But he only stood there, watching her with hooded eyes, distant, a stranger.

"Come on," Wes said, his gun still aimed at her head. He nodded to Brendon. "Let's go. You're both with me."

WES KEPT HIS FACE IMPASSIVE AS he herded Nat and Brendon across the deck. His mind was racing from a torrent of emotions.

He had seen her die, had seen the missile's rainbow of fire arc toward her.

She should have died.

There had been nothing he could do, no way to recall the drone missile, no way to stop the inevitable from happening.

Watching that rocket fall was like watching the world end. He had braced himself against the helm, said a prayer, and closed his eyes.

When he opened them, he saw a brilliant flash light up the ocean and turn the sky white, bright as a sunny day, a day Wes had never experienced before, a day from the time *before*, a bright brilliant day.

Which should have been impossible, because there could be no light in a world without her.

And yet Nat was still standing there, surrounded by the flash of white, blinding light.

It was her.

She was the light.

Somehow, she'd torn the missile into a thousand shards. She'd saved herself and everyone left on that ship.

Lovely Natasha Kestal.

Wes saw her as he'd seen her the first time at the casino, when she'd stolen his chips and taken firm ownership of his heart, and he remembered her face when he had kissed her, and the words she had said to him that had burned into his soul.

I love you, I love you so much, but I can't.

Her dark hair fell below her shoulders, and she was wearing some sort of black slim-fitting leather, with a shield strapped to her back and a sword holstered on her side. She was as beautiful and dangerous as she had always been, now even more so.

I can't.

Then he realized she was standing in the middle of a burning ship, and he had to get her the ice out of there. The *Colossus* was slowly sinking, its deck covered in debris, and there were holes in its hull.

"SHAKES! GET ME AN INFLATABLE!" Wes ordered, planning to head over to the cruiser as quickly as possible. He radioed the *Colossus*. "THIS IS LIEUTENANT WESSON! STOW YOUR WEAPONS, I REPEAT, STOW YOUR WEAPONS!" He couldn't take the chance that one of the grunts would fire on Nat, even though it looked as if she could take care of herself. He nearly fell down the stairs, stumbling over the risers as he hurried from the command tower to the deck.

Shakes and a group of soldiers were already lowering a boat into the water, and Wes squeezed between a pair of the younger recruits. "Tell Farouk to set a course and follow us," he ordered Shakes. "And get ready," he said meaningfully. This might just be the opportunity they were looking for, a way out of the bind. In chaos was opportunity, a wise man once said.

Wes steered the small motorboat over to the burning ship. "Keep your weapons holstered. The smallmen are unarmed and, well, *small*. There's no need to shoot anyone," he ordered.

"What about that girl?" one of them asked. "And that white-hair with her?"

Wes squinted. "I'll take care of them."

They snuck on board from the aft to find the crew had abandoned ship, and the deck was covered in smoke and fire, littered with spent cartridges, shattered guns, and shrapnel, pilgrims scrambling into lifeboats. It was then that he realized he'd been so focused on Nat that he hadn't even seen her drakon. Where was the mighty beast hiding, and did it matter? He wasn't afraid of her drakon. He wasn't afraid of her.

Wes had just made it on deck when he saw Nat, covered in that orange fire, Brendon next to her. Brendon said her name, and the fire died.

Just like that.

She didn't see him. She was facing the *Goliath,* which was steaming their way. He'd seen her break iron chains, toss slavers into the sea, turn that missile into dust. If he didn't get to her quickly, she would tear both ships apart.

He wanted to call to her but he had soldiers by his side, and any one of them could kill her with a bullet. He had to do this himself.

So Wes put a gun to her head and told her to follow him.

Now Nat was walking right in front of him, so close that he could reach out and touch her, but instead he had to content himself with admiring her graceful silhouette, the way her belt hugged her small waist, how pretty her dark hair looked tucked behind her ears, exposing her long, white neck.

She had no business being on this ship.

Maybe even in this world.

"Lieutenant?" one of his soldiers asked.

Wes snapped to attention. He had almost forgotten that he had a crew to command. "You two, find the captain, see if he's still alive, and if he is, get him down here. Bark, Stuffin, and the rest of you, go belowdecks, secure the holds, find fire suppression equipment, put out the flames, and get this vessel in order."

The crew scattered, and Wes made a few calculations and punched out instructions to Shakes on his handheld, using the secret code they'd shared during countless covert missions. Within moments, they were Jekyll and Hyde once more.

"Wes, where are you taking us?" Brendon asked meekly. "Is Roark with you? Shakes?"

He didn't answer. He had to pretend not to know them, not to care about them for now. He saw Nat look over her shoulder at him questioningly, but he had to keep his distance for her safety. He was in command, and she was the enemy. He tried to appear indifferent, stolid, but he caught her gaze and for a moment it was like nothing at all had happened to tear them apart. They were back on that island shore, and she was in his arms, and he'd just kissed her. It was all he could do not to kiss her right there.

Nat—

But the clanking of boots from the stairway above brought him back to the present. Wes looked up and found the captain of the *Colossus* staring down at him, several soldiers right behind him holding their guns. "About time you arrived, Wesson," he snarled. Wes remembered him from training at the base; his name was McCleod and he had a nasty way about him, one of those sickos who took sadistic glee in the pain of others.

Wes saluted the captain, since he outranked him by a few stripes and they were still on the same team, or at least he had to pretend to be. "Taking these two to my ship; we've got room in our hold. I told your boys to worry about getting this fire under control."

"No, this ship is done, we'll ride over with you," McCleod said.

Wes had a feeling it wouldn't be easy to get his friends back on his ship. "There isn't any space on the inflatable, sir. I'll send another for you and your men."

"Nonsense, leave the prisoners behind. We were taking them in peacefully when they began firing at us, and now look at this mess. Better yet, shoot them both and be done with it." He turned to his men. "Shoot these two and round up the rest. Come on, Wesson."

Wes moved to shield his friends when, out of nowhere, the captain began to choke and the guns flew out of the soldiers' hands, shattering against the bulkhead.

The same white-haired sylph that Wes had seen from a distance appeared from the shadows as one by one McCleod and his men fell to the floor, clutching their throats, clawing at their own skin.

"No!" Nat cried in horror. "Faix—no!"

But it was too late. The captain and his soldiers were dead, they were sprawled on the deck, their faces purple, suffocated and bleeding from the cuts on their throats made by digging their nails into their own skin.

Wes stepped over their bodies and pointed his gun at the white-haired stranger. "I don't know who or what you are, but don't you make a move until I say so."

The sylph only smiled, staring fixedly at Wes. He raised his hand and Wes cocked his gun, the two of them at a standoff until Nat came between them. "Stop it!"

The sylph turned to her and lowered his hand.

"Thank you," she said, and whispered something in his ear. She turned to Wes. "Are you all right?"

"Yeah, your boyfriend didn't do any damage to me, sweetheart," he said, annoyed at how intimate Nat seemed to be with this creature.

She reeled as if slapped. "He's not my—"

"HEY, ICEHOLES, SOMEONE CALL A CAB?" It was

153

Shakes, from the deck of the *Goliath,* as the cruiser powered next to the burning *Colossus.* Farouk waved from the bridge, Roark next to him. Brendon yelped. "I knew it!"

"GET OVER HERE!" Wes yelled back. There were too many pilgrims on the *Colossus* to fit in the remaining lifeboats. He had a new idea and he needed his boys to help, and to secure any soldiers that remained on the ship.

"You—" he said, turning back to the white-haired sylph. "You didn't have to kill them. We would have been able to subdue them."

"Perhaps. But I could not take the chance. Now there is enough time for the pilgrims to make their way to the gate of Afal. I saved their lives," Faix said, his long hair rippling in the wind, his eyes cold and distant.

"You can't save lives by taking others," Wes said, his knuckles turning white as he held his gun. It didn't matter which side they fought for; those soldiers didn't have to die that way. "Whoever you are, you're a sad excuse for a sylph," he said, thinking of Liannan and how she would nurture even the smallest wounded animal back to life.

"That's no sylph," said Brendon, piping up from behind them. "He's a drau."

22

THERE WAS A STUNNED SILENCE ON the deck as everyone stared at Faix. Drau were a legendary and vicious race. They cared for nothing and no one, and their power knew no bounds nor restraint. The white-haired man stared back at everyone with his beautiful but fearsome silver eyes, and his words projected into everyone's consciousness.

The smallman is correct. I am drau. I was here when the world was young, when drakons and their rydders filled the sky. I will remain here until the end, until the very stars expire and this world is just a memory.

I am drau.

I am Faix Lazaved, Messenger to the Queen of Vallonis. We are the first and the last, and you are right to fear me, for all the stories about my people are true.

I can kill with my mind.

My heart is made of ice.

"Faix! Stop it!" Nat yelled. "Stop scaring everybody! These are my friends."

She turned to their ashen faces. Wes was staring at her like she was a stranger, and it hurt to see that betrayed, shocked look on his face.

"You're with him?" Wes asked.

"Yes, but—"

He nodded, cutting her off, unwilling to hear more.

She didn't want to explain everything in front of everyone, and especially not in front of Faix. Couldn't Wes see what a joy it was for her to see him, to hear his voice, to know he was alive and safe?

Wes raised his gun and pointed it at Faix again. "You'll leave the rest of these soldiers alone or answer to me," he said, as the remaining crew of the *Colossus* came out of the shadows, their hands raised in surrender.

"Your weapon will not hurt me," Faix said.

"Can't hurt to try," Wes said with his signature cocky smile.

"Wes, please. Don't. He was helping me. We were looking for Liannan. She was calling for help. I thought she was here. I *heard* her."

"She's not here, Nat," said Brendon. "We haven't seen Liannan in weeks, nearly a month."

"But that can't be," she said. "The call came from here." Still, as confused as she was about Liannan, Nat saw that Wes and Faix were still eyeing each other warily, and she knew she had to act quickly to defuse the situation. Faix had shocked her with his speed, his ruthlessness. He'd snuffed out lives as easily as blowing out candles, but Faix was her guide, her teacher—and her friend.

Drau or not, she thought of him as a friend.

She had let him into her mind, let him into her consciousness, forming a bond that was not unlike the one she shared
with her drakon.

"You should have told me," she said to Faix. "You should
have told me what you really are." The drau were creatures of
myth, the most powerful and terrifying race on earth, or so
the legends went, but he was also her friend and he had lied
to her about what he was.

"I did not mean to deceive you. I have always been myself.
Drau is your word for us, you divide us into sylph and drau,
but we are one and the same. Drau is merely an older word
for our kind," he said. "Your people fear us for good reason.
But you must know I would never harm you or your friends."

"Right," Wes said sarcastically.

"You fear me, Ryan Wesson. You see me as a romantic rival, I take it? An interesting proposition, I will agree. She is a
wondrous girl."

Nat colored, but she knew Faix well enough to know he
was no more attracted to her than he was to her drakon. While
there was friendship between them, there was no chance of
romance from either side. No. Faix just wanted to taunt Wes,
to piss on his territory, so to speak. *Boys.* Drau or mortal, they
were all the same. The two of them locked eyes to see who
would blink first.

Wes slowly dropped his gun. "Fine."

"A wise choice," Faix said, returning his stare. Then he
blanched and put a hand to his temple.

"What's with him?" Wes asked.

"I don't know—Faix? What's wrong?"

"It's nothing," Faix said, recovering his composure. His features were at once more serene, impassive. She knew he was lying, just like he had about the charm around his neck. She'd never seen Faix react in such a manner. Even when they were alone in the small boat, gunfire in the air, their ship sinking, Faix hadn't seemed the least bit worried.

She caught Wes staring at her, but when she met his eyes, he looked away again. She wished they were alone, wished she could talk to him without Faix peering into her head. But since that wasn't possible right now, she turned to Faix instead. "I trusted you."

"And you can continue to do so," he said, smoke hanging in the air, waves crashing against the cruiser. There was soot in his hair and on his face, and for the first time Faix no longer resembled the bright and perfect sylph, the wise and ageless mentor she had known. "You and I are the last of the rydders. Many in Vallonis believe the rydders are born to fight, that we are creatures of violence, warriors who are best kept outside Apis. But I disagree. We can be more than warriors, more than a vehicle for flame and destruction. You can control the fire and dread that lives within you. You have seen it." His eyes blazed when he spoke of the flame. He was a warrior, a man who would kill if needed. Her teacher and mentor was gone.

"You killed them without warning," she said. "Is that something rydders do?"

"When it is necessary."

"And was it?" Wes said.

Roark had climbed on board from the rope ladder on the

far side of the deck, and Brendon had run to him. The small-men were embracing, their eyes teary, grins wide. Dirt clung to their faces and clothes, their hair was plastered with sweat, but their happiness was apparent to all.

Nat wished her relationship with Wes was as easy. How did it get so complicated so quickly? He was standing only a few feet away from her, but she couldn't talk to him, couldn't even move closer to him, and he was unwilling to look at her. This was not what she dreamed of when she'd pictured seeing Wes again—the two of them surrounded by smoke and flame, with the bodies of the dead on the floor, the remaining soldiers cowering, the pilgrims' moans, a white-haired drau between them.

I love him.

I love him, and this is all I can have of him.

Of course it was. This was her life. This was always her life. She didn't know why she ever expected it to be any different. No matter how many promises they made to each other, she belonged to the Blue and he to the gray lands. They could never be together, and the faster they accepted that, the easier it would be.

From below came the echo of gunshots, breaking the awkward silence, and Nat, for one, was almost glad for the interruption.

Wes winced. "The last of the *Colossus* crew, probably," he said. "I'll handle this my way. We take everyone alive. You, stay here," he ordered Faix. He whistled to his crew. "Use iron on him if he moves."

"What about me?" asked Nat quietly. "Am I your hostage, too?"

23

BEFORE WES COULD ANSWER HER, ONE of his boys ran up, sweaty and scared. "Lieutenant! There's a soldier who's barricaded himself in one of the cells and won't come out. Told him we were from the *Goliath,* but he won't listen."

"That's what I thought," he said, still keeping a close eye on the drau who hovered too closely to Nat. The drau who had called himself a *romantic rival.* Was Nat seriously with that white-haired icehole? Had the whole world gone completely mad? "Okay, I'll deal with it."

"No—he said—he wants her," the boy said, pointing to Nat. "He wants to talk to the girl. He won't surrender otherwise. We've tried but he won't listen to us. He wants to see her."

Wes caught Nat's eye briefly and raised his eyebrow. He had misgivings about it, but it seemed easier to agree than resist the request for now.

"You don't have to go with him, Nat," the white-haired man—the freezing *drau*—said to her in what was way too proprietary a tone for Wes's liking.

"I'll go," she said.

Wes nodded as if he couldn't care less. He motioned to the stairway and Nat headed down. Belowdecks, the lights were off, and the corridor was beginning to flood.

"So if he's not your boyfriend, who is he then?" Wes asked, his voice low. He knew he shouldn't say anything—that he had no right to say anything—but he couldn't help himself.

Nat turned around to look him in the eye. "He's just a friend."

"You're friends with drau now, is that it?" He raised his eyebrow and his eyes sparkled to show he was teasing her, trying to ease the tension. "I don't see you for months, and this is what you do with your time?" He was unable to stop himself from teasing her, just a little.

"Like I said, I didn't know," she said. "It's complicated . . . and what about you? What have you been up to . . . *Lieutenant*?"

But gunfire lit the corridor and he didn't have time to answer. The sound was deafening. Sparks flew as bullets peppered the hallway. Wes ducked and covered Nat with his body, pressing both of them against the wall, glad to have the excuse to touch her for a moment, even if someone was shooting at them.

I missed you.

They were so close he could have kissed her cheek, and he could feel her body tense underneath his.

I missed this.

The corridor shook with the sound of bullets ricocheting. Wes yelled, his voice echoing down the length of the ship, "THIS IS LIEUTENANT WESSON, CAPTAIN OF THE

GOLIATH! I ORDER YOU TO DROP YOUR WEAPON AND SURRENDER!"

There was a deafening silence. Followed by more gunfire.

"Wes," Nat said. She'd said his name for the first time, and it set his every nerve ending on fire. "Be careful," she whispered.

He held her gaze. "Aren't I always?" But his heart beat painfully. *Whoever that icehole was up there, she still cares about me.* The thought made his face flush, and he forced himself to look away.

One. Two—

"I REPEAT, DROP YOUR WEAPON!" he called, as he burst into the hallway, firing his own.

"YOU HAVE THE GIRL?" a voice called from the open doorway.

Once again Wes looked at Nat, who shrugged. "She's right here with me, buddy," he called.

"Okay," said the voice, with palpable relief.

"Is it only you in there?" asked Wes.

"It's just me," said the voice.

This was going to be easier than he thought. "All right, toss out your gun."

The cloud of smoke cleared and a rifle flew out, skidding on the floor. A stout soldier followed, walking out with his hands up and his head down.

"What the hell is this all about?" Wes asked.

The boy looked up, from Wes to Nat, wide-eyed. "Is it really her? The girl? The one who destroyed the missile? The one everyone's been talking about? The rider?"

"Drakonrydder," Nat corrected, stepping forward. "How do you know about me?"

Wes smiled drily. "Yeah, that's her," he said to the soldier. To Nat, he said, "Seems you're quite the hero these days. The grunts all tell stories about your black-winged friend and the girl who rides on his back."

"They do?" Nat sounded amused.

"It *is* her." The soldier stood inches from Nat, his gaze filled with admiration, with awe. He looked hopeful but intimidated, like a little boy standing before his hero. The soldier's hand wavered as he offered her a handshake. "I want to join you," he said, his voice trembling. "I want to follow the drakonrydder."

"Her name is Nat. And she's with me," Wes said smoothly. "So I guess you are, too, now. What's your name, soldier?"

The kid looked around fifteen years old and twenty pounds overweight. Wes hadn't seen many overweight kids in the RSA. Food was a luxury; only the wealthy could afford to eat too much of it.

"Ice Cream Cone, I mean, Chip. Chip's my real name. Chips Win. I know it's a dumb name, what can I do, my parents worked in the casinos. The guys call me Ice Cream Cone, Cone for short." He spluttered out the words, nervous or embarrassed. Probably both.

"How'd you get that handle? You eat all the hot fudge squeezers on your boat?"

Cone blushed, which probably meant he had. Wes was amused but tried not to show it.

163

Back on deck, Shakes had rounded up the rest of the *Colossus* crew and was working with Brendon and Roark to ferry the last of the pilgrims into the lifeboats heading toward the *Goliath*. Without having to tell them, his boys already knew what they had to do. Wes had promised Shakes they would get out as soon as they saw an opportunity, and this was it. They were giving the pilgrims their cruiser—with the larger boat, they would be able to survive the perils of the black oceans, and their odds of reaching the Blue improved markedly.

"Hey, Nat," Shakes said with a ghost of a smile. "Welcome back."

"Shakes!" she said, and gave him an affectionate hug. Wes was irritated to find that now he was even jealous of Shakes, if only because Nat seemed to have no problem showing her affection for *him*.

Get a grip, man.

His friend winked at him and let Nat go. Shakes always knew exactly what he was thinking. He'd better, since they were running out of time.

"Head back to base, don't follow us," Wes said to the remaining soldiers of the *Colossus* and the *Goliath*, whom they had dumped into the last inflatable. "You only have enough fuel to get back there, so don't waste your time. If you want, you can join us like Cone here. We're going AWOL, and you'll be fugitives, but we need good men. I'll take you on."

There were no takers.

"Fine." Wes nodded.

Next to him, Nat turned pale and gripped his arm. "Liannan!" she said, her eyes closed. "She's calling me. We need to find her."

"Liannan?" Shakes said urgently. "You know where she is? She's alive?"

"Yes." Nat opened her eyes. "They're keeping her alive for now . . . but she doesn't have much time."

24

NAT OPENED HER EYES AND STARED at the group of friends who surrounded her—Wes, handsome and severe in his gray lieutenant's uniform; Shakes, now a skeleton of his former self, sallow-skinned under his scraggly beard; Brendon and Roark, hopeful but wary; Farouk, keeping his distance a bit; and Faix, standing apart from the group, his silver eyes glittering like icicles. She might as well be looking at a patchwork quilt made up of clashing, tattered, mismatched rags.

Half of them hate the other half.

Still, they were familiar, and they were here to help. And help was what she needed more than anything else right now.

"Liannan needs us," Nat said, raising her voice. "She's so scared."

"Where is she?" Shakes asked, red-faced. "You said she didn't have long to live . . ." He choked on his words. The possibility was too difficult to talk about. Nat understood, because she felt the same way.

"She's a prisoner somewhere, but her call faded before I

could focus. I thought she was here." Nat sighed. "I need your help again," she said to Faix.

"We must not act rashly," said Faix. "We answered the call and it brought us here, where she is no longer. It could be an echo, or some sort of deception."

"I *heard* her," Nat argued. "There has to be a reason the call brought us here." *Maybe Liannan wanted me to find Wes,* she thought. *Maybe she sent me here first.* The thought made her blush. *But why would she do that if her life was in danger?*

She tried again. "I know we can find her this time. Faix, please."

"Who's blondie?" Shakes growled, casually holding his gun as he turned to the silver-haired Faix.

"Nat's new friend," Wes said. "Fake the Drau. Or something."

"Faix," said Faix, with a withering look. "Son of—"

"Save it, Fake Blondie," said Shakes.

Faix did not smile. Nat tried not to. "He came here to help," she said. "And he could basically kill you with one breath, so I'd watch the jokes."

"Must be some breath," muttered Shakes. Still, he backed away.

Nat shook her head. "You don't get it. Liannan's call brought us here, and I was only able to focus on it with his help." She had to make them understand that even if they couldn't trust Faix, they needed him, especially if they wanted to find the missing sylph.

And she knew that, more than anyone, Shakes did. Now he looked almost contrite. *Message received.*

Nat closed her eyes again, straining to hear Liannan's soft

voice. It was there, a faint echo, muffled, most likely by an iron cell that dampened her magic.

"Faix," she said. "Can you help me find her voice again?"

Faix shook his head, and Shakes looked like he was about to murder him.

"So Fake Blondie won't help," Wes said. "Maybe we can convince him otherwise." He cocked his gun.

The drau looked annoyed. "You misunderstand. There is no need for violence. I will aid you in your quest to find your friend."

"Thank you, Faix." Nat smiled.

"I was merely expressing my concern that perhaps this call that you hear is not what you think it is."

"And what are you, the expert on fake calls? That seems pretty convenient, doesn't it, Fake?" Wes turned his gun over in his hand, polishing it with the edge of one uniform sleeve.

Faix ignored Wes. "If you insist, Nat, you must do as before, open your mind to mine, and together we will find her."

Nat nodded, and she noticed Wes looking uncomfortable at the idea. She could only imagine what he thought about her merging consciousnesses with a drau, especially Faix. But there was nothing else to be done; this was the only way.

Faix held his hand out and she took it, closing her eyes before she could see the look on Wes's face.

With every second, she could feel Faix's power amplifying the call.

Nat, can you hear me? Don't let them—

The words died but the image remained. Nat could see it

clearly now—Liannan, standing with her back to her, wearing a white robe and looking out a small window with iron bars.

Nat opened her eyes. "She's in a holding cell. In a prison that overlooks some sort of a temple with a statue of a white elephant in front of it."

"That's the Grand Temple of the High Priestess of the White," said Roark. "The one in New Kandy's Red City." The country used to be called Sri Lanka, a tropical island nation in the continent that was once called Asia, but nothing of the country remained after the Big Freeze, other than a few icons from its past that the white priesthood had adopted for its own.

"Are you sure?"

"There's only one," said Roark. "We know it well. It's where they take the marked, and afterward . . ." He shrugged, but Nat knew what everyone knew. Afterward, the people who were brought there were never seen again.

Wes looked grim. "Eliza's in the Red City base as well. Looks like that's our next stop."

Shakes nodded, hope returning to his eyes again. The happy-go-lucky guy was still in there, hidden beneath all that pain, and she was glad to see it.

"We're coming with you. We came to help Liannan," said Nat.

"We?" Wes said. "I don't think the boat's big enough for that so-called friend of yours."

"They're all set, boss," Farouk said, meaning the rest of the pilgrims had been transferred to the *Goliath*.

Wes nodded. "Good work." He yelled over to the former hostages huddled on board the deck of the ship. "You guys know how to drive that thing?"

One of the smallmen nodded.

"Ten minutes," Shakes said.

Ten minutes to what? Nat wondered.

Wes nodded. "Okay, you guys, get out of here!"

"Wait!" a voice called from the *Goliath,* then another and another. "Where is she? Where is the rider?"

Wes turned to her. "They want you. Looks like everyone does these days." He sounded bitter, and Nat didn't like it.

She ignored his remark and pushed her way to the railing. Across the water, the pilgrims stood in a group, their arms raised in farewell. "Thank you." One by one, they murmured their thanks, blessing her and wishing her luck on her journey. *"Bless the drakon. Bless its rydder."* It was the same song that the birds had sung to her on her first trip across the ocean.

They honor you, Faix sent.

She nodded, a lump in her throat. She was a drakonrydder, a protector of Vallonis. She'd waged war on their enemies, fought on the black waters, taken risks without seeking thanks or praise. When she went to battle, she only knew rage and fury. But now she understood. When she fought the drones, she fought *for* these people, the faces she'd never seen. Even if she did not know them, they knew her, and they thanked her.

Slowly, she, too, raised her hand in farewell.

The rest of Wes's team were helping stack the bodies, saying a few words of blessing before putting them into the water. She joined Wes, who was standing by the railing and supervising the task.

"What happened to that drakon of yours, by the way?" he asked. "You traded it for the drau? Because I have to say, I think you got the short end of the stick here."

She inhaled sharply and tears sprung to her eyes.

When he saw the hurt look on her face, his frown softened. "I'm sorry. Is it . . . is it okay?"

"We were hit by an iron bomb and it was hurt badly," she said. "It's in Vallonis—in the Blue—healing."

Wes's face softened, letting her know he cared. "Will it live?"

"I hope so," she said meeting his gaze, letting him see her pain, the worry in her eyes. Her voice trembled. "Faix says it will. That once it's whole again, it will join me."

He nodded, but his eyes darkened again at the mention of the drau. "Look, I can't have him on my team. They're killers, drau. I've met their kind. They'll do whatever it takes to get what they want. I won't do that. That's why I left the military in the first place. I threw away my career, a half-decent life. I didn't want it, I didn't want to be like your *friend*."

Nat took a deep breath to respond, but Wes wasn't done.

"I know what you're thinking, that he's helping you somehow, but believe me, he's using you, I don't know what for, but trust me, that's what they do. I took a job once, ferrying a drau out of Ashes. He paid upfront, acted polite, thankful, humble even. I snuck him out of a hospital, kept it secret, kept it quiet. I stowed him in the trunk, but he panicked as we reached the hospital checkpoint. He popped the trunk, killed the guards, and killed one of my men. Said he didn't need my help anymore, then took his watts and he left me to die. I got out, but I learned my lesson."

"You don't know him. We all suffer, and we all have our reasons for what we do," she said.

"Nat, his reasons are the wrong reasons. He'll get you killed, he'll get us killed."

"But he's with me."

"Yeah, you made that abundantly clear," he said bitterly.

"What does that mean?" she asked sharply.

"It doesn't matter."

"'It doesn't matter'?" she asked, forcing him to look her in the eye. "All those things you said to me before you left? All those promises?" Her heart broke just a little every time he looked away from her. "If that doesn't matter, then what does?"

She saw a flash of pain on Wes's face, and then he shrugged. "People say stuff all the time. It's not as if they mean it. I got caught up in the moment."

"I guess so," she said coolly. "I guess I did, too. But I'm going to help find Liannan. She reached out to me. I can't let her down. And Faix isn't going anywhere."

Wes frowned and didn't respond.

Nat sighed. She wished he wouldn't act like this, pretending he didn't care for her. But maybe it was for the best. What kind of future could they have anyway? She belonged to Vallonis. Wes was a boy from New Vegas. They had both walked away from each other once, and maybe he was right: What did it matter?

What could it? So why was her chest aching? But if he could stand it, then so could she. She could stand to not touch him, to be apart from him. She could, she really, really could, she told herself, even if all she wanted to do was put her hand in his and lean on him, feel his heart beating against hers again.

Faix sidled up to Nat. Wes looked sourly at the two of them. Nat wondered if he would really leave them behind, if Wes could say good-bye to her so casually after everything they had been through, without even giving her a chance to explain.

Finally, after the silence between them had turned from awkward to uncomfortable, Wes made his decision. "Look, if the two of you are going to join us, there are some ground rules. This is my crew and my command. You obey orders. We don't kill and we don't hurt anyone unless it's truly necessary. The world's fallen apart, but we haven't," he said. "I'm not in the business of killing kids."

Faix regarded him gravely. "Our opinions differ, Wesson, but I will abide by your rules. Anastasia is important to Vallonis. I am here by the order of the Queen to protect our last drakonrydder."

"Oh yeah? You're her bodyguard? Is that it?" Wes asked, annoyance and jealousy written all over his face.

Nat shook her head at Faix. *Don't spoil it. Stop taunting him.*

The drau looked amused. *Why not tell him what you really feel, as he is dying to know. Look at how angry he is because you are acting indifferent.*

She pushed Faix out of her head, unwilling and too stubborn to listen.

Wes cleared his throat.

"Thank you. We accept. We will join your crew," said Nat. "How far is the Red City?"

Wes sighed. "Two weeks, depending on the oceans, the trash, and the waves. It's hard to predict these things."

"Two weeks in one of those?" she asked Wes, motioning to the lifeboats.

Wes barked a laugh. "We wouldn't last two days in one of those." He looked up at the sky, searching for something, and Nat did the same, wondering what he was looking for. They heard it first, a loud whirring sound of blades cutting through the air, and a few minutes later a black helicopter appeared, hovering above the boat.

"That's our ride," Wes said with a grim smile. He hit his comm. "Shakes, you ready?"

"Roger that," Shakes replied. "Right behind you, boss. Almost finished packing."

"With any luck we'll be in the Red by tomorrow morning," he told Nat. "Listen, make sure your friend does everything I tell him, otherwise I *will* leave you both behind. I've got a bird to catch."

PART THE THIRD:

REAPING DAY

Often, for undaunted courage,
fate spares the man it has not already marked.

—BEOWULF

25

THE HELICOPTER LANDED ON THE DECK, like a fly on honey. Wes straightened his uniform and ran a hand through his hair, still unused to how short it was. Time to work. He counted twelve men on the chopper, guns in hand, visors, full body armor. Had someone snitched? Were they onto him?

Relax. It's just protocol.

Probably they'd just assumed they were landing in a hostile situation. Which they were, even if it wasn't the kind they expected.

A full strike team had arrived, and all Wes had was his wit and uniform, two loyal soldiers who were tired and hungry, a couple of smallmen, and of course Nat and that white-haired friend of hers. The two of them could probably waste the entire crew without blinking an eye, but that wasn't the way this was going down.

Wes planned to take control of that helicopter as easily as slipping a wallet out of someone's pocket or tricking a mark during a shell game—two things he had no problem doing.

Which cup held the ball? Whichever one you didn't pick. He'd had to steal every single thing he needed in his life, so he had lots of practice. From a limousine to take him to El Dorado to a chopper to take them to the Red City, and in the end he'd probably have to steal Nat away from that pretty boy, no matter what she said about them being only "friends."

That drau is nobody's friend.

He wasn't sure it was the right idea to take them along; he didn't trust the drau. But there was no way he was leaving Nat behind, and more than that, he couldn't leave her with *him*. The protector of Vallonis had her own protector. But after those horrid things he'd said to her, it wasn't as if Nat was going to fall into his arms anytime soon.

People say stuff all the time. It's not as if they mean it.

Wes wished he could erase the memory of even imagining those words, let alone saying them.

He could be such an icehole sometimes. But he didn't know what she was doing with the drau and he didn't want to think about it. He couldn't help but notice how alike they were, a matched pair, both of them in leather armor and carrying swords. *He's just a friend,* she'd sworn. And yet she couldn't leave Faix. Worse, she had defended him after he killed all those soldiers—boys and girls their age, some younger. And now she was looking at the white-haired motherfreezer like he was the second coming. Her Fake Blondie protector.

Wes snorted.

Excuse me while I fake vomit.

Wes looked anxiously at the *Goliath,* which was speeding away. Good. The pilgrims would make it to the Blue. Now all he had to do was get his crew safely and peacefully onto this chopper without hurting too many people.

Soldiers began to jump from the chopper, landing on the deck and fanning out, assessing the situation. "We got a distress signal," their sergeant said.

"Yeah, from me."

"You're Wesson?"

"Yeah."

"What the ice happened here?"

"Pilgrims shot at us as we tried to take them. They took out most of the crew and McCleod."

"Where are they?" the soldier asked, looking around at the empty deck.

"We gave them to the sea. Listen, I'd love to chat, but I need to get my team back to base and report to Bradley. I have some wounded soldiers here." He gestured toward Shakes and Farouk, who attempted to look critical. Cone, the fat kid they'd taken on, looked pale and frightened. Which wasn't a stretch for him.

"These your hostages?" the soldier asked, motioning to the smallmen, Nat, and Faix.

"Yeah," he said. "I got orders to take them back, too."

"Right, it's reaping day at the market, I remember," the soldier said. "Davey will take you back to base."

"No—I've got our own pilot. Command said you guys need to stay here to make sure they don't come back . . . secure the area."

The sergeant nodded and Wes ushered his crew into the chopper. Shakes went first, got in the pilot seat, put on the headphones, and started fiddling with the instruments. Then Farouk and Cone. Brendon and Roark shuffled on, followed by Nat and Faix.

The soldiers stared at the tall, white-haired boy in the black armor.

Faix stared back, his silver eyes glittering.

"You a drau or something?" the soldier asked. "Hey, man, look at his eyes! They just turned silver!"

"Naw, that's no drau, that's just a freak," the other soldier said, laughing as he poked Faix on the arm with the butt of his rifle.

"Leave him alone," Nat said.

"What are you, some kind of drau groupie?"

"Hey, it's the—it's the witch—the one—you know—the one who rides that thing!" the other soldier said excitedly. They leered at Nat, jockeying to get next to her. One of them took his handheld out and started taking pictures. Nat winced at the flash, and frowned as the boys crowded around her.

"She's pretty hot," one said. "Hey, Wesson, maybe leave this one behind for us, huh?"

"Knock it off," Wes growled, annoyed. "Don't even think about it." He knew Nat could take care of herself, but it didn't stop him from feeling protective. Besides, these kids didn't know what they were getting into. Nat's eyes were flashing angrily, and he'd seen what she could do when she looked like that.

Don't. Not here. Not like this.

One of the guys slung his arm around Nat's shoulders, and another groped her back, and that was all it took. "Don't touch me!" she yelled, pushing the soldiers away, and the scene dissolved into chaos.

Wes dived into the crowd around Nat, pulling the soldiers away from her, and one of the boys punched him right in the chin. Shakes and Farouk ran out of the chopper, along with the smallmen, to join the fray. Faix remained still, watching. For a bodyguard, he didn't seem too handy.

"DON'T SHOOT! DON'T SHOOT!" Wes ordered the group. He was still hoping to get out of this with his hands clean. "NAT!" he yelled, just as a snarling female soldier hit her from behind with her gun. Wes threw the soldier who was punching him to the ground and ran to her.

Nat was rolling on the floor, holding her shield to block another soldier's kicks. Wes jumped on the boy and began to pummel him. But they were losing, the chopper crew had full gear on, and in quick succession the smallmen were stunned, Shakes and Farouk were badly beat up, and he couldn't fight every one of them himself.

"Round 'em up, round 'em up!" the sergeant barked.

The soldiers moved to restrain them, holding out the shackles, but before they could touch any of them, each and every member of the strike team slumped to the ground, unconscious.

Wes looked down at them, and when he looked up, he met Faix's eyes.

The drau was serene. "I didn't kill them," he said mildly. "They are only asleep." The soldiers were lying on the deck, their mouths open, their eyes closed or rolled to the back of their heads.

"Well, you could've done that before we all got beat up, huh?" Wes asked as he helped Nat up. He checked the bruise on her cheek, which was already fading. "That icehole," he said, and he wasn't sure if he meant the guy who had groped Nat or the drau. Maybe both.

"It's okay, I can take care of myself," she said stiffly, moving away from him to stand next to Faix.

Great.

The three stood for a moment in uneasy silence, massaging their bruises, stretching their necks. Wes helped Shakes to his feet. A line of blood dribbled from Shakes's beard. Farouk lay on the deck, stunned, with Brendon and Roark attending to him. "He needs a healer," Roark said. "I think he has a concussion."

Faix knelt by the fallen soldier, murmured a few words, and gently placed his hands on his forehead. Farouk woke up and blinked his eyes.

Cone stuck his head out of the chopper. He had remained inside, scared to fight. "Is it over?"

No one answered him.

"Help me carry these soldiers to the hold," Wes said, gesturing to the one nearest the open doorway.

"Let me," said Faix. He followed Wes, taking the nearest soldiers and dragging them into the cell two at a time. Nat and Shakes carried the fourth. The rest of the team made quick work of the task, and they laid the soldiers next to each other in neat rows.

"They'll wake up soon; I used a rather gentle spell," said Faix.

Shakes looked skeptical.

Faix shrugged. "At least in my opinion it was gentle."

Wes tossed a case of MRSs into the room with them along with his satellite phone. "They can call for pickup when they do wake up."

Behind him, Shakes and Farouk were loading the chopper with supplies from the ship's kitchen. Brendon and Roark had already dug into the wafers. "Look! New flavors. Roast beef!"

Wes caught Nat's eye and for a brief moment they smiled at each other before looking away again. He knew what she was thinking. It was just like before. Now all they needed was Liannan.

26

NAT WATCHED AS WES WIPED MIST from the chopper window. Outside, snow covered the soft hills of the New Ganrajayan coastline. They'd been flying for hours. To mask their escape, Wes had removed the chopper's radio and satellite tracker, and smashed the black box recorder and the backup GPS. Shakes was flying blind, keeping the helicopter soaring low, below radar, and fast. Wes had done everything he could imagine to cloak their escape from the RSA, and Nat hoped it was enough.

Wes was sitting next to Shakes in the copilot's chair, the one that Farouk usually occupied, and Nat understood it was because he was avoiding her. Wes didn't trust Faix, and by extension, he didn't trust her, either. He hadn't said a word to her since they left the deck of the *Colossus. Boys.*

Nat knew he was jealous of Faix, but there was no reason to be. If only she could make him understand that she held no secret romantic attraction toward the unmasked drau. Faix was beautiful, but he was also foreign, ancient, strange. He was a guardian, a teacher, a mentor, a link to Vallonis's past and her heritage, and that was all. But there was no way to explain that to Wes if he refused to talk to her. He didn't even seem to want them on his crew, and had only taken them on grudgingly.

Next to her, Faix had retreated into a blank silence, his eyes open but glazed. He looked as if he was meditating. Perhaps he needed to rest. Magic was like any other kind of energy; magic had a tithe, when used it had to be replenished. It had limits. Even the drakon flagged, even the drakon needed time to heal. She reached out, tried to touch Faix's thoughts, but found only silence. His mind was closed to her for now.

Fine.

She left him alone. She wanted to learn more about her power, about Apis, but she understood his need for privacy. Liannan's call had interrupted her training, and she was eager to try again. As they flew through the clouds, Nat concentrated on her empty palms, trying to imagine a flame arising from deep inside herself. *The fire is within you.* Faix had made fire without a drakon, and said she could do the same, but how? Nat fixed her gaze on her empty hands, trying to conjure the feeling of fire and heat, to create something from nothing, to spark a flame without flint or match.

Nothing. She balled her fists in frustration, then unclenched, exhaling. Faix had said she could not let her emotions get the best of her. She would have to learn control, to use her power and exercise it at will, not as an unpredictable, violent, raging impulse.

Nat closed her eyes, searching for the drakon, across the many miles between them and the deep earth in which it was buried. *Where are you?* She felt so empty and alone without it.

She waited patiently for an answer, sending the same call again and again. Finally, a familiar jolt of power came rushing through her body, electric, the connection between them sparking once more. Her drakon was healing. Vallonis was nursing it back to life.

I am here. I have never left you.

A puff of smoke appeared, dancing on the palm of her hand. *The fire is within you.*

"What are you doing?" a voice interrupted her.

She looked up to see the new kid, Cone, watching her with widened eyes. "Did you do that? That's cool."

Nat closed her hand, feeling a little self-conscious to have been caught playing with fire, and the puff of smoke disappeared. "Just practicing."

Cone nodded as if she had just confirmed something.

"Can I ask you something?" she said.

"Sure," he said, weaving his fingers into a steeple, then quickly pulling them apart.

"Why did you want to follow me?"

The young boy chewed his lip and looked out the window, down at the inky waves that swirled between continents of ice. He squirmed uncomfortably in his seat. "There's nothing to live for, the world's done. Toast. We're drafted into the military, then spit out when they've used us up. All there is to eat is glop, all there is to drink is Nutri. There has to be something else out there. They lied to us. The Blue is real. There's . . . magic out there. Magic that will change the world. You're part of it, and I want to be part of it, too. Better here than stuck on that cruiser, that's for sure."

She smiled. "So you've gone AWOL. Wes is a bad influence."

"No," he said. "Not AWOL. I've done something better: I've died. For all they know, I was sucked into the black waters with the rest. I'm free. I can start again. I can fight, but this time I get to pick my side."

"I'm sorry about your friends," she said softly, thinking of the crew of the *Colossus* who had choked to death on the deck, felled by Faix's power.

"Those weren't my friends. I was new to this unit, and excuse my language, but they were a bunch of motherfreezers. They would have killed you without blinking if they'd had a chance. I don't want to be like them. I want to be brave. I want to be like you."

"I'm just as scared as everyone else," said Nat, leaning against the cockpit wall. "I just don't dwell on it that much. But thank you for believing in me," she said, the cabin feeling small. Nat smacked her head on a panel latch when she tried to back away from the kid.

Cone smiled. "I have to believe in something." Then he closed his eyes, too tired for more conversation. He slunk back into the tiny chair, trying to find a comfortable position in a seat that wasn't designed for comfort.

Nat noticed that behind her, the smallmen were sleeping on each other's shoulders, their heads touching, Roark snoring softly. They were all exhausted. She leaned back in her seat and was asleep before her eyes had closed.

When she woke up a few hours later, Wes was conferring with Cone and Farouk about the map. The frozen spires of

New Kandy loomed in the distance; they had arrived at their destination. "Are you sure?" Wes asked Cone.

"Yeah, the markets are over here, on this island off the mainland: They call it the Red City because sunset turns it red. It's the only place in the world that still gets a bit of natural sunlight, right before dark. That's where the guys said the base is." Cone said, pointing to a spot on the map that was unfolded on his lap.

"So we'll land over here," said Farouk.

"No, it's too risky and too near the base. I want to keep this chopper hidden so we can use it to get out of here," said Wes.

"What's over there?" asked Farouk, pointing to an unmarked area on the mainland.

Cone shrugged. "As far as I know, nothing. That could be good."

"No, that's too far to the ferry," said Wes. A boat made daily runs from the mainland to the island where the temple complex was located. They would need to make the trip from the landing site to the ferry on foot, but once they got off, it was only a short hike to the markets.

"How about over here?" Wes pointed to the other side. "What's that?"

"Ruins of the old city. They built Kandy Two on the other side," said Farouk.

"Okay, we'll land there. There will be room to hide this thing, and it's not far from the port."

Shakes landed the chopper behind a few burned-out buildings covered in snow and ice. The boys pulled their identifying stars and ranks from their collars and cut the name tags out of their pockets. Runners often wore military surplus, and once they were done, they'd look like just another ragtag team sent to collect trinkets from the markets for their rich clients.

"Here, let me," Nat said when Wes struggled to pull the lieutenant's stripes from his shoulder.

She put a hand on his arm and pulled delicately, her breath catching in her throat at how close they were.

"Thanks," he murmured, still unable to look her in the eye.

"You're welcome."

"I think you should stay behind, all of you," he said abruptly, meaning Nat, the smallmen, and Faix. "It's too dangerous. You know what they do in the markets, so close to the temple. We can't take that chance."

Nat's cheeks burned. "We're here to help." She brushed lint from Wes's uniform.

"And you'll be helping by staying safe," Wes said, adjusting the buttons on his jacket. "If we don't make it, you guys need to find Liannan and get out of here." He was using his commander's voice now, the one that sent men to battle. In spite of her irritation, she liked the ring of it, the authority it held. He had a day's worth of stubble on his jaw and the look of a man who hadn't slept in days, but was trying to keep the exhaustion off of his face, trying to appear brave.

"Cone, can you fly this thing?" he asked.

The big kid stood, looked at the pilot's seat and nodded. "Yeah," he said. "I flew one of these in basic."

"Good. You stick with the chopper, too," Wes said. He reached for the latch; he was going, leaving. The door inched open, cold air swept through the cockpit.

"How will we know you're all right? You threw out all the radios," she said, the freezing air turning her breath to white mist.

"Yeah, too dangerous, as they monitor all the open channels," Wes said, still fingering the latch. "But I got an idea. Your friend can read minds, right?" asked Wes, gesturing to Faix.

Nat nodded.

"Then he'll know if we run into trouble," he said, with a slight cheeky grin.

"I will," said Faix, who had awoken from his dreamlike state.

"I still don't like it," she muttered. She knew he was only looking out for them, but she wanted to stay close to him.

Wes yanked the latch, sliding the chopper's side door fully open, motioning for the others to go. Shakes and Farouk loaded their packs with provisions. They put up their hoods against the wind and left the chopper. Wes was next. He was leaving her again, and the ache in the hollow of her chest intensified.

He smiled as he fixed the straps on his gloves and lowered the hood over his face. "Don't worry about me, Nat. Like you, I can take care of myself," he said, echoing the words she often said to him.

"Don't," she said softly. "It's not funny."

"I didn't think it was," he said mildly.

They stared at each other. Maybe it was just too overwhelming to see one's beloved after months of wishing and hoping and dreaming. They were too shy, unsure if the other still felt the same as before. And so they had reverted to their sharp tongues, to their cool façades. When underneath, her heart was burning. And the way he was looking at her right now . . . like he couldn't believe she was there, like he wanted to eat her up, kneel at her feet and ravish her, all at the same moment—*if only he would*—

God, she loved him. Future or no future. Even with all the broken promises. What was a promise anyway? She wanted him. *I want you, Ryan Wesson. Always and forever.*

Now she just had to swallow her pride and admit it. *Wes, come back to me,* she wanted to say, but the words wouldn't come out.

So he shrugged, broke her gaze, and soon he was gone with the rest, lost to the snow.

27

IT WAS HARD TO LEAVE NAT AGAIN, almost worse than before, because at least the first time they had parted with a kiss and a promise. This time it was as if she didn't even care what happened to him; she barely even said good-bye. Wes gritted his teeth, his cheeks burning from the cold wind, and swore that he wouldn't let that happen again. What kind of game were they playing? This was not how he imagined their reunion, but then he hadn't accounted for her drau bodyguard, either. He had been kidding about having that guy read their minds; he didn't want that creepy consciousness anywhere near his. And while it hurt to leave her behind, he knew she was safer there, away from the greed of the crazed High Priestess and the flesh markets that sold *every* kind of meat—to eat, use or abuse, from bed slaves to powdered bones.

He led his team onward, passing the ruined debris of yet another glorious city from the past. Offshore, a cruise ship rested on its side, its hull wrapped in ice, waves pounding the warped metal. This had been a resort town once, in the time *before*. A century ago, families vacationed here. They rode Jet Skis and made sand castles. Wes and his boys picked their way through the snow, passing ancient souvenir stands filled with warped postcards with pictures of blue skies and cheerful umbrellas dotting the now-frozen shore.

A child of the postapocalypse, Wes could never shake the feeling that he had arrived too late to some grand party, that by the time he'd been born the lights were off and the dance floor was scuffed and littered with stubbed-out cigarettes and empty champagne bottles—the remainders of a party the likes of which the world would never see again. Not that he'd ever been to that kind of party, but he'd been to enough Studio 54 nights at Ice to make the connection. Although at the bar, patrons only smoked electronic ciggies and drank champagne-flavored Nutri. Nutri Bubble, it was called, and it tasted gross.

Farouk eyed the ancient cruise ship. "Bet there's some great swag on board. When that cruiser sank, people ran off, left everything behind." Farouk was always looking for souvenirs, for stuff he could sell in K-Town or on the black markets. Silverware or old computer parts could buy him a weekend in Ho Ho City. The kid was too easily distracted.

"We'll swim for souvenirs after we've found Liannan and Eliza. For now, let's focus," Wes said. He didn't know how long Eliza had or if she was even alive. But moving quickly gave them a better chance for a positive outcome. Command wasn't known for its efficiency, and Wes was counting on a few days before they freed the helicopter team and Bradley discovered that he had gone AWOL. Of course, Wes had always planned to break the agreement, but he had wanted to do it at the right time, when he held all the cards, when he knew Eliza was safe. But he was playing a losing game, and he was down to his last stack.

Wes and his team sloshed through the muck, past a shopping mall submerged in a glacier of black ice. Beyond the mall stood the skeletal remains of a few hotels and office buildings. Storms had ripped the windows from their frames, so only the columns remained, the steel red with rust.

The road they were taking crested a hill, and across the water they saw an island with a mountain in the center, its snowy peaks lost to the gray clouds. At the base of it was a shiny white temple with a statue of an elephant in the front courtyard.

"The Grand Temple; it's built right against the mountain," said Farouk. "In front of the temple is the market where you can, uh, buy things."

Things.

Talismans created from the bones of the marked. Their ashes were turned into "magic powder," their bones used as good-luck charms. Wes felt a chill from the very thought while next to him Shakes looked furious.

"Your clients risked the black waters to visit this place?" asked Wes.

"Not really. Most just send runners to buy goods from the market that they bring back to the domes. Wife needs a fertility treatment or some other miracle cure or potion the priests sell. But the bigwigs talked about it all the time, how visiting the Red City was high up on their bucket list. Shopping at the markets, and taking a turn at the abattoir."

"Abattoir?" Wes asked.

"Yeah, some kind of activity the priests run. Not sure what it is, supposed to be some kind of maze or something, or target practice maybe; they kept talking about the 'white hunt,'" said Farouk.

"Huh." Wes didn't like the sound of that. "I guess we'll find out soon enough."

"I guess so. You know, boss, that little move we made in El Dorado means I'm banned from New Veg. They'll have my head for busting up that limo." Farouk laughed, once, because none of it was really very funny. "Icehole."

Wes couldn't even manage a smile. "I don't think any of us are going back when this is over." He turned to Farouk. "I appreciate it, man."

"You should; this job doesn't even pay," Farouk said with a grin.

Shakes laughed. "Charity begins with Ryan Wesson, haven't you learned that by now, 'Rouk?"

"You kidding? I'm, like, the president of that charity." Farouk held out his hands. "What else do you want from me?"

"You'll learn." Shakes clapped him on the back.

"Yeah, I'll learn it the way I learn everything."

"The hard way?" Shakes held up his fist.

"No doubt." Farouk pounded it.

"You two iceholes done?" Wes rolled his eyes, but he felt gratified to have his friends with him, and wished he could offer them something more than just a life on the lam if they were lucky enough to survive this rescue. "All right, anyone asks, we're runners working for Diamond Jim," he said. "He needs some luck to put in his lucky dice."

"DJ? Didn't his casino burn down last month?" asked Shakes.

"In a ball of flame. But no one out here knows what's going on back home. The name might buy us some credibility," Wes said.

Farouk tapped the gun on his shoulder and nodded. "Should be a cakewalk."

"Like the rest of this?" Shakes quirked an eyebrow.

"Yeah, I'm a freezing baker," Wes said, with a sigh. He looked at Shakes. "Practically management material."

They left the ruins and came upon the new city. New Kandy was similar to New Vegas, a metropolis that bloomed in the ice around a desirable commodity. But if Vegas was in the business of marketing hope, luck, desire—a chance to win against the odds—New Kandy trafficked in darker stuff. It flowered beneath the mountain, at the foot of the white temple, and the hotels and inns that ringed the city served the needs of the tourists and the runners who came to buy the goods gleaned from the magical dead.

It was a racket, to be sure, just like New Vegas.

Only the stakes were higher.

Wes couldn't help but feel a chill up his spine as they entered the city proper, following a road that led to the port. The streets were filled with white-garbed priests and their acolytes, runners in their usual hodgepodge garb, slavers with their tattooed faces, swarms of soldiers giving everyone a cautious eye. The whole place weirded him out. *Between Dorado and NV and here,* he thought, *I'd pick the ocean full of garbage.*

The pier at the end of the road was new and shiny, cast in stainless steel to resist the toxic waters. The priests had cleared the debris and ice from the area around the pier. With the snow absent, the trash gone, the place looked half civilized.

They joined a group waiting for the ferry to arrive, made up mostly of runners like them, scraggly teams of ex-military types, who didn't blink an eye at their presence. Wes was glad for the company. Runners kept their mouths shut and didn't ask stupid questions. He sipped on a green Nutri Veggie and popped open a burger squeezer, trying not to wince at the puddinglike texture. Not too long after they arrived, a ferryboat appeared on the horizon, emblazoned with the words TEMPLE TRANSPORT on its side.

Easy enough.

As the boat drifted into the dock, sailors wearing white jackets leapt from the ferry, tossing ropes, mooring the white ship. Planks were drawn and connected, and soon tourists were exiting the ferry. Most were civilians, and their snug-fitting white heat suits and oxygen helmets said they were wealthy. These were the ones who literally could not breathe the same air as the rabble, air that was too toxic, too common. They were probably from the dome cities like El Dorado. This was an adventure for them, a taste of how the other half lived.

Wes couldn't help but hate them, and stifled an impulse to break their silly helmets. He overheard a few of the tourists talking about a "good hunt" and boasted about getting one "right between the eyes," and the queasy feeling in his stomach returned. It had to be some kind of illegal safari, although it was unclear what kind of game preserve could exist here. There was only that mountain and the temple.

Once the tourists were off the boat, the priests in the white jackets drew a second plank, opening a lower hold. Steerage passengers disembarked, runners in gray flack jackets and winter-white camouflage like theirs.

Finally it was time to board. "How much?" Wes asked when it was their turn.

"Everyone is welcome to visit the temple," said the temple representative on the dock, a fat, smiling young priest with a face full of white powder and chalk on his hands. "But it will cost extra to sit on the main level."

"Fine, we'll take last class," said Wes, taking three tickets that gave them access to the lower berth.

As they settled into the bowels of the boat, Wes, who didn't believe in anything but the cold, said a little prayer to keep his sister and his friends safe. He didn't know to whom he was praying, as religion hadn't been part of his upbringing. He thought he might have been praying to Nat's drakon. At the very least, the drakon had saved them once, and Wes could see no reason why it couldn't again.

Cakewalk, he thought, dropping his head into his hands.

28

So Wes was gone, again. Nat tried to tell herself it wasn't a big deal. Caring was hard, apathy easy. When she was a prisoner at MacArthur Med, her superiors had made her believe she was incapable of emotion, of any compassion or attachment. As she stood outside the chopper, watching him disappear into the mist, behind the tall snowbanks, leading Shakes and Farouk toward the ferry port, she *wished* she were incapable of any feeling. *Patient unable to love*, the doctors had written in her chart. She wished they had been right, because then she wouldn't be feeling the hurt she was feeling now.

Nat felt a comforting hand on her shoulder. Faix was standing next to her.

You should have told him how you felt, he sent.

I know, but I was too proud to admit my feelings, she replied.

I once thought as you do, and suffered for it. One day, he will be gone, and only your regret will remain.

She blinked away her tears. Faix was right. Life was too short and time too precious to waste. The next time she saw Wes, she would tell him, even if it meant she would be vulnerable, even if it meant acknowledging that she was the weaker one.

Love does not make you weak; it is the absence of it that does, sent Faix. "But alas, I must leave you for now," he said, in his speaking voice. It was then that she noticed he was wearing new armor, gleaming white like his hair, and had a long sword strapped to his back. Shaping the ether must come in handy when you needed a change of wardrobe, she thought with a smile, even though she was disconcerted by his announcement.

"Leave? Why? Where are you going? Back to Vallonis?"

He shook his head. "Someone whom I have been looking for called to me while I was resting."

"Who? Don't tell me I'm not your only student?" Nat tried to smile, but the thought of Faix leaving any of this to her alone was already making her heart pound.

"Remember the spell book I told you about, the one that was used in the binding of magic to the world? The one that is locked in the Gray Tower?"

She remembered. *"The Archimedes Palimpsest."*

He nodded. "I saw something in a dream while we were flying. I think I know where the thief is hiding," he said, looking like a ghost in the snow, his hair blending with the swirling flakes, his pale skin icy.

"Where?"

"Somewhere beneath that mountain"—he nodded, motioning to the island across the way—"very close by."

"And you can't wait? What about Wes? How will we know

if they run into something they can't handle? You were supposed to monitor their thoughts."

Faix's eyes glittered with amusement. "You can do the same."

"I can't."

"Yes, you can; you've shut them out deliberately because you *can* hear them. But now you must listen for them."

Nat felt a little abashed that he knew she was pretending she wasn't gifted with the same power. She had meant to tune it out, not wanting to pry, but now that she felt she had permission, she could hear them clearly. Shakes, thinking of Liannan, hoping to find her soon, worried, anxious, yet excited to be reunited with his beloved; Farouk, bitching to himself about the cold, but shouldering on, wondering when they would be able to eat. Wes . . . that was strange . . . she couldn't hear Wes . . . why was that? Maybe because she wanted to hear him so badly, or maybe she was protecting herself from knowing how he felt about her, as it would be too much like snooping. She could tune into Shakes and Farouk, and that was enough.

"Never underestimate your power," Faix was saying. "I have seen the fates in the glass. You remain the hope of Vallonis. Before it disappeared, I was able to read a few words from the palimpsest. 'The Resurrection of the Flame will light the world,'" he said, tapping her collarbone. "Take care, Nat. You are nothing like the small insect for which you are named." His mouth twisted into something close to a smile.

"Faix—" She felt bereft suddenly, to think of losing him, too, so soon after Wes.

"Take heart: If I am right about this, it will change everything for the better, and we will surely see each other again. This is not good-bye, only farewell." Then he was gone, disappearing into the ether as simply as winking out a light.

Roark stumbled out of the chopper, blinking his eyes. "Did I just see . . . ?"

"Yeah. He left," she said, feeling terribly alone.

"Good riddance."

She shook her head. "You still don't get it. He's fighting for the same thing we are."

"What is that? I forget." Roark smiled.

"For us. Everyone. For the survival of the Blue. To fix this broken world," she said softly. What did Faix mean by that? That she was the hope of Vallonis? That her fire would light the world? But there was no time to ponder, for there was movement on the horizon. She squinted. "Do you see that?"

"Aye," Roark said, fingering his dagger.

A white military truck moved in the distance—the blizzard, acting as a camouflage, made it hard to see until now. "How many?" Nat whispered.

"Too many for us to handle," Roark replied grimly.

"Let's get back in the chopper," she whispered. "Maybe they won't see us." He nodded, and they crept back into the helicopter and closed the door.

"What?" Brendon asked, when he saw their faces.

Cone was about to speak when Nat put a finger to her mouth and gestured out the window. The stout boy's face turned crimson with fear when he saw the truck. They all held their breath as it moved past them slowly.

Roark and Brendon huddled together in the first row of seats. The smallmen had spent weeks in a detention center, where they'd endured long hours of isolation, little food, no sunlight. She wanted to console them, but she didn't know how. She'd never had a mother, a family. *Help them stay alive— that's all I can do.* Nat felt claustrophobic, and her legs ached from crouching. She hoped the truck would pass soon, and after what felt like an eternity, she stuck her head above the seats to try to see outside.

"Looks like we're okay," she said, just as a gloved finger tapped the windowpane.

"Open up," a hoarse voice called.

Nat looked down, now understanding that she hadn't seen the truck anywhere because the soldiers had come on foot and surrounded the chopper. *Freeze it. Rookie mistake.* She and her friends would be captured unless she acted quickly, just as Faix had done when he'd disarmed the soldiers on the navy cruiser.

Use the ether. Use your power.

She imagined their guns torn from their hands, flying through the air, the soldiers knocked out cold in the snow. But when she opened her eyes, they were still standing there, more irritated than before.

Don't hurt us. Go away. Leave us alone.

She tried again, but the soldiers remained where they were, stoic, immobile, their guns cocked and ready to fire.

Freezing ice!

"Open up, I won't ask again," the soldier warned.

Faix was wrong. She was powerless and weak on her own; she couldn't even keep her crew safe for half a day. She opened the chopper door before they blasted their way inside.

Sometimes surrender was the only option.

29

THE BOAT DOCKED AND DISCHARGED
its passengers, and Wes and his team shuffled out with the
rest. Farouk had uncharacteristically complained of seasick-
ness during the trip, and the minute they set foot on land,
he retched all over the snow, the sickly glop smelling of que-
sadilla foam and Caffie-Nutri (the super-caffeinated flavor
popular with the younger kids: Caffie-Nutri! Twice the fun!
Twice the excitement!).

"Yum," said Shakes.

"Ice you," muttered Farouk, wiping his mouth with the
back of his hand.

"Stop squabbling," Wes ordered, tense as they joined the
crowd headed toward the line of white plastic tents in front
of the temple gateway. The famous flesh markets. *Was this
where Eliza and Liannan had been brought?* It wasn't as he had
pictured it at all. He had assumed it would be dirty and dis-
gusting, filled with cannibal outlaws and whimpering slaves,
meat of questionable origin hanging on hooks.

This was nothing of the sort. The brightly ordered streets were filled with pristine white tents, their wares displayed behind glass cases set on gleaming white tables. The products themselves were packaged mostly in white Styrofoam boxes. Discreet signs read CHARMS, POWDERS, or VICTUALS. Towering above the market was a surprisingly tasteful and tall structure built from the purest white Carrara marble. The white temple was sleek and angular, its base carved from the side of the mountain, its peak stretching as tall as the first low cliffs.

"Where's the RSA base?" asked Wes. "Cone said it would be right here. Farouk, go check it out."

"Let's keep going," said Shakes, narrowing his eyes at the people crowded around the outdoor market. The white tents whipped in the wind, and the heat elite pawed through the products on the tables, fingering trinkets, holding them up to the light. No matter how white and clean and pure everything looked, the place had an air of sterility and death. The white marble and polished steel tables were reminiscent of a morgue or a butcher's shop.

The whole place made Wes's stomach churn. He couldn't watch tourists picking through charms and talismans as if they were candy, when, in fact, they were handling the bones of the dead. The priests wore white powder on their skin, covering their hands and faces. It looked like talcum powder, but Wes couldn't be certain. *Could be bone dust*, he thought with a shudder.

But whose bones? The marked? People like my sister?

"Sylph powder! Sylph powder here!" hawked a nearby seller.

This priest wore silvery hair extensions woven into his gray strands. Wes didn't want to think about where they came from.

"What the hell is sylph powder?" growled Shakes.

"A skin treatment," the priest said with a gleam in his eye. "Make your skin shine like theirs, eh? Or for your lady back home?"

Shakes lunged for the man, putting his hands around his neck and throttling him. "I'll give you freezing sylph powder!" Farouk and Wes had to restrain him as the priest shrieked for the soldiers' protection.

"It's not her," Wes whispered fiercely, hustling his friend away. "It's not Liannan. Nat said she was alive, that they're *keeping* her alive. We'll find her, okay? It's not her. Calm down, or they'll get us before we get to her."

Shakes took a deep breath and stopped fighting. "Okay."

Wes nudged one of the runners crowded around a display of glass charms, a young kid no older than fourteen with zits on his chin, an ugly scar on his cheek.

"What's that?" he asked.

"Eye charms. Look at the colored iris inside, it gives luck to the wearer," the kid said. "They're popular where I'm from."

Wes made a face. "Yeah? Well, where I'm from, those make you look like an idiot." Which wasn't exactly truthful, as New Vegas was full of eye charms. Better than a rabbit's foot.

The kid shrugged. "You getting one? No? Okay. More for me," he said as he scooped up the charms and paid with his watts.

"What's happening over there?" Wes asked, motioning to

the side entrance of the marble tower, where a group of tourists was lining up, many of them carrying weapons of some sort, automatic rifles, deadly-looking knives, even crossbows.

"Line for the abattoir. Isn't that why you're here?" he asked, sizing up their guns. "It's reaping day. The white hunt."

"Right. So we just line up, then?" Wes asked. "It takes you right inside the temple?"

"Yeah, pretty much, but you go through security before they let you in," the boy said. "If you check out, you get to play; if not . . ."

"If not?" Shakes asked.

"If you don't pass the test, you don't get to leave." The boy chuckled. "It's no big deal. They don't want some lockhead ruining the party. I'm sure you losers will be fine, you guys don't look like anything but a bunch of Vegas donkeys." He ran off then, catching up to another group.

"Heatbag," Shakes muttered. "How'd he know?"

Farouk returned. "I asked around about the RSA base, and everyone just laughed at me or looked at me funny. I don't get it. It's got to be around here; there are enough soldiers here to field an army. What about you guys?"

"We're getting in that line," said Wes. "Whatever it is, it takes us inside the temple where Eliza and Liannan are."

A dozen or so unarmed white-cloaked priests flanked the entrance. Cameras dotted the ceiling to let the visitors know they were being watched. The real security was probably nearby, scanning the video feed, waiting to pounce if something went wrong.

A white-robed priest with a third eye tattooed on his

forehead welcomed them. "We are blessed to have so many of you partake in the white hunt today." He smiled broadly. "As a reminder, once you have made your shot, please follow the signs to the exit and allow the next person to have their chance. If this is not your first time, please follow me; otherwise, remain here for the mandatory inspection."

The groups separated accordingly, and Wes and his boys were among the few who remained.

"Are you all together?" the priest asked. "What is the purpose of your visit?"

"We're here for Diamond Jim; he needs a few more of his lucky dice," said Wes.

"Ah, the Diamond Casino, of course." The priest nodded. "Welcome. Your first time in New Kandy?"

Wes nodded, and the three of them were sent to a small room to the side where a young girl with yellow eyes and a fearful expression stood alone in the middle of the room. She greeted the three boys with a nod.

"Arms up," she said.

Wes raised his hands. Shakes and Farouk did the same.

She closed her eyes.

Wes wondered what was going on. What kind of inspection *was* this anyway? Then he felt a painful jolt in his head, as if stung by a laser or a force of some kind, and he batted it away angrily until it subsided.

Get out of my head.

The girl opened her eyes. "Who did that?"

Farouk shook his head and Shakes shrugged his shoulders. "Do what?"

"We don't know what you're talking about," Wes said coolly. "Can we go now?" He wasn't even sure what she meant—that thing? That thing where he batted the dark away? Was that what she meant?

He wasn't even sure he could say what had happened.

He had acted out of instinct and hadn't even realized he'd done it until it was gone. But what had he done exactly? His hands trembled and his head hurt as a wave of sickness overwhelmed him.

The priestess looked up at the camera in the ceiling and shook her head. In a moment, the entrance to the room was barricaded with priests holding weapons and iron shackles.

"What is it, beloved?" an older priestess asked, her voice feverish with excitement. "What have you found?"

The girl pointed to the boys. "One of these three is marked."

30

"GOOD HUNTING," THE SOLDIERS SAID to each other as they surveyed their hostages.

"Reaping day, too. Priests will be happy to see you, tiger eyes," one of them said, chucking Nat's chin before cuffing her wrists with heavy iron shackles. "You'll make a nice little eye charm, won't you?"

Nat grimaced as an image came to mind suddenly, and she saw herself lying on a marble slab while a white priest plucked her eyes from their sockets and placed each one in a hollow glass charm for a wealthy woman to wear when she hit the slots in New Vegas. *Blood running down the white stone.* Nat had seen those eye charms all her life, but she thought they were fake, made in a factory in Xian. She wanted to throw up.

"What've we got here?" an older soldier asked.

"Two pint-sized and a marked girl," the boy replied.

"What about you, fatty?" he asked. "You marked, too?"

"No, sir," Cone replied.

"Deserter, huh?" the captain said, noticing Cone's uniform.

"No—I . . ."

Before the boy could finish protesting, and without a moment's hesitation, the captain shot him in the face.

Dead as snow.

Cone fell to the ground with a thud, his blood red and thick, covering the white beneath him.

Cone!

Nat was too shocked to scream. For a moment, the iron bonds on her wrist stretched to breaking, then snapped back together. She fell to her knees. *He was just a kid. He hadn't even had a chance to fight yet. And they killed him because he wasn't marked, wasn't magic like us. If they'll kill ordinary folk like flies, what will they do to us?*

Brendon and Roark were speechless. They looked up at Nat, their eyes wide with fear and bewilderment. She shook her head. He was just a boy who'd wanted to follow the drakonrydder, who'd believed in her, and she'd failed him.

"Come on. Get in the truck," one of the soldiers said, leading them to their vehicle, a modified Hummer like the one Wes had used to transport her out of New Vegas.

"Where are you taking us?" she asked the soldiers as they were led inside the cargo hold and made to sit on the floor of the truck. She was still shaking from seeing Cone murdered right in front of them.

"You'll see soon enough." The boy smirked.

"Let's hope they can run fast," another snickered. "Tourists like a bit of excitement."

Then the doors slammed, the truck lurched, and they were

off. The road was bumpy; the constant jostling made her feel nauseated. From the window, she could see that they were heading out of the ruins and into the city limits.

"Help us! Help us!" she cried.

Roark and Brendon banged on the iron bars as well. "Help!"

The streets were crowded with tourists, runners, hawkers, and priests in their white cloaks and powdered faces. She spotted the runners first—shaggy young guys with a weary, grizzled air, guns slung over their shoulders. Was Wes one of them? Where was he?

A few people in the crowded streets looked up with curiosity, but no one helped. It was as if screaming captives were a common sight in New Kandy, and knowing the rumors about the city, maybe they were.

The truck entered a tunnel and everything went black. There were no lights inside the cargo hold, and iron made Nat feel physically sick, like she couldn't even properly think or speak. She was unaccustomed to complete darkness. She had lived for months with the drakon at her side, its fire lighting the sky, its flames keeping the cold and darkness at bay.

She struggled against her shackles, trying to imagine them destroyed, breaking them down to their molecules, to see their atoms spinning so she could turn them into something else. She could do this. She had broken iron shackles before. But it was as if Cone's death had numbed her, weakened her, and all she could accomplish was a little rattling of her chains. Maybe that was the idea. The captain had killed Cone as a warning, to make sure the rest of them remained cowering and submissive.

If that was the case, it had worked.

Finally the truck stopped, and the sound of the lock turning echoed in the small chamber as the latch released and the back doors swung open. A soldier motioned them forward.

Nat stepped out of the truck, clenching and unclenching her fists, looking around wearily. Roark came next, blinking his eyes against the darkness, then Brendon, who was coughing.

They were in some kind of building, and the soldiers herded them toward a flickering light in a far corner. Nat was surprised to find the walls looked familiar. These were the white stone walls and the concrete floors that she had seen in her vision of Liannan. The endless corridors filled with prison cells, the cries and screams of the pilgrims. On the far end was another hallway, and above its arch were engraved the words SACRIFICE IS FREEDOM.

A priest walked over to the three of them. "We are blessed to have you. You honor us with your presence. We hope to be worthy of your sacrifice."

My sacrifice?

Mine and Cone's and Liannan's?

The whole gray world?

Would any of it ever be enough?

Nat spat in his face.

The priest smiled and licked the liquid from his lips. "A taste of the divine."

The soldier herded them into one of the cells and locked the door. "Put your hands up to the bars," he ordered, holding up a key.

Nat did, and he took off the handcuffs. He did the same to the smallmen. Then the soldier left them alone in the cell.

She slid down the length of the wall and put her head in her hands. Where was the rest of their team? Did they find Liannan? Was Wes nearby? They had come to rescue their friend and now needed rescue themselves. *Some mission,* she thought, and an awkward chuckle bubbled up from her chest.

"What's so funny?" Brendon asked.

She told them.

He gave a faint grin. "Yeah, we suck." His red curls covered his face, and Nat had to remind herself that the smallman was older than her, even though he looked so young. Roark's greater bulk made him appear less childlike, but she sometimes mistook him for someone half her age as well.

"It's all right, we always get out somehow," Roark said. "They haven't gotten the best of us yet." He put an arm around Brendon and kissed his forehead.

Nat was glad they had each other. She wished she had Wes by her side, too. To die without seeing him again was too awful to contemplate.

If only she'd been brave enough to tell him what she was really feeling. If only . . . What if she never saw him again? What if he died without knowing? What if she did?

And where was Faix? He said they would see each other again, so that had to mean they would survive this, whatever it was. She tried to sense Mainas, but the drakon did not respond, which wasn't surprising since Nat was surrounded by a suffocating amount of iron.

They were going to die here if she couldn't figure out what to do.

Sacrifice is freedom. She didn't want to stay long enough to learn what that meant, but she had a feeling she already knew.

Eye charms.

Reaping day.

Tourists like a bit of excitement.

This was how the priests killed the marked. It was a bitter truth. They had others do it for them—for sport—as entertainment. Ending her life would be someone else's great adventure. *I hope they enjoy the sacrifice.*

31

WES AND HIS TEAM HAD BECOME prisoners just as quickly as they'd been welcomed with open arms. *If you don't pass the test, you don't get to leave,* that young, obnoxious runner had told him. *One of these three is marked.* But who? Him? Shakes? Farouk? His friends were just as dark-eyed and powerless as he. No, this only meant the priests were on to them; they'd seen them arrive in the chopper, and somehow they knew Wes and his boys weren't who they said they were.

"You're making a huge mistake," Wes said, as the guards disarmed and quickly ushered them down into the bowels of the temple. "Look at our eyes! We're not marked!"

"The Beloved is never wrong," the priest said. "Do not fear, your sacrifice is an honor, and in sacrifice you will find freedom."

As they were hustled into their cells, he saw soldiers every-where: guarding doors, keeping an eye on tourists who were being led to another room. So many soldiers—this place was crawling with military.

Then he realized why Farouk had only encountered laughter when he asked about the location of the base. The base wasn't near the temple. The base *was* the temple, or the temple was the RSA base. He didn't know why he didn't realize it sooner.

It was all so simple.

We've got a base out there, a place to get rid of those we no longer need.

The military used the white priests as a cover to dispose of the marked captives once they were no longer of use, *and* profited from their deaths.

Wes felt ill. At least he knew where Eliza was now.

"Welcome to the abattoir. You bless us with your sacrifice," said a disembodied voice. Wes and his team were standing shoulder to shoulder with the marked victims, whose brightly colored eyes were glowing in the dark. They looked thin, pale, undernourished. They were all in some kind of holding pen before the labyrinth. Across from the corridor, dimly, he saw a second pen with even more prisoners.

He couldn't see much; the maze was built into the caverns beneath the mountain, and their footsteps echoed on the hard surface. The echoes suggested a larger space, a vast nothingness, but looking up, he saw another path carved above theirs, where silhouettes lingered in shadow, men and women holding rifles, perched on catwalks, dangling above the path, just waiting for the poor saps who would run below.

This wasn't a hunt, this was a slaughter. It was then that he remembered "abattoir" was another word for "slaughterhouse."

There were dozens of victims with them in the pen, and Wes gathered his team around him. "Okay, listen up, once those gates open and they let everyone out, don't run. The best way to stay alive is to find a place to hide. When the track clears, we need to get up on that ledge somehow, take one of their weapons, then find the exit."

"I don't want to die," Farouk said.

"I know," Wes consoled, but Farouk couldn't shut up.

"I'm not freezing joking when I say that. Like, I really, really don't want to die," the younger boy said.

Wes grabbed him by the shoulder. "You won't, icehole, I promise. Hide, and when I give the signal, come out."

"LADIES AND GENTLEMEN!" intoned a voice from above. "THE WHITE HUNT IS ON! REAPING DAY IS UPON US! GODSPEED AND GOOD LUCK TO ALL!"

The iron bars creaked open, releasing the prisoners. As the marked fled the pen, Wes noticed that the bars to the second cage hadn't opened. He guessed the organizers were staging the prisoners' release times, saving half of the marked, so they could release the remaining captives later. Perhaps they didn't want to choke the maze with kids, or maybe they just wanted reaping day to last a little longer.

Red lights flickered above the maze. The caverns beyond were carved with swirling niches, deep hollows, and winding passages: places where the marked could hide, for a time, from the snipers. It looked as if the passages were designed to prolong the hunt, to make the snipers work for each kill, to increase the hunters' pleasure.

The prisoners scrambled into a maze of caverns, dashing as

fast as they could, the hunters above running and whooping after them. Just as planned, Wes and his team held back, and soon found a shallow crevice to hide in.

All around them, the marked victims screamed as hunters picked them off one by one. The floors ran slick with blood and the tunnels echoed with cries of death and victory. It was a stampede that quickly turned into a massacre.

"We need to separate," Wes said, panting. "I'll go right, you guys go left. Give the signal once we find the exit. Got it?"

Shakes and Farouk nodded.

Someone shot at their feet. Wes looked up to see a hunter smile. The man was gray-haired and deeply tanned, like the men he'd glimpsed in the Dorado. Wes gave him the finger and kept running. He didn't look back to see if his friends had made it; he had to assume they had. They were too fast and too smart to be shot by some thrill-seeking tourist.

It had been a good call to hide at the beginning. Once he started running, he couldn't stop. The tunnels were long and twisty, and once in a while they opened to a huge space. If he could just keep out of those pockets and hide in the smaller tunnels where no one wanted to go, he would be safe.

Lucky for him, the tourists were awful shots. There was another one now, sighting him with his scope, fumbling with the lens. While the guy was trying to figure out how to target, Wes climbed the rocks and ripped the rifle out of the tourist's hands, then pulled off his oxygen helmet, too. The guy screamed, as if breathing the moldy air under the cavern was going to kill him.

Wes knocked him on the jaw.

"I should shoot you right now," Wes said, putting the rifle in the guy's face, pressing it against his nose.

"Don't. Please don't."

"Which way out?" he asked. "WHICH WAY?"

"That way," the tourist said, pointing to a path that led deeper into the cavern.

"What do you think I am, a sucker?"

"No—no—there's a door there, a staircase, it will take you to the surface, I swear. It's the only way out of here. Please don't kill me. Please don't kill me."

Wes pushed him away and ran. He had to get his friends first. He whistled the signal and waited. Shakes whistled back, then Farouk. Two more whistles to let them know the exit was on the right. He'd meet them there.

Then a few more bullets grazed his shoulder. Another hunter, a better shot, and this one didn't stop firing. Wes raised his stolen rifle and pulled the trigger. He squeezed once, twice, but nothing happened. The rifle was jammed. A bullet from the tourist's rifle pierced his leg. Wes tossed aside the jammed rifle as he collapsed to the floor in shock, and then the pain set in. The hunter closed in for the kill. This was it. This was how he was going to die, in this dark cavern, alone and bleeding.

"WES!"

He looked up.

It was Nat. She was crouching in a nearby crevice. "Here! Hurry! Hurry!"

With the last ounce of energy he had left, he crawled, dragging himself toward her, and she pulled him into the safety of the hidden cave as the hunter kept firing, bullets ricocheting against the stone, preventing them from escaping the cavern or approaching the cave's narrow mouth.

She took him in her arms and he could smell her hair, the heady scent of smoke mingling with the sweeter scent just below, which always reminded him of home. She was here. It was as if he had dreamed her up, the one person he wanted to see so badly, right in front of him. If it was a dream, he didn't want to wake up, and if it wasn't, he was glad he wouldn't die alone.

32

NAT HELD WES IN HER ARMS. "YOU'RE
not dead yet, come on, don't be a drama queen," she teased
gently as she helped him sit on the rocky floor. He was bleeding and cold to the touch, probably from shock. "Donnie, we
need to make a tourniquet for his leg," she said. She knelt
down and peeled back the fabric of his pants where the bullet
had hit him. It was an ugly gash, but clean.

Nat, Brendon, and Roark had been hiding since the hunt
started, deciding to wait it out before trying to find a way off
the killing floor. She thought they'd been targeted until she
realized it was Wes who had been shot right in front of her.

Brendon handed over his kerchief and, together with Roark,
fashioned a bandage on Wes's leg. Outside their hidden cavern,
the hunter had stopped firing and moved on to easier prey.

"Where are Shakes and Farouk? They're not—" she asked,
fearing the worst.

"They're meeting us at the exit. I found out where it was
before that heatbag shot me." He smiled at the smallmen and
thanked them for dressing his wound, then looked around.
"Where's Cone?"

She shook her head. She couldn't say it.

His face changed, and his eyes looked pained.

"I know. I'm sorry. I couldn't keep them safe . . . they surrounded us, and they killed him because he was a deserter and wasn't marked. Right in front of us."

"It's not your fault," he said softly.

Hearing those words broke something inside her, and this time it was Nat who fell into his arms. Wes seemed surprised at first, but he held her, letting her grief wash over him. He was a bulwark, a rock, someone she could lean on who wouldn't break underneath her sorrow. "Nat," he said huskily, wiping away her tears with his fingers.

"Yeah?"

He smiled. "People say stuff all the time. They don't mean it. I'm sorry . . ."

"Shut up," she said, and then she didn't wait anymore. She pulled him close, tugging on the cords of his hood so that he had no choice but to lean toward her. She breathed into him, happy to find a haven in this madness. He put his hands against her face and kissed her, slowly at first, as if savoring every moment, and when she opened her mouth to his, their kisses turned urgent, breathless and dizzying.

When they finally stopped, he was smiling. "I should have done that earlier."

"I can't argue with that."

"I missed you," he said.

"Me too. More than you know."

"Really?" He was grinning broadly now.

"Really."

"Good." He picked up her hand and kissed it, his lips soft against her skin.

"Are you guys done? We're kind of tired of trying to pretend we didn't just see that." Roark snorted. "Although the nausea will remind us."

"I don't know, I rather enjoyed it," Brendon said wickedly.

"You and me both, man." Wes winked. "Now, what do you say we bust this joint?" he said, as he tried to stand and winced.

Nat slung his arm over her shoulders. "Can you put any weight on it?"

"I'll have to," he said.

"That's okay, I have you," she told him. "Did you find Eliza?" she asked.

He shook his head. "What about Liannnan?"

She sighed. "We'll find them. I know we will."

One by one they left the safety of the niche and headed down the narrow, winding cavern, Wes hobbling along, leaning on Nat as they inched their way out. Wes gave the signal again, and was relieved to hear both Shakes's and Farouk's responses. Nat was starting to think they could actually get out when a voice boomed from above, along with the familiar click of a gun.

"Not so fast."

They froze. Nat looked up. There was a hunter right above them. But this one wasn't a tourist—she recognized that voice and wanted to flee. It was Bradley, the commander. As if they needed any more confirmation that the RSA was behind this whole enterprise.

He was savoring the moment—that much was clear.

"Look what we have here. A two-for-one special. The girl who can fly and the boy who always says no. Oh, wait, and two littles to add to my collection. Maybe I'll wear their tiny little bones on my medals. I hear they're particularly lucky for finding food." He aimed his gun right at Wes. "I have no idea how you got here, Wesson, but you are exactly where you need to be."

"Say good-bye, ice trash." He squeezed the trigger.

It was like everything happened in slow motion. Nat stared at the bullet that was whizzing its way toward Wes's heart. She'd been here before; she had saved him from death once already. That first time, on the black water, she had no idea what she had done. She had no idea how her love had saved him from death.

But this time she did.

She looked up at Bradley. There was no emotion on her face and she felt none in her heart. Not fear. Not anger. *Control* was the key to her power, Faix had told her. Control was the essence of her power.

The fire is within you.

She saw the man who had tortured and used her, the commander who had forced her to steal children from their mother's arms, who was going to cut down her friends one by one, starting with the one she loved most.

But she felt no rage, no anger, no fear, only a supreme sense of herself, of calm and logic.

Control, Faix had told her.

Wes was still leaning on her shoulder, still smiling at her.

Maybe, to tap into your power, all you need to do is think of me.

Those were his words on the black ocean, when she had saved them the first time.

Faix was right, but not completely. Having control was not enough. Emotion was also part of her power, and love was stronger than fury, stronger than rage, and it was her love that she used now. Her fierce and abiding love for Wes, for Brendon and Roark, for Cone, who had died too young, for Shakes and Farouk, still hidden in the maze, and her love for her drakon, buried underground but alive inside her.

The fire is within you.

The fire burned deep in her soul, white-hot, as bright as daylight, and she screamed as she unleashed it onto the commander, melting the bullet he had sent toward Wes and setting him ablaze. Setting the cavern afire. Burn down this temple. Burn down this house of horrors.

White fire that could burn rock and melt stone.

Drakonfire.

"RUN!" Wes yelled, pulling her and the smallmen toward the exit, where Shakes and Farouk were already waiting. When they got there, they found that the force of her blast had opened the doors, and they all ran.

Inside the maze, the killing floor was burning as the marked victims ran out, as the screams of the hunters echoed through the tunnels.

33

WES LED THE TEAM OUT OF THE MAZE
and into the temple, rushing past the terrified priests who
ran from them. A few soldiers tried to stop them, but even
they ran when they caught sight of Nat. Beautiful Anastasia
Dekesthalias. The Resurrection of the Flame.

"Why are they screaming?" she asked.

"Because you're covered in fire," Wes told her, awed. She
was standing in the middle of a bonfire, covered in the hot
white light, just as she had been on the deck of the *Colossus*.
Her face and her skin and her eyes were glowing.

"I am?"

She held up her hands, amazed at the sight of the flames
that danced on her skin. She looked afraid, and so, without
thinking, he took her hand and held it. "Let it burn," he said
softly. "It's beautiful. You're beautiful." He touched her cheek,
her hair, and bent to kiss her through the flames.

The fire did not burn him, only tickled and caressed his
skin like warm feathers all over his body. She looked into his
eyes and smiled, and he knew they understood each other.

The marked victims were coming out of the second pen, the

cage that hadn't opened at the start of reaping day, and when they saw Nat covered in fire, they blessed themselves. *Bless the drakon. Bless its rydder. Bless the fire that will light the world.*

"Liannan," Shakes said hoarsely, interrupting the two of them. "Where is Liannan? Did you find her?" Shakes's desperation reminded Wes he was there for someone, too. Eliza.

Nat shook her head, and the flame disappeared. She was just Nat again—the armor was gone, and she was dressed simply in black jeans, worn boots, and the flannel shirt she wore on the first night out of New Vegas.

Wes raised his eyebrow. "What other costume changes have you got under there?" he asked. "Because I have a few ideas," he said with a grin. "And they're all hot."

"Shush," she said as they ran down the hallway after Shakes. "But what did you have in mind?" she teased.

"Liannan!" Shakes yelled, pushing into the crowd, scanning faces, looking for a sylph, finding one, then another. "LIANNAN!"

Wes skidded to a halt. "Listen, I've got to check the cells for Eliza . . . she's here somewhere."

Nat nodded. "I understand. Go. I'll stay with Shakes."

"Take Brendon and Roark, I'll go with Farouk," he said. "We'll meet you guys at the entrance in five."

"Right," she said, motioning for the smallmen to follow her. Farouk ran to Wes's side.

She turned away when he caught her hands again.

"I don't want to leave you," he said. He didn't want to let go.

"You won't. Not ever. I'll always be with you," she said, squeezing his hands. She stood on her tiptoes and kissed him again, then unlaced her hands from his. "But Liannan and Eliza need us."

He nodded. Of course they did, it was why they were here in the first place. "Liannan needs our help, but the only person Eliza ever needed saving from was herself," Wes muttered.

Then Nat turned away from him. "Shakes—I think I know where Liannan is. Hurry!"

Wes watched them disappear down one of the marble hallways, his heart beating painfully in his chest.

"Where to, boss?" Farouk asked.

Records. There would have to be records on file somewhere. Prisoner records. Lists. He couldn't go searching the whole place for her cell; it would take forever, and he would be too late again. "The office—come on. There have to be some manifests. She just got here."

They found the office in the front rooms. It was abandoned, the priests having fled, and the whole temple was beginning to fill with smoke. Wes flung open file cabinets, hurling files and folders every which way as he searched for his sister's name on the documents. Where was she? Where was Eliza? Had they killed her already? Was he too late?

Farouk booted up the computer. He banged on the keyboard and scrolled through the screens.

"What've you got?" asked Wes, looking over his shoulder.

"Prisoner transport from El Dorado. Couple weeks ago. This is it. She must be on this list." Farouk ran his finger down the screen, looking through the names. But there was nothing. No Eliza.

"She's not here," Farouk said, fingers flying on the keyboard again as he tried a couple more searches. "That's weird. Your hacker said she was in the program, right?"

Wes nodded.

"But there's no record of Elizabeth Wesson anywhere. Not even in their main file. She's never been a prisoner of the RSA. I don't get it."

"What do you mean?"

"She's not in any of the detention centers. See? Those are blacked out, but I was able to get through the firewall to figure out the names of the people they're holding—"

"Yeah, yeah, get to the point."

"There's no record of her anywhere in the system."

What did that mean? She'd been on the transfer list in El Dorado. And Bradley had threatened him with his sister's death to get him to accept his commission.

"Check the blacklists," he insisted.

Farouk shook his head. "I already did. I went there first."

"Do it again!"

Farouk typed a few letters on the keyboard. The screen flashed with FILE NOT FOUND. ERROR.

Wes shook his head. "Maybe they purged the records."

"Maybe. But I doubt it, there's always a trail."

Wes felt a sick sensation, and he remembered what he'd said to Nat. *The only person Eliza ever needed saving from was herself.* There was something wrong here . . . something didn't add up, and he had a dark, terrible suspicion that he knew what it was.

34

"WE'LL FIND HER," NAT TOLD SHAKES, who had run ahead, opening cell doors one after another, calling Liannan's name. "She's here. She's really here."

She heard Liannan's voice in her head so clearly, it was as if the sylph were right in front of her. *Nat, hurry! Hurry! Nat!* The priests and soldiers had abandoned their posts, and tourists ran in all directions while the marked victims, unshackled and unrestrained, trained their power on their former captors, helping the fire grow, letting it burn.

"They must have kept the sylphs in a special place," Roark said, "since none of them were in the maze with us."

"Good idea," Brendon said, huffing next to him.

"Shakes! We need to go this way," Roark said, motioning to stairs that led away from the prison cells. "These pens open up to the maze, and there were no sylphs on the killing floor."

Shakes nodded, his face pale and anxious. The fire was contained in the lower levels for now, but was beginning to lick at the walls and the stairway. "We need to hurry!"

Roark had guessed correctly. The four of them arrived on

the next landing, finding another hallway full of cells. When Nat used her power and forced the doors open, sylphs began to walk out of their prisons. Some were blind; others were fingerless, some limped. They were all bald, their beautiful hair shorn to the scalp, and Nat remembered the silver extensions the priests wore in their hair.

Shakes gagged. "Motherfreeze it," he whispered.

"Liannan of the White Mountain?" Brendon asked. "Do you know where Liannan is?"

One sylph shook her head, rubbing an eye that was no longer there, another scratched at the place where an ear had been cut from her head. When no one recognized Liannan's name, Nat felt her heart drop. Then she heard it again.

Liannan's melodious voice. Clear as glass.

Nat, come to me.

Nat.

Her friends made their way through the mob of sylphs, looking for Liannan, but Nat turned the other way.

She heard her friends scream Liannan's name. She heard them barge through a cell door, heard Shakes's sob. She heard Liannan cry, "Vincent!" Liannan always called Shakes by his real name; she was the only one who did.

No.

That was wrong. She heard none of this.

Liannan was still calling her. Drawing her to the other hallway, the one at the far side of the temple.

"Nat, where are you going? Nat!" Shakes yelled from the other side of the room. "She's in here! We found her! Nat!"

But Shakes was wrong.

Liannan was not in that cell; she was down this hallway.

Nat didn't look back. She knew where she was going, where she would find her friend.

She opened the door and walked underneath the archway.

SACRIFICE IS FREEDOM.

35

"KEEP CHECKING!" WES SCREAMED AT
Farouk, unable to accept that there was no record of Eliza
anywhere in the system, anywhere in the marked program.

It couldn't be. Eliza Wesson was an RSA prisoner. She had
been stolen from her family as a child, taken in a fire. That
was what he had believed, that was what he wanted to believe,
even if he knew the truth. As he had told Nat that night on
the slave ship, the truth was, he had no idea what had happened to Eliza.

Eliza could be scary sometimes.

She wasn't very nice.

Eliza was a weaver. She made you believe things that
weren't true.

Nine years had passed since he'd seen his sister. The girl
he'd known then was a child, angry, confused, and often mischievous. He had made his share of mistakes, done stupid
things, but Eliza had always been different. Even at seven,
there was something wrong with her.

For nine years he'd tried to forget that side of her. He wanted to remember the sister with awkward smiles who wore bright colors. Those memories were hazy—perhaps he had idealized Eliza. His only souvenir of their childhood was a photo, a picture of a little girl in a puffy snowsuit standing next to a snowman. He was in the picture, too, his chubby arm slung around his sister's shoulders. She was happy, smiling.

That was the sister he had come to save, his last remaining family in the world. His mother would never forgive him if he gave up on her. It was the reason he had left Nat at the Blue several months ago, the reason he had brought his entire team to follow him into danger and ruin.

Because he had to find out what happened to her. They were twins, but Eliza had always been his little sister.

"I'm telling you, boss, she's not here," said Farouk. "I'm sorry."

Wes banged his fist on the desk, making a huge dent in the middle. "LOOK AGAIN!" he roared. When he saw the fear in Farouk's face, he apologized. "I'm sorry—but she has to be here. The system is wrong."

Wes shook his head. His hands were shaking, and his eyes were watering. His head hurt. He didn't know what to do.

There was a scream from across the hallway. Wes exchanged a glance with Farouk and they bolted out of the room.

Shakes emerged from one of the cells, carrying Liannan in his arms. She was weak and pale, and her golden hair was knotted and tangled. The six-pointed star on her cheek was throbbing.

Wes felt a flash of joy to find her alive, but Shakes—that

scruffy beanpole of a boy with a crooked beard, who should have had a smile on his face as wide as the ocean—was visibly distraught when he saw Wes.

"What's wrong?" he asked, even though he knew that everything was about to fall apart.

That Shakes was about to confirm the dark, awful suspicion he had shoved to the back of his mind.

"Wes," Liannan said, her voice a whisper. She was the one who had screamed, he realized, and she hadn't screamed in fear but, like him, had let out a roar of frustration. "Wes . . . you have to help Nat."

"Nat. Nat . . . what do you mean . . . why? What's happened?" he asked, his heart thundering with fear.

"Nat's in danger—"

"Where is she?" Wes asked, crazed. "What are you talking about?"

"Wes, listen—she used me to call her here. I tried to deflect it, I sent the call somewhere else, I sent Nat to you, to find Roark and Brendon, hoping it would delay her while I tried to fight her. But it was no use. She's so strong. She bled me, used my blood to mask the iron in a magic bomb that brought down Nat's drakon. Because it's Nat she wants. It's Nat she's wanted all along."

"Who wants her? What are you talking about?" asked Wes, even if he already knew exactly what Liannan would say before she said it.

"Lady Algeana Penthos, High Priestess of the White. She's your sister, Eliza Wesson."

PART THE FOURTH:

CHILD OF VALLONIS

The cave you fear to enter
holds the treasure you seek.
—JOSEPH CAMPBELL

36

FOR A MOMENT NAT WONDERED WHY SHE
was walking alone in an empty hallway. She had been following Shakes, Roark, and Brendon, and in her distant memory,
she recalled them calling her name. Telling her to turn around,
that she was making a mistake. But she did not hear them, or
if she did, their words did not make sense.

All around her, the temple was burning, the fire from the
killing floor making its way upward, consuming everything in
its path. She climbed up one set of stairs, then another. She
heard the screams and the terror, but underneath the screams
she heard something else.

A voice calling for her.

Liannan's voice.

Like a key fitting into a lock and opening something inside
her, drawing her to this place. She forgot about her friends,
she forgot everything. There was only this place, and the voice,
and the call she must answer. Nat realized she had been here
before. She had been in this place, had walked through its
white marbled walls.

She followed the voice to the top of the mountain.

She found the door with the golden lettering and opened it.

Faix stood in the room, his mouth open in a silent scream. But Nat could hear neither his voice nor his thoughts in her head. All she heard was the voice, soothing her, saying her name again and again, blocking her from hearing or understanding anything else.

"Why, Faix," she said, "what are you doing here?" Her own voice was sleepy and slow as her mind struggled to make sense of her surroundings.

Why was she alone?

Why was Faix looking at her that way? Why didn't he speak?

As if she were awakening from sleep, suddenly she saw that something was terribly wrong here. His white armor was dirty and torn, and his nails were black with dirt. His silver eyes were gray and the necklace he wore around his neck was gone. He looked strangely bare without it, almost exposed. Nat shook her head, but the image remained.

It's not right. It's like the broken bridge all over again.

Faix shouldn't look like that. This shouldn't be happening.

Nat tried to compose herself. "Faix, what happened? Faix?"

But instead of answering her, Faix fell to the ground, his own long sword bursting through his chest as he was impaled from behind, and his sapphire blood spilling on the floor.

Nat saw but she could not see, not really.

Sapphire blood.

She watched the sword push through her lost friend's heart as a child watches a storm from the window.

Bluer than tears, Nat thought. *Bluer than the Blue.*

Faix fell to his knees, then pitched forward at her feet. The sapphire stain ran across the stone.

Faix is dead.

Faix.

My Faix.

She felt as if the air were leaving the room.

She felt as if her own heart were pushing and pounding out of her chest.

She felt as if she'd seen this all before.

Because I have.

It was then that Nat realized the room she was standing in was the same one she'd seen in her vision all this time. The chains on the wall, the blood pooling on the floor, a white-robed girl in the corner.

She had seen this. She had thought the girl was Liannan, that Liannan was calling for help.

But the girl was not Liannan, and Liannan had not been crying for help, not at all, but had been sending her a warning, garbled and suppressed by her captor, who had used her to draw in their prey.

Nat! Don't let them fool you! I need you to listen to me! Save yourself!

The white-robed girl tossed away Faix's sword and stepped over his body. Like the rest of the priests, she had white powder on her face and hands, and a third eye drawn on her forehead. She had thick brown hair and her eyes were as cerulean blue as the blood that she had spilled. She was beautiful and terrible, and she now wore Faix's necklace around her pale neck.

Nat wanted to rip it from her throat as she watched. This

thing—this heartless beast—had stolen Faix's heart, and it was all Nat could do not to repeat the trick.

But it wasn't just that.

Something about her was familiar, the shape of her nose, her long, thin hands.

"Do you know me, Anastasia?" the girl asked. She looked at Nat strangely, with interest, as if she'd only just noticed her in the room.

"Eliza!" Nat gasped. "You're Eliza Wesson."

"That was my name once," she said, staring at Nat with contempt. "Before. When I was weak."

Nat said nothing.

Before, she thought. *When you did not need to steal hearts because you still had your own.*

The girl's blue gaze was steady. Unnerving.

"But not anymore. I am Lady Algeana Penthos, High Priestess of this temple."

Lady Algeana of the Dark. Eater of Souls. Destroyer of Worlds.

Eliza bowed her head with a smile.

"But that would mean . . . that . . ."

"Yes," she said, amused. "Poor Bradley thought he was recruiting me into the program when he found me. Thought he could make me into one of his little fire-eyed puppets. Silly man. I might as well have tied strings to his arms and made him dance." Her smile broadened as she relished the thought. "Did you enjoy killing him? That was my gift to you when I had no more use of him. I told him to go into the maze, that he would surely find someone there he was looking for."

Nat backed up against the wall. There was something

dreadful about Eliza, a gray darkness, a dank, seeping poison that swelled up from what should have been her soul. "You're a murderer. You kill your own kind. I don't understand. Why? What happened to you?"

Eliza lifted her chin. "They have to die. It is their honor, to feed my power, when they die as innocents in the maze I capture the essence of their souls," she said. "My priests sell these worthless tokens to the rest of the population, but what they don't know is that each time a marked person dies, their power adds to my own. I claim it for myself, as only I can do." Her eyes were blazing now. "I am more powerful now than I have ever been. The worlds I weave, my illusions, are no longer ephemeral; they have substance. I can weave fire that burns—ice that freezes. A good trick, yes? Turning nothing into something. A lesson I learned as a child."

Nat was paralyzed. She couldn't move as Eliza took the rough chains and locked her hands in them. The chains that had never once been for Liannan, but were always for her.

I'm such a fool.

Eliza raised an eyebrow. "I saw you in the glass. The last drakonrydder of Vallonis. Anastasia Dekesthalias. The Resurrection of the Flame that will light the world," she said. She tugged the chains tight, drawing blood from Nat's wrists. "If only I had known you were already in the program. I ordered Bradley to bring you to me that night you left MacArthur, but you slipped away. So how was I to find you now? And how would I get you to come to me? But then we captured the sylph . . ."

"Liannan. Her name is Liannan." Nat couldn't help herself. *Her name is Liannan, she is not one of your toys, she is my friend.*

Eliza shrugged. "And suddenly, it all fell into place. I would use her blood to mask the bomb, and her voice to call you here. She was so very handy. But I had no idea until we caught her that you knew someone . . . someone close to me."

"Wes," Nat said miserably.

"Yes, my sainted brother, Ryan, who refused a commission when Bradley first offered it. Bringing all those pilgrims to our temple could have at least proved his usefulness. But no. He was too good for that, he would never do such a thing."

Of course he wouldn't, Nat thought.

"Wes always needed to believe in himself as the hero."

Because he is one.

Eliza sighed. "I heard he was back in New Vegas, so I put my name on a blacklist, made sure he saw it. It seemed to be the only way to get him closer. I wonder if he liked all those little touches. My 'room.' The bunny. I never had such a toy, but he wouldn't remember, he's much too sentimental."

"Kind." The word is "kind."

"He had to believe I was their prisoner, even though he knew better. He had to think I was in danger. It was the only way to draw him out. He's always been a gullible boy."

"Loyal." The word is "loyal."

Eliza dismissed her brother with a flick of her pale wrist. "Then those silly children set fire to the dome. But we got Wes anyway," she said, her lips parting, white teeth glistening. She motioned to Faix. "I thought he would bring you to me, too, if he had, maybe I would have let him live."

"You used them all to get to me. All my friends . . . ," Nat said. Eliza had hunted them down, each one, had brought them all here to die.

"What are friends for?" Eliza asked. She picked up Faix's sword from the floor. "He was my teacher, too. Did he ever tell you about his favorite pupil? Did he start your lessons with the violin? You thought it was your idea, but it was always his. Faix. Give the Queen my regards, tell her I got her message." She laughed, kicking Faix's body so it rolled into the blue blood.

"I called him to me, felt his presence the moment you landed on the island. Told him I was ready to change. And of course he came. 'There is still time to repent,' he said. 'The Queen still loves you. *I still love you.*' I called them Mother and Father, did he tell you? How can one be more than a thousand years old and so stupid?"

THE WEAVER
AND THE QUEEN

THROUGH THE FIRE, THROUGH THE SMOKE
and flame, she saw the boy and the girl huddled in the corner.
Twins. She hadn't known there would be two children, as she had
seen only one in her mirror. Which one? The boy looked afraid, but
his sister stared back boldly. The girl had sapphire eyes and a swirl
on her shoulder. A weaver.

It was the girl.

A decision was made.

She was the one.

The one they had come to steal.

In the century since the ice came upon the world, the people of
Vallonis sent scouts into the gray lands to search for the source of
the corruption, with no success.

Then, sixteen years ago, the Queen beheld a vision. A vision of the one who would save them. A child of Vallonis born in the gray lands who would be able to unlock the tower that held the Archimedes Palimpsest. The child of the Queen, imbued with her spirit and power for a new age. The mirror showed them the child in the flames, and they stole her from her family when she was seven years of age.

The Queen and her loyal consort, Faix Lazaved, brought the child to Apis to live with them. She became like a daughter, a child to replace the one she had sacrificed for Vallonis.

They believed Eliza would be the one to recast the spell, to fix the frost and the darkness that had seeped into its making and set the world aright.

Faix declared he had never had a more apt pupil. He was so proud of her. Eliza was a fast learner, and took easily to her daily lessons of magic. She learned to shape wondrous creations out of the ether. This stolen child was everything they'd hoped for. They called her their star child, delighting in her cleverness, her talent, her sorcery.

Three years ago, they sent Eliza back to the gray lands with the key to unlock the Archimedes Palimpsest and bring it back to Apis.

But Eliza never returned to them.

Instead, there was news of more violence and darkness, of a shining white temple governed by a cruel mistress. News that their people were being tortured and killed, herded to their deaths by armies in gray, and turned into dust by holy men and women in white.

Eliza Wesson was not the child they thought she was.

Heartbroken and defeated, they came to the conclusion that there could be only one explanation.

They had stolen the wrong twin.

37

WES COULDN'T UNDERSTAND WHAT
Liannan was telling him; it hurt too much even to try. The
whole world was burning around him, and somehow the story
burned him more. His sister was the High Priestess? Eliza
was behind this temple? The one who ordered the white hunt?
Who gathered marked pilgrims to this place only to slaughter
them? The priestess who worked with the RSA? How could
that be?

Eliza was mischievous and delusional, cruel and thought-
less, but she wasn't a killer, she wasn't a cannibal.

Was she?

"It's been nine years, Wes," Liannan said, standing now
and leaning on Shakes's shoulder. "People change. Sometimes
for the worse." The sounds of fire and fury were only growing
stronger. They needed to go.

Wes tightened his fist, but there was nothing to strike. Not
here.

"Where is she?" His voice was strangely cold, as if it belonged
to someone else. Someone whose sister did not threaten all he

loved along with the world they lived in. "Where's Nat? What does Eliza—my sister—want with her?"

"She went up the stairs," Brendon said. "We couldn't stop her. She was like someone possessed."

Wes moved to the door.

Roark put a hand on Wes's arm. "This place is burning down. We have to run. You can't go after her—we can't lose you, too."

But Wes shook him off, pausing long enough to grip Roark by the shoulder. "Try to get one of the ferryboats. Wait for me at the dock. I'll come back with Nat. And I can handle my sister. I promise."

"Wes," Liannan said gravely. "Eliza's not your sister anymore. You have to remember that. She'll use everything and anything to fight you, to get what she wants."

He nodded and ran up into the burning building, up into the smoke and flame, to find his love and his shame, his future and his past—at least, the one who held it hostage.

Enough.

The stairs were black with flame, but Wes kept climbing; he wouldn't leave Nat behind, and if they were going to die here, they would die together. He found the doorway and burst into the room. The chamber was hewn from the stone, a round room ringed by arched windows and encircled by a wide terrace.

Nat was chained up to the wall, her arms spread out like wings, wrists and ankles shackled.

Powerless as a pinned beetle. A broken bird.

A girl stood in front of her.

Eliza. My sister.

He recognized her bright blue eyes along with her thin nose, her sharp chin, the features that they shared—and yet her face had somehow gone wrong, slightly twisted, the nose too long, the chin too pointed. Even as a child, she had always been annoyed when their mother cooed over his good looks.

"Eliza."

Her name seemed to rankle her. "You may call me Lady Algeana. And you may kneel."

Wes didn't move.

Brother and sister stared at each other. He didn't recognize this stranger in front of him. He wanted to find his little sister, but she was gone for good: The snow had hardened into ice.

Wes smiled.

If there was one thing he knew, it was how to handle ice. He'd spent his whole life working it. Hard, he knew. Soft, that was more difficult to understand.

Try again.

"You've grown up, Lady Algeana." He clenched his jaw and tried not to glance across the room at Nat, hanging from chains, uncertain if she was alive or dead, awake or unconscious.

"Surprised?" Eliza said with a shrug. She brandished a gleaming blade.

Careful.

Eliza was beyond saving, and he could see that as clearly as the sword she held under Nat's throat.

THE SCROLL
AND THE KEY

SHE HAD BEEN BORN ELIZABETH
*Alexandra Wesson, sister to Ryan Andrew Wesson, in a frozen city
glittering with casino lights. But the name they had given her in
Apis was Algeana Penthos, the girl who would take away their
sorrow. The Child of the Stars. Daughter of the Earth. Light of the
Moon. Dearest Savior. Angel.*

*On the day that she was to fulfill her destiny, she said good-bye
to the two people who loved her the most. By the people of Vallonis,
they were called Queen and Teacher. But to her, they were Mother
and Father. She would not fail them. She would accomplish what
no one in Vallonis had been able to do since its return. She would
find and unlock the Gray Tower and recover the missing scroll, the
missing spellbook, the Archimedes Palimpsest.*

The journey was rough and hard, she was hungry and tired,

but she made it up the tower. She placed the key into the lock and opened it.

But the scroll lay behind a wall of impenetrable mist.

She screamed in frustration and unleashed the full force of her rage upon the wall, but it did not dissipate. The mists held.

The scroll, the spellbook, the Achimedes Palimpsest, was out of her reach.

Her failure was devastating and immense. It could only mean one thing. She was not the Queen's child. She was not Faix's hope for the new world. She was no one. She had failed them. They would not love her when they found out. They would blame her for being the wrong one.

She could not return to Apis without the scroll.

And in her failure, her anger grew.

She had no idea who she was now. She was not the Bright Star. She was not the Earth's Daughter. She was nothing, just another marked victim of the gray lands. Just another piece of ice trash.

She hated who she was and hated everyone who was like her.

Her birth parents had been afraid of her, and her adoptive parents in Vallonis had only loved her for what they thought she could do.

But what if Nineveh and Faix found out she could do nothing?

That she was no one?

That they had been wrong about her?

Would they still love her then?

Impossible. No one had ever loved her. Or if they did, they did not love her enough. Not her mother, who died too young, or her father, who was too tired to make an effort. Not her brother—she *would not think about her brother—no. Not him. She would forget she even had a brother.*

She hated this world and the hope that the White City had instilled in her, the hope that had died in her heart that day.

This world was nothing, and one day, she would destroy even the hope they held for a new one.

For Eliza had seen a vision in Avalon's Mirror, a relic from the second age.

The Resurrection of the Flame that will light the world. A vision of drakonfire covering the earth. A baptism of remaking, golden and bright.

Eliza vowed to make that fire her own.

She would burn down the Gray Tower that held the scroll so that all hope was lost forever.

38

NAT'S HEART SOARED AT THE SIGHT
of Wes, his uniform burned at the edges, his face flushed with
heat and fear. It was unnerving to see him picking his way
around his sister. And strange to see their two faces, so alike
and yet so completely opposed.

Two mirrors, she thought. *Not mirror images. Mirror opposites.*

His eyes flickered from Eliza's to her own. Nat tried to lift
her head, to smile, but she found she was shaking and her
body would not obey.

"What do you want with her?" Wes asked. "Leave her alone,
Eliza. Leave my friends alone."

"My dear brother, just like when I was little, I want everything you have and more," she said as she placed the drau's
blade right below Nat's chin.

"I have nothing. You have everything." He edged nearer to
them. Eliza pressed the blade forward, and he froze.

"True. I have everything. Now." She smiled. "Now that you
have foolishly brought me the drakonrydder, and for that you

have my gratitude, brother." Eliza's mouth twitched. "And her fire is mine to command."

That was it. That was what Eliza wanted all along.

My drakon.

With Wes in the room, Nat felt her anger grow. Her blood began to burn until her chest caught fire.

You took Faix.

You stole his heart.

You spilled the blood of Liannan.

You will not have my drakon.

Nat closed her eyes and drew from the fire. She felt her power return, flooding back to her, making her almost sick with joy. "*Your* drakon? *Your* fire?"

The Lady Algeana took a step back as the metal on Nat's wrists began to bubble and smoke.

"Think again, bitch," Nat said, and burst from her shackles, hurling Eliza across the room with a single great roar of flame. "That was for Faix," she said. "And this one is for me."

DRAKON MAINAS.

I CALL YOU FROM THE EARTH.

RETURN TO YOUR RYDDER AND VANQUISH OUR FOES!

The fire is within me.

I am the drakon and I am the flame.

She could call her drakon from anywhere on earth and it would answer. That much she understood now. It was only a matter of time.

And fire.

Orange, incandescent flame appeared outside the temple window. The clouds churned, forming a vortex in the sky, and in the center of the swirling clouds, she saw a hint of black, a dark shape growing larger. Nat recognized the churning maelstrom. It was a door, a portal. She had used such a portal when she and Faix traveled from Vallonis to the black ocean. She recalled his words: *In the gray lands, the doors to Vallonis are few as we must protect our country, but a door from Vallonis to your world can take us anywhere.*

Now her drakon was coming through one such door, heeding her call, traversing the portal to reach the mountain base. The black spot at the center of the vortex grew and grew, a dark center that quickly obscured the gray clouds.

It had healed completely; it was back to its full strength now and able to travel through time and space to get to her and not a second too soon.

The drakon sprang from the vortex; flame issuing from its maw. The creature's white-hot fire shattered the windows of Eliza's chamber; it vaporized the door. Flames danced across the walls and Nat fled, Wes at her back, through the place where the door had stood, out onto a terrace, on the top of the mountain, where the drakon hovered in the air, its dark wings unfolding, its green and gold eyes flashing. The drakon roared and its fury made the mountain tremble.

The creature raised its wings, descending on a plume of air, its talons gripping the terrace stones as it landed.

The creature howled, tucked its wings to its sides and craned its long black neck.

My drakon self.

"There you are," crooned Nat, stroking its hide, marveling at its scales, their surface mottled like coal, rocky and sharp. Black, translucent wings unfurled from the creature's back, blocking the sky, casting eerie shadows on the ground. Rents and jagged scars littered the beast's wings. This was a creature of war, its body scarred from combat, every inch of its hide armored and gnarled, but it had healed. Its claws raked ribbons in the stones. The creature huffed and breathed, its every movement a tremor. Sulfur and ash swirled in the air. Nat felt the flame's heat engulf her, and it was good. It felt like the sun, like a thousand suns rising at once, warming her.

Eliza was out on the terrace and she had backed away against the far wall. But instead of cowering before the great beast, she only laughed louder. "You think you can burn me, rydder? Let's see how you fare against your own kind." Then she took the necklace from her neck, a charm held by a golden claw, and smashed it to the stones.

A white flash shot through the air.

Smoke and ash formed a swirling white cloud, a cone of light and frost gathering around the broken pendant.

A figure emerged from the cloud, a scaly, glistening creature.

In the place where the red pendant had smashed against the terrace floor, a white drakon unfurled its translucent wings.

The creature's neck unwound from its torso, revealing jagged scales and a thorny mane.

Pink eyes glared through nictitating membranes.

The white drakon bared rows of silvery teeth.

A beard of horns disentangled from the creature's jaws, the spikes swaying as the creature's neck extended.

It grew larger and larger, rising against the gray clouds, casting shadows over Nat and her drakon. What was this? A drakon in a bottle?

But Faix had said his drakon was dead . . .

There was no time to argue, for the white drakon was very much alive, and hissing.

Eliza laughed and swung into its saddle, brandishing the drau's sword. "Call your drakon, rydder. Let's see how you fare against Gria." Then she flew up through the smoke and into the sky. The white drakon roared at his new freedom, beating his wings faster and faster.

Nat and Wes watched it go.

"Wes," she said, pulling him close. "You've got to get out of here."

"Did you miss the part about the other drakon?"

"This is not your fight," she said gently.

"She's my sister." He looked down at Nat. "Or she used to be my sister."

"That thing is no one's sister." She shivered.

"I can't leave without you," he said. Nat knew it was true. She knew she had to make him go.

"Eliza . . . ," Nat began.

Wes touched her lip. He understood, in his soldier's heart. She did not need to explain it, not to him.

"Go get her," he said, and he knelt so she could use his knee as a stirrup as she leapt upon her drakon's back, gripping its black hide, pulling herself to the nape of the drakon's neck. "Come back to me."

She smiled. "I will." The scales shifted beneath her. The drakon tensed its leg muscles; it hunched close to the ground before springing upward, bounding into the sky.

Fire swirled in her chest, in her throat. She was whole again and astride her drakon as they flew high above the temple mountain, above the city of towering hotels. Nat gloried in being part of everything once again, the cool air, the wind rushing against her cheeks as they soared over the city. A white flash cut through the sky. The air darkened; she saw scales. The white drakon shimmered in the clouds, then vanished. Nat pursued, Drakon Mainas pounding its wings.

She heard a crash, the sound of glass fracturing. Nat jerked her head upward. Beyond the lip of the nearest tower, the white drakon soared into view. Its claws broke the white stone and shards shot through the air, tumbling out of the sky.

What had just happened? Faix had a drakon hidden in his charm? A white drakon?

And how did Eliza know to break it?

Nat blinked, and her drakon pitched right, turning, craning its neck, folding its wings to avoid the debris. The white drakon whipped its tail, scattering rubble from the building in all directions. Mainas turned away just in time, dodging a shower of steel and glass the drakon had torn from the building and tossed toward Nat. The sky was a blur of white scales and frantic motion.

A sudden roar nearly shook Nat from her seat.

Dive, Nat cried. *We must flee.*

Nat fled and the white drakon pursued. She flew low over

the streets of the market, then rose, pivoting, diving through the city of glistening towers, hoping to find cover, a place to hide. Nat heard a crunch, the whining of steel bending beneath the white drakon's claws.

Looking back, she saw Drakon Gria lift a couple of armored trucks and toss them into the air toward them. The drakon had picked up the heavy trucks with no effort or exertion, throwing them into the air like snowballs.

The first crashed into the street below them, a miss. The second sailed so close, Nat felt its wind against her face.

Faster. Faster.

Her drakon rolled and dove, soaring between the towers, struggling to evade the pursuing white beast. She looked for narrow streets, places the larger drakon could not pass, but it was no use, the creature was closing in.

Stop running, she thought. *Fight. You twice bested a drone army, armadas fell beneath our flames; we can beat this creature.*

Nat and her drakon changed course and met the white drakon head-on, breathing fire, turning one of the towers into a black ruin. The building collapsed and Nat rolled away from its path. The white drakon, close behind, turned too late. The creature crashed through the tower's crumbling frame, its wings tucked above its back to protect its rider.

The white drakon screamed, its rage doubling as steel and glass pelted its scales. Drakon Gria pierced the cloud of debris, rising above the fallen tower, strips of flesh torn from its wings, boiling metal dripping from gleaming scales. The creature shook off the wreckage, clearing molten metal from its skin. Drakon Gria spread its wings, revealing Eliza, alive and unharmed. Drakon Mainas moved to pursue, but Nat held back her mount.

She spied something in the distance. Not a drakon, something smaller. She saw a lone figure dashing through the streets—a boy, dodging the wreckage, seeking cover. Wes.

What is he doing? He's going to get himself killed.

While her attention was distracted, the white drakon recovered; its wings sent furious winds rippling toward her. Nat forgot about Wes; she forgot about everything except her mount. Nat sent her drakon spiraling toward the safety of narrow streets, hoping again to evade the drakon's pursuit, but when she flew into an alley, a building began to collapse right ahead of her. It was too late to turn back. The crunching of steel and glass rang in her ear. No time to dive, to evade.

Fly into it, she told her mount. *Do it.*

Drakon Mainas did not hesitate, the rydder and its mount trusted each other, they were one and same, and so they soared through the tower, unharmed, their bodies passing through glass and steel, the drakon's flame melting the obstacles, clearing a path for Nat and her mount.

They soared upward, emerging into the light and the snow.

Nat gasped. On the far side of the wreckage, the white drakon hovered, waiting.

The creature screamed and a hurricane of brilliant, scintillating white shot from the creature's mouth.

And burned her with cold.

39

WES RAN OUT OF THE TEMPLE AND INTO
the surrounding city, following the battle and following Nat.
He flattened his body against the wall of a tower, protecting
his head as an avalanche of debris clattered to the street. A
gleaming tower collapsed, glass and steel billowing in all directions. Dust filled the air and he closed his eyes, feeling the
smoke in his lungs. He coughed, wiping his eyes clean before
rushing into the alley.

He found cover beneath the eyebrow of a shaded entry.

Where is she? Where's Nat?

A roar shot through the streets, the sound of bolts ripping,
concrete exploding. The drakons were above him, in a dog-
fight above the city. Debris crashed to the street, exploding
as it hit the pavement, destroying the sidewalks and benches,
falling on the screaming tourists, the market. Soldiers had
abandoned their positions, jumping into boats, trying to get
as far away from the fighting monsters as possible.

Wes spied the white drakon. The creature swooped low,
close to the street, picking up trucks and tossing them into

the air. He followed the arc of the truck and saw it strike a building, just barely missing the black drakon. He saw Nat for a second, but she disappeared when the black drakon rolled, turning sharply to avoid the barrage of vehicles the white drakon had thrown at it.

It was unlike anything he'd ever seen.

Wes hoped Shakes and the others were safe by the dock. If they weren't at the dock already, he didn't see how they could get there. The drakons were tearing New Kandy apart, turning the streets into canyons of molten metal and glass.

Something heavy struck the windows above him, and glass dust showered down. He clamped a hand to his mouth and nose, kicked open a buckled metal door, and found shelter in an abandoned lobby. Pulverized glass and aluminum filled the smoke-saturated air. He wiped dust from his face, and his leg was throbbing with pain. When he bent to tie the tourniquet, his hand came up red with blood.

Freezing hunters.

Wes picked up his sniper's rifle and looked through the scope, tracking the white drakon. But it was hard to see through the haze, and he was worried about hitting Nat and her drakon instead.

The dust cleared, and he shoved open the door and darted into the street. He scanned the sky, heard distant roars. He dashed through an alley, through smoke and snow. He caught sight of the white drakon hovering.

Where are you now, Nat?

Wes hid beneath an overhang, shielding himself from the white drakon's gaze. Eliza was sitting on the white drakon, her blue eyes blazing; she tugged at the reins, and the white drakon climbed into the clouds. He lost track of the creature. He heard the beating of its wings, the tortured sounds of steel ripping and stone breaking, but he could not see the drakon, so he followed the creature's roar, the breaking of glass and stone, his heart pounding, his body sweating beneath the heat suit. He unzipped his jacket; he was burning up.

He dashed through empty streets, past the overturned tables and broken tents, struggling but most often failing to follow the white drakon. Whenever he approached, when he neared the drakon, the creature would turn suddenly or arc upward and disappear. Wes would scramble, trying to follow, dashing down alleys, peering through archways, but found nothing.

There was a tremendous roar, and through the clouds he saw the two drakons. White and black, engaged in a duel to the death.

The white drakon opened its jaws, enveloping Nat and her mount in a storm of white. Down below, Wes felt the white drakon's breath, icy cold, as formidable as the black drakon's flame.

Wes felt the cold all around. He had felt this same cold before. He knew where it came from, who had caused it, and the feeling was familiar, the sensation that nothing was quite what it seemed.

After all these years, the memory had not yet faded. He would never forget that moment. The night he had lost Eliza.

There had been a fire, just like this. A cold fire, one that chilled to the bone, that turned breath into ice. And that's when he knew.

It wasn't real.

The white drakon wasn't real.

None of it was real.

It was just another of Eliza's illusions. She had woven a great story, crafted a drakon out of the air to fight Nat's. Her power had changed. It had grown. He didn't know how she had accomplished this feat, but he sensed an evolution. Eliza's tricks, her illusions, were no longer ephemera. The drakon wasn't real but even so it had substance. Her illusions had the power to kill and to destroy—the damaged city was real, and the destruction was real.

His sister, the weaver.

Teller of tales.

Weaver of lies.

She had always wanted to do more with her power, to exceed her given abilities, to weave deadlier and more potent worlds.

When they were little, Eliza would make puddles appear out of nowhere and he would trip, or she would make ghosts dance in the darkness of their bedroom. More than once she had set kids on fire, just to watch their reaction, to see them squirm as they tried in vain to dampen the illusory flames. She'd tricked him a few times, when he wasn't paying attention, but she'd never hurt him. Not much, at least. Not everyone was so lucky. She'd once made a glass door look open when it was closed. A girl, maybe eight, nine years old, hit the glass, shattering the pane, blood on her hands and face.

The night Eliza disappeared, the night of the fire, she had told him she was going to do it. *Someone is coming for you,* she'd said. *But I won't let them take you away. I will burn down the house before they do.*

He didn't believe her. Eliza always said stuff like that. But frightened and curious, he had stayed up that night, waiting. After midnight, he heard noise, confusion, yelling. A wild flame lit their room, a blaze so bright, it hurt his eyes.

But there was no heat. Only cold, and he'd known it wasn't real.

Nothing she did was real; it only felt real, only smelled and tasted real, but it wasn't real—or at least it had not been real when they were children. Wes had not seen his sister in nine years; she was seven when they last spoke. Those years, the time they had spent apart, had changed her; Eliza's power had grown. He tried to recall the night she disappeared, the iridescent light, his bedroom, his bed, aflame. And now, for the first time, as if he had repressed the memory on his own— or maybe Eliza had blocked it—he remembered the figures who had come that night, who had come to take her away.

The tall woman in white with the sad eyes who stared at the two of them.

Twins? she'd said. *I did not see two in my mirror.*

It's me, Eliza had said. *It's me that you want!*

Then they were gone and Eliza with them.

This isn't real. Stop it. Stop her.

He could do it.

Whatever this was, whether it was real or not, he could stop this.

He could stop Eliza's power.

He could do it when he was a child and he could do it now.

He felt a release of pressure, a ringing in his ears, and a red trickle of blood began to flow from his right nostril. Pain washed over him, but he did not relent, he had to keep fighting, fighting back against the cold that threatened to take them all.

40

THERE HAD BEEN NO TIME TO ACT, no moment to counter the white drakon's strike. *I will not die—not like this,* Nat thought, but it was too late. The white drakon was upon her. It had unleashed a blast of ice, cold enough to freeze her bones into glass, but just before the cold could hit, it halted in midair and moved around and away from her as if she were protected by a bubble.

Nat was safe inside a shield that blocked the white flame, sitting inside an impenetrable barrier. The white frost fell harmlessly against the swirling orb and did not touch her. She was unaffected even though she was at the heart of the cold fire.

Nat sat, transfixed by the flames, her drakon's wings flapping, the creature suspended above the city. The white drakon poured its flame into the air, throwing its hatred and its madness into the white cloud, its cold flame billowing like an icy hurricane. Nat did not flinch or move. She sat, motionless, like a stone fixed in a babbling river, the frost flowing like water around her.

Then she saw him.

Wes, standing in the middle of the street, looking up at her, his face pale and his eyes red-rimmed, blood pouring out of his nose, dripping onto his shirt.

He was doing this somehow. He was shielding her from the cold, holding back the deadly frost.

The cold fire began to close in on itself, and now it was Eliza who was screaming in terror. The cold consumed her, and in an instant, as quickly as it had appeared out of the charm, the white drakon disappeared.

And Eliza plummeted to the street.

41

WES SAW ELIZA FALLING. HE SAW HER
disappear into a haze of dust and smoke. When he reached
the place where she had fallen, he saw a pile of wreckage,
broken pieces of marble, dust, snow, and ash left over from
the battle. Wes scrambled through the pile, shouting his
sister's name. "ELIZA!" He needed to find her. He hadn't
known she would fall to the street when he shattered her
illusion. He hadn't had time to think. His only thought had
been to save Nat. He didn't mean to hurt his sister. He was
angry and furious and horrified to find who she had become, but she was still family. He couldn't leave her here,
lying beneath the wreckage, gone and forgotten. In spite of
what she'd done, he still thought he could help her.

Right before her drakon had disappeared, right before
it was clear that he would win, that his power—whatever it
was—would be able to push back the cold that she had created, she had called to him.

"Ryan," Eliza had whimpered. "Ryan, don't, you're hurting
me. Ryan!" And it was the voice of the sister he remembered.

Eliza, nine months old, when they still shared a crib.

They said twins had a secret language, and he had always felt special because he was one. He had a sister. His parents weren't rich, they couldn't have afforded a second child license, and just by luck, they had rolled the dice and come up snake eyes. Two children.

Eliza, at three, with her chubby fingers and secret giggle.

"Don't do it, Ryan, please. Don't hurt meeeee."

Wes had almost given in, had almost stopped fighting her, when he remembered Liannan's words. *She will use anything and everything against you.* Even his love for her. He had brought his crew, his family, to the far side of the world to find her.

He had said good-bye to the girl he loved so he could fix what was broken inside of his sister.

"No one ever loved me, because I was different, because I was marked," she told him while they fought, cold against shield.

"That isn't true, Eliza. We all loved you, Mom, Dad, me. You were loved. You just didn't see it. You never understood that we didn't love you *in spite of* your power; we loved you *because of it.* We were proud of you. We loved you."

And he pressed the shield forward until the cold cracked, until he had used everything in his power to destroy her. She was gone. Eliza was no more.

Now he stood in the middle of the pile where his sister had been and wept bitter tears at her passing. He was alone in the world; there was no one left of his family.

Then he felt a soft, warm breeze on his back. He turned around.

Nat had arrived on her drakon. "Wes!" she called, sliding off the saddle and almost falling.

He ran to her and she jumped into his arms. He held her so fiercely, he didn't think he would ever let go. She bent down to kiss him and slowly slid down the length of his body.

"You're covered in blood," Nat said.

Wes looked down. There was blood all over his shirt, on his face, his hands. "It's okay."

"You did it," she whispered. "You saved us."

He nodded, too tired to speak. The wind had stilled, but now snow was falling, burying them in soft white flakes.

"I'm so sorry about Eliza," she said.

He nodded. There was nothing more to say. She was his sister and he loved her and now she was gone.

Nat took his hand and helped him up so he could sit behind her on the drakon's back. "You all right?" she asked, turning around.

He grunted.

"I'll take that as a yes," she said, digging in her heels so that the drakon soared into the sky.

"Whoa! Take it easy," he said. Wes had never flown on the back of a drakon before, had never been this high off the ground. *The world is not the world I knew,* he thought.

Beneath them, the whole gray earth seemed to pitch and roll back and forth. The sea and the grid of the city slid about, miles below, as if he and Nat and the drakon were the one fixed point in all the universe.

Maybe we are, he thought as his head ached and his own blood dripped down his throat.

He did not know anything, not anymore.

His sister was not his sister, but his enemy was not only his enemy, either.

The story of his life had slid apart and broken into pieces. He tried to catch them, but his head hurt and there was so much blood.

He could almost hear his sister's voice in his head—not the Lady Algeana's, but his sister's. Eliza's.

Try. Look.

What do you see?

What is really there?

He opened his eyes and saw.

Everything is smaller from up here, but somehow more vast.

We crawl like ants on a leaf, but the leaf stretches all the way to the horizon.

Wes dropped his head and let the air and the sea blow past him.

He was a creature of the earth, and he preferred the ground, its solidity, or the sea, as he knew how to keep balance even as the waves moved underneath him. But this—this was not the earth that he knew. This was something else, something new and different and wonderful.

Wes was tired, so tired, and he leaned against Nat's back and closed his eyes.

He had done it. He had defeated the Lady Algeana, had used his power against hers.

My power, he thought. *I have power.*

Why, and why now?

Where did it come from?

Had he always known, or was it something he hid even from himself, like the memory of the night his sister was taken? Was it something he had pushed away, if only because he never wanted to be like her?

He couldn't accept that Eliza was truly dead or that he had killed her. He hadn't wanted that for his sister, he had not meant her harm, he had only meant to keep her from destroying Nat.

He was so very tired.

But it was okay. He was with Nat, and they would be together now. Whatever happened, nothing would separate them.

Wes held on tightly and vowed never to let go.

The earth can keep rolling. I have the one piece that matters. It's not going anywhere.

Nat's not going anywhere and neither am I. Not anymore.

We are fixed.

Together they flew to the only ferryboat left on the dock, where their friends were waiting.

42

Liannan had wrapped Faix in white. The drau was as beautiful as the day Nat had met him, and when she knelt to say good-bye, she felt his presence in her mind.

Faix? She sent him the word, because she could not let go of him, either, not yet. *Not Faix.*

I stored my energy for this, he sent, and an image came to her then. A city hidden behind smoke and fog, its walls overgrown with vines, monsters creeping in its shadows.

This is the Gray Tower hidden in the Dark City.

You must do what Algeana could not. You must travel there and recover the Archimedes Palimpsest. *The child of Vallonis should be able to penetrate the mist in order to recover the book of truth.*

Be well, Anastasia Dekesthalias. The time of ice and frost is over. The Resurrection of the Flame will light the world, and I wish I had lived long enough to see it.

"Faix," she said. "I'm sorry we doubted you." *That I doubted you,* she sent.

There is no need for sorrow. Only hope must guide you now. When you recast the spell, you will need these. Nat glanced down at her hand and found a small gray key and the same small golden charm that Faix wore around his neck. Whole.

So that had been an illusion, too.

It returned to its rightful owner. It carries the tree of life. One of the last remnants of Atlantis. Go to the Gray Tower. Find the Archimedes Palimpsest. Recast the binding spell. Take away the ice and the frost and the corruption. Light the flame. Make the world anew.

Promise me that.

She shook her head, overwhelmed by the thought of doing any of those things without the drau by her side.

I will miss you as well, he sent back, as if from very far away.

Don't go. Faix. Not yet. Her eyes blurred. *What if I can't?*

You can and you will, Nat who is nothing like a gnat. I can promise you that.

With those last words, his voice faded from her head one last time.

Nat felt tears running down her cheeks.

Good-bye, Faix.

"I'm sorry," said Wes. "I know he was your friend."

She nodded. So many friends had been lost today. She would remember them all, write their names in her heart, each one a memory of a true sacrifice.

"Where are we going?" she asked as the ferry began to move beneath her.

"Wherever you need to go," replied Wes, still holding her close. They stood by the railing together and watched the temple city burn in the distance.

Nat told him what Faix had told her. "He thinks the Queen stole the wrong child," she said to Wes. "That you are the child of Vallonis. Your magic is the ability to dispel magic—you have an immunity to its workings."

"As I am the opposite of my sister?" He shook his head.

This was their strange reality now.

Nat touched his cheek with her fingers. "You will be the one who can recover the palimpsest."

He cocked an eyebrow. "Well, I *am* extraordinarily talented."

"You know what this means?" she asked, pushing her lips up to his ear.

He shook his head.

"That you and I belong together," she whispered. She pulled back her head, smiling. *The girl from the Blue and the boy from New Vegas.* "See, Wes? You kept your promise. You came back to me."

"You just want me to kiss you again," he teased with a laugh.

"So what if I do?"

"Happy to oblige," he said, and so he did.

He was still kissing her when it happened.

His face changed, turning gray, and his body began to convulse uncontrollably, blood seeping out of his eyes, his nose, his mouth, and he collapsed in her arms.

"Ryan!" she screamed. "Ryan, what's happening?" she asked. Her friends crowded close to her. Shakes was yelling,

Liannan was waving her arms, Brendon and Roark were by her side, catching her, breaking her fall as she struggled underneath the dead weight.

"Get him water!" Roark yelled, while Brendon wanted hot towels and Liannan chanted healing incantations.

But Nat remained frozen in fear.

For she knew what this was.

This was the price.

Wes had saved her from Eliza's spell, but at what cost?

Magic has a tithe. Faix had taught her that much.

Magic was like any other kind of energy: When used, it had to be replenished, or it could be strained to its breaking point. It had limits, and Wes had met his.

She could almost hear Faix sending the words. *Everyone must pay. None are exempt. The sun rises and the moon sets. The oak breathes out what the wren breathes in.*

Nat began to sob, her tears falling on his face, as he shuddered and twitched and finally his body stopped shaking, his skin was gray and she could not see if he was breathing.

It was as if everything that was happening all around her was happening so slowly. Wes was lying on the deck of the ferryboat, and Shakes was pounding on his chest, trying to jump-start his heart, while Liannan breathed into his mouth.

I should be doing that, Nat thought dully. *I should be breathing life into him.*

But somehow she knew that it wouldn't matter.

That no matter what she did, Wes would still be cold and gray.

This couldn't be happening. Not to Wes. Not when they had finally found each other again. She could save him. She had saved him before. Her love was stronger than this. "You're not dead. You can't die. Wes. No. This isn't how this ends. This isn't the end for us," she said fiercely, holding his limp body in her arms.

But there was no time to mourn.

"NAT!" Roark screamed, pointing to the sky.

She glanced up.

Drakon Mainas was soaring above them, and had unleashed a roar of flame directed at their boat. It lit the bow on fire, and Shakes and Farouk moved quickly to put it out.

MAINAS! WHAT ARE YOU DOING? STOP THIS!

Then she saw. A white-robed figure sat astride the drakon.

Eliza. She had somehow used her power to survive the fall and to hide from Wes.

There are other ways to steal drakonfire. Eliza smiled. *Give my brother my regards in hell.*

It was another illusion. It had to be. Eliza was playing with their minds again, making them believe something that wasn't true.

She called to Mainas.

But there was no answer, and the black drakon continued to dive and roar, lighting fires as quickly as her friends could put them out.

MAINAS! TO ME! But it was no use, and all she heard in her head was white noise, a blanket, muffled, just like the garbled call from Liannan. Her bond with her drakon had been compromised. The connection between her and the great beast was weakened. What happened?

"The iron bomb," Liannan said. "It poisoned your drakon, fraying the bonds between you. It allowed her to be able to command it. It thinks she is you."

"And it's not the least of our problems," said Shakes, looking up at the sky.

Nat followed his gaze. Drones streaked through the air, howling through the gray clouds. Then another rumble, not a drone but something else.

A shell exploded in the air above them and a tank rolled into view, into the blasted streets of New Kandy. The treads slowed, the motor idled. A hatch opened and a figure emerged.

A boy wearing army gray peered at them through thick goggles. He tore off his helmet and pulled down his goggles, and they were confronted by a familiar face with short platinum hair they called "drau style" back in New Vegas.

Avo Hubik. The Slob. The onetime slaver had returned to the army. Behind him, more soldiers approached, along with two more familiar faces. Daran and Zedric Slaine, with sneers upon their faces. Back from the dead and ready to take revenge on the crew who had wronged them. More armored vehicles rolled into the streets of the city as a fleet of drones darted through the air.

Her drakon was stolen. Wes lay dying in her arms. And the military had arrived to recover its base.

Now it was all up to Nat, to steal back the victory they had worked so hard to win.

ACKNOWLEDGMENTS

We'd like to thank all the wonderful people who made this book possible, starting with our lovely and wise editor, Jennifer Besser, and publisher, Don Weisberg, along with everyone at awesome TEAM PENGUIN, especially the crack editorial team who helped us make our deadline: Arianne Lewin, Katherine Perkins, Kate Meltzer and Anne Heausler—we are truly grateful for your diligence and dedication to the series. Thanks for saving these two freezing iceholes from plummeting into the void. Big kisses to Elyse Marshall, Anna Jarzab, Shauna Rossano, Emily Romero, Erin Berger, Courtney Wood, Erin Toller, Scottie Bowditch, and Felicia Frazier and her amazing team of sales reps. We are so lucky to have you guys on our side!

Thank you to our agents, Richard Abate and Melissa Kahn at 3Arts, who make sure the lights are always on at our house(s).

Thank you to Steve Stone for the amazing new covers.

Thank you to our dear friend Margie Stohl for all the supportive words and for just being brilliant in every way. Thank you to all our fabulous friends in New York and Los

Angeles—we would name you all, but only Margie helped with the book. Thank you to our families.

Thank you to our readers who have thrilled to Nat and Wes's story, thank you for your tweets, GIFs, Tumblrs, e-mails, Facebook likes, Goodreads reviews, and crazy enthusiasm for the series. See you at the grand finale!

TURN THE PAGE FOR A PREVIEW OF
THE THRILLING THIRD BOOK . . .

HEART *of* DREAD, BOOK THREE: GOLDEN

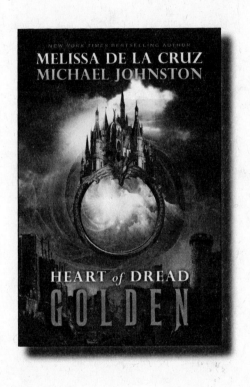

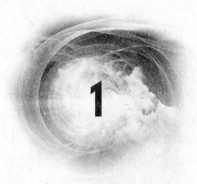

1

THE RUINS OF THE WHITE TEMPLE
burned in the hazy distance, and from high above in the clouds,
Nat could see the unholy city of New Kandy covered in a blanket
of smoke, its tall towers now mere black skeletons.

The city was on fire.

Death was in the air, all around her. Nat could feel the grim
grip of fate cut deep into her bones. She knew it by the stench of
the ash, the burning cinders in her eyes.

Ruination had come for them, for all of them.

Then the buildings' silhouette seemed to sway, as the vision
wavered, flickering in and out of sight. Nat blinked her eyes and
gritted her teeth, forcing the connection to return. For months
she had used her drakon's powerful gaze to scan the horizon for
enemies, to prepare for any hidden ambush, to notice changes
in the battlefield that no mortal eye could hope to observe. That
was the nature of her duty, the right of her destiny.

Or so it had been.

But now the thread between them was fraying fast, as a new

bond was being forged between drakon and rydder. Helplessly sidelined, Nat found herself not where she should be—high above the clouds with her mount—but rather, sitting on the deck of a ferryboat, watching as her one true calling was stolen from her.

Because an imposter rode atop Drakon Mainas.

An imposter, and a murderer. A threat not just to Nat, but to the entire world, and any hope for its future.

Not to mention, a danger to the drakon itself.

Eliza.

She was to blame. The Lady Algeana, formerly known as Eliza Wesson, the child who had been stolen from her home by the people of Vallonis in order to save their world. But Eliza was the *wrong* child and she had grown up to become no one's savior.

Quite the opposite. She had taken what was not hers to take, and now everything lay in ruins as the result.

Nat could feel Eliza's heels digging into Mainas's hide, urging the creature to fly faster and higher away from the battle, fleeing from its true mistress. Nat fought back, desperately attempting to regain command of her drakon.

Mainas! Stay!

Do not leave me!

You're making a mistake!

Nat felt a rage in her core burn as hot as the flame that swirled around the drakon's heart—and for a moment Eliza's hold slipped and the drakon reared, frantically attempting to buck her off her seat, lashing with its head and tail, shrieking with anger and pain.

But only for a moment.

Nat was too far away, and Eliza too strong, and every

thunderous wingspan and passing second widened the gap between them.

I am your mistress now. Eliza's calm voice cut through the smoke and fire. *You are mine to command.*

Nat had to strain to hear the sound of the wind rushing beneath her drakon's wings, to feel the cold air around its scales. The thread between them was tearing, like fibers quickly spinning apart, unraveling what had been fiercely knitted together.

She held on as hard as she could to the drakonsight, gazing down upon a dark, burning landscape, at the remnants of a broken city, where at its edges, a battalion of tanks rolled across the blistered earth like ants converging on a hill.

Then it was gone. *No . . . not yet . . .* She had to hold on to her drakon. *Drakon Mainas!* she called again. *To me!*

Nat followed the slender thread that led back to the mind of the monstrous green-eyed and black-scaled creature that was her own twin soul. She burrowed into its thoughts, screaming for it to hear her, to recognize her as its avatar.

We are one and the same, drakon and rydder! I am Anastasia Dekesthalias. The Resurrection of the Flame. The girl on your back is an imposter. You have been deceived!

Return to me! Mainas!

There was no response—only the dull ache of loss.

And then, abruptly, it was over.

The thread between Nat and her drakon snapped, and her vision disappeared into complete darkness. Eliza had finally succeeded in cutting the cord.

Nat lost her drakonsight. She no longer felt the pounding of the creature's heart, the strain of its muscles; its fury was no longer hers to command and unleash. The drakon was gone and Nat was alone.

She had lost her mount once before, had even sent it deep into the ground willingly, to heal after a fierce firefight during her guardianship of Vallonis. But this was different. Something elemental was now broken and torn inside her—as if a piece of her very being had been taken away, and she was blinded, rendered deaf and mute. Senseless.

Drakon Mainas!

She screamed, even though she knew he couldn't hear her.

A moment later, Nat opened her eyes to the world around her, still unable to focus. Everything looked fuzzy and gray, now that she had lost the keen eyesight of her drakon.

Reality was not something she wanted to come back to. Not yet. It was too hard and too cold and too painful. She had lost too much.

Where am I?

Snow was falling. That was one clue. She could smell it, even taste it. It was in her hair, on her filthy clothes, mixing with the ashes from the battle. She heard tanks—another clue. They were rolling through the streets, from the sound of the rattling treads.

Beyond that, she could pick out the slightly higher pitch of the drones buzzing in the air above them. Like flies gathering around her location as they would around a dead body. Which is what Nat herself would soon be, if she stayed here where they could find her.

And where is that again?

The deck of a ferryboat.

Nat's eyes snapped into focus, and she found herself staring up at the stricken faces of her small, tired crew. Shakes crouched next to her while the smallmen, Brendon and Roark, held on to each other. Liannan's head remained bowed, her silver hair falling across her face. Farouk stood frightened and grief stricken, his hands clenched at his sides.

And something else. *Someone else. A dead body.*

She looked down at the boy in her arms. Ryan Wesson lay motionless, as frozen and gray as the floor beneath him.

It all came rushing back to her—the battle with Eliza, Wes using his newfound powers to dispel his sister's illusions. Victory and escape were in their grasp, until Eliza suddenly reappeared on Drakon Mainas's back while Wes had collapsed on the deck. Shakes had tried to jump-start his heart by pounding on his chest, but nothing had worked.

"Wes!" Nat cried, her tears making tracks through the dirt on her face. It seemed unreal, this moment. His lifeless face. The weight of his still body.

This couldn't be happening. *Just a moment ago, we were kissing—how can this be?* Now his lips were blue and his eyes were closed. He had saved them all from Eliza, but at what cost. Magic had consequences to its use. He couldn't wield its power without hurting himself, and no one could have imagined the toll it would take on him.

I didn't think it would do this. He couldn't have known, either.

Not that it would have made any difference to Wes, she knew. Nat stroked his cheek. He would have fought for her to the death, no matter what. But he didn't have to. She didn't want him to.

He didn't have to die.

He can't.

"Stay," she said, telling him the same thing she had said to her drakon earlier. "Don't leave me." She put a hand on his chest, willing whatever power she had left to flow into him, to keep him alive even just a moment longer.

Nothing happened. There was no spark of life in his pale face.

It was useless. She was useless.

"Nat, he's gone, and we need to move, they've spotted us," said Shakes gently, with a hand on her shoulder. "Roark—help me cast off the lines, Brendon, to the wheel, Farouk, see if you can get that engine running."

The boys exchanged uneasy glances as they swiftly carried out Shakes's orders.

Liannan caught Shakes's pleading look and moved quickly toward Nat. "Hey," she said softly. "There's nothing you can do for him anymore. And we need your help if we're going to get out of here alive."

Nat said nothing. Ashes in her mouth. Numb. Spent.

"Wes would want that, Nat. Don't make his sacrifice meaningless. He needs you to be strong. He wants you to live."

Nat ignored her. She ignored them all. They'd all given up on Wes, but she wasn't going to. He couldn't be dead, he couldn't leave her, not now. Not so soon after they'd found each other again.

She pressed harder against his chest, willing his heart to beat. Willing him to make his way back to her side.

She could live without drakonsight, without drakonlimb, without drakonwing. But she could not live if Wes did not.

The deck vibrated underneath her as the boat's engines sputtered to life—and then died just as quickly. Shakes cursed. "What the ice is going on back there?"

"Pipes are frozen solid," yelled Farouk from below. "And we can't get a fire started in the coal bin!" The ship had been retrofitted with a steam engine when its owners hadn't been able to fix its electric one.

"Nat, come on," cried Liannan, running toward the back of the ferry. "Help me to conjure a flame!"

But Nat remained still. Without her drakon, there was no fire left in her, she was sure of it. She was unable to move, unable to breathe, as Wes's heart remained silent underneath her palm.

His heart had stopped and now hers was shattered.

She was no use to anyone. She couldn't keep him alive—she had no drakon, no fire, no power of her own. She was nothing, she was nobody.

Dimly, she heard the RSA forces swarming around the broken city, recapturing the marked who were once prisoners in the White Temple, the very people Wes and his crew had just set free. Rounding them up one by one.

It was all for nothing.

A gunshot cracked in the distance, and Nat jumped. She turned to see—and from afar, she saw a body fall to the ground with a hard thump.

No. They weren't rounding up the prisoners.

They were executing them.